DUMB SHOW

DUMB SHOW

Mike Johnson

Press

99% Press,
an imprint of Lasavia Publishing Ltd.
Auckland, New Zealand

This edition published 2016
First published by Longacre Press, 1996

www.lasaviapublishing.com

ISBN: 978-0-473-37818-9

About the Author

Mike Johnson, fabulist and poet, is recognised as one of New Zealand's leading and innovative writers. He lives on Waiheke Island and teaches creative writing at AUT University in Auckland. His first novel, *Lear: The Shakespeare Company Plays Lear at Babylon*, was short-listed for the New Zealand Book Awards, his novel *Dumb Show* won the Buckland Memorial Award for Literary Excellence and he won the Frances Kean Award for his short story *Magic Strings*. His first book of poetry, *The Palanquin Ropes*, was co-winner of the John Cowie Reid Memorial Competition.
You can find more of his published works at **www.lasaviapublishing.com**

Also by Mike Johnson

Novels
Zombie In A Spacesuit, 99% Press, Auckland.
Hold My Teeth While I Teach You To Dance. 99% Press, Auckland.
Travesty. Titus Books, Auckland.
Stench. Hazard Press, Christchurch.
Counterpart. Harper Collins, Sydney.
Lethal Dose. Hard Echo Press, Auckland.
Antibody Positive. Hard Echo Press, Auckland.
Lear: The Shakespeare Company Plays Lear at Babylon. Hard Echo Press,
Auckland (republished by 99% Press, Auckland).

Shorter Fiction
Back in the Day: Tales of NZ's Own Paradise Island, 99% Press, Auckland.
Foreigners. Penguin Books, Auckland.

Poetry
Two Lines and a Garden, 99% Press, Auckland.
To Beatrice: Where We Crossed the Line. Pie Press, Auckland.
Vertical Harp: The Selected Poems of Li He. Titus Books, Auckland.
Treasure Hunt. Auckland University Press, Auckland.
Standing Wave. Hard Echo Press, Auckland.
From a Woman in Mt Eden Prison & Drawing Lessons. Hard Echo Press,
Auckland.
The Palanquin Ropes. Voice Press, Wellington.

Non Fiction
Angel of Compassion. TP Press, Auckland.

Children's Fiction
Kenni And The Roof Slide, Illustrated by Jennifer Rackham. Beansprout
Press. Auckland.
Taniwha. Illustrated by Jennifer Rackham. Beansprout Press. Auckland.

Preface for the 2018 edition of Dumb Show.

Dumb Show was first published by Longacre Press in 1995, and was my fourth novel. It remains my most critically acclaimed work to date, winning the Buckland Memorial Award for literary excellence. It was reviewed widely and positively throughout the country. It took me four years to write and what I remember most was the struggle I had with the form, the structure, and the satisfaction I felt when it finally came right. Longacre engaged in a thorough editorial process, resulting in a text I have made no attempt to change in this republication. It was my first novel written on a computer, an Apple Mac Plus.

Dumb Show is set in my childhood home of the Canterbury Plains, and very much evokes that atmosphere, and although it is not directly autobiographical it is informed by my own experience. The way readers have taken the book has varied. One reader described it as 'the darkest novel I've ever read,' while Iain Sharp described it as a 'grand domestic comedy.' To me it remains an emotional landscape of luminosity and intensity, and it is wonderful to see it in this elegant new edition.

Mike Johnson Waiheke Island January 2018

To Canterbury with love

Contents

Judd and the Pig

JUDD KNOWS there is Pig about; the signs are unmistakable. A full sized beast will leave a trail through the scrub, and fresh turned earth where the roots are youngest. Yesterday he found a patch on Scrubby Flat so recently rooted that some of the dislodged stones were still damp on their upper side.

- Pig'll seek lower ground before bad weather, Uncle Honk says.

The path he is following is more imaginary than real; not so much a path as the most practical way up the Dog-leg, following old sheep trails along the ridge. Below to the north lies the farmhouse, snug and peaceful-looking in the bend of the Dog-leg, a tiny replica attended by a dinky tractor and barn; Grandfather's glass tower shines like a jewel perched on matchsticks and blocks.

Up ahead, around domes of smooth, exposed rock, ranges Mut, chief pig dog to look at him, heading for the first summit, the Knee of the Dog-leg. Judd quickens his pace, holding the heavy binocular case hard against his side.

- Where is't, boy? Where is't, can y' find it?

Mut whines and comes running back to Judd, ears perked.

- You'll find it f' me, won't y'?

Mut laps air in assent, turns, and runs off up the ridge, looking importantly to the right and left and back to Judd again. It is generally agreed at the house that Mut is a stupid dog, however good a hunter Uncle Owl may claim him to be. Much more stupid than the sheep dogs; that is Uncle Honk's conclusion. Grandfather says it's something to do with the shape of the dog's head; red-setters are bred for their looks, creating a narrow skull too small to house their brains. As a consequence of their brains being squeezed up inside these tiny skulls, the dogs act stupid, running about and forgetting where they are. Uncle Owl insists however that Mut is the best rabbiter he's ever had. - The dog never stops movin. It'll flush im outa the densest bush, he says.

But pigs are another matter.

- Where is't, boy?

Mut looks around, assuring him that if there were any pigs lurking about he would scare them right out of the rock. He'd hole one up until Judd came in with the knife like Uncle said to do and finish it off with an underarm into the belly. - Go f' the belly, that's the softest part.

Judd doesn't think they'll find it up on the Dog-leg, but it is the best place to start to look. As he gets higher, he can clearly see the lower section of the foothill bending out into the plains to the east of the house, protecting them from the south, blocking their view of the plains to the east and north east. From the Knee, which Judd is approaching, he can look east down the lower flank of the Dog-leg to the plains, or west, back up into the teeth of the mountains and Snowy Peak up the back of beyond.

Mut looks about expectantly. Perhaps a pig will jump up and wave his tusks at him. What would Mut do then? Run like a bastard most probably.

- Find it! Judd puts all the urgency into his voice he has heard from Uncle Owl when there is a rabbit or deer nearby. Mut keeps on swivelling his head, having no better idea of where to look than Judd. It annoys Judd to see such rank stupidity in a dog, for Mut doesn't even know what he is looking for, he is only pretending. To really hunt for pig he needed to bring Tonks, Peg or Billy, real pig dogs, but Uncle Honk would never agree to that. - Working dogs are not pets, he'd say. A stupid dog deserves scragging.

Judd heard him tell Uncle Owl about a man who wrapped wire around a dog's balls, hooked it up to an electric fence and turned on the current. The result was the subject of some amused speculation in which bottles of home brew played a prominent part. Uncle Owl told Uncle Honk about a man who nailed a neighbour's dog to a tree, still alive mind you, because it got into his chicken yard. He was a Greek of course. Uncle Honk told Uncle Owl about a man who got so angry with his dog he broke its jaw so it couldn't eat. It ran around dangling its jaw at food and water and died of dehydration.

Somehow Judd can't imagine Mut in any of these extremities; the animal is hardly worthy of such exalted tortures. Hardly worthy of more than a casual boot in the arse, which happened regularly if Uncle Honk was about; he never seemed to learn about Uncle Honk.

Mut does his best to respond to Judd's tone, going into a state of hyper-alertness, jumping from one vantage point to the next, ears pricked high, turning, giving him a frantic look.

Judd laughs and throws a rock at him.

- Stupid animal!

- Dumb bitch of a dog.

- Put yr tongue away or I'll cut it up f' bacon.

The rock hits Mut on the flank as he skirts to evade it, his hind legs scraping against the rock beneath; he turns his head to give Judd a desperate, guilty look.

Judd laughs harder. It may be difficult to imagine fancy tortures for a turd-brain like Mut, but it isn't hard to imagine an accident. Mut losing his footing on a rock. Mut falling into a crevice. Mut with his back broken, feebly waving his legs in the air like a cockroach. Mut with his head crushed in, bleeding from the ears. Mut with his underbelly ripped open and his guts spilling out like a dead pig. Mut with his arse hanging out the other way. Mut crushed, broken and bleeding in a million different ways.

The pleasure these images afford him pale however beside the imagined pleasure of finding a pig. And finding some way to kill it. He hasn't quite figured that bit out yet since his own pocket knife is too puny for the job. Maybe someday he'll find a knife lying around, and if he does there'll be a use for it alright.

He sees it: a big black boar with tusks like dirty ivory and fiendish little piggy eyes. Eyes as pink as a baby's. Bigger than a man, since its belly would be fatter and covered with short, sharp dark bristles. He sees himself dragging it back down to the farmhouse, maybe using Mut in harness, although the dog is probably too stupid to know how to pull, and dumping it in the yard the way Croak the cat would dump dead rats at the kitchen door.

That'd wipe the grin off their faces.

The dog sheers away as Judd scrambles up onto the Knee and gratefully drops the binocular case to the ground. Mut stands a few feet back from Judd, watching. From where Judd stands the upper Dog-leg follows the line of the river winding back into the mountains. The Knee is a knoll, a fortress of rock from which he can survey the surrounding territory and plan his strategy. Below him, to the west, is the toy house, barn and yard. He can see the clump of macrocarpas where his father works on the fence; he can even see old Wakefield the bull calmly at work on the grass beyond the macrocarpas. Beyond the farmhouse, the bed of the river shows as a great white bone bent around the Dog-leg at Rocky Heads, following the northward march of the Alps before turning east to the plains.

He clambers to the top rock on the Knee and surveys the territory of the Dog-leg. He's got nothing more to go on than a hunch that the pig has holed up somewhere here, making expeditions down to Scrubby Flat to forage. Lots of hollows and little caves, gorse gorges and escarpments up here for pig to hide, but the ground is too hard and tussocky, shale and flint, to follow a trail, especially when the hillsides are half covered with old sheep tracks anyway. A smart pig would know all this, know the benefits and the risks of abandoning the beech forest or the denser bush of the lower mountain slopes, and weigh it all up in its piggy brain. - Pigs are smart, Uncle Honk says, and they can think on their feet, which is more than you can say for some humans. There's plenty of stories about smart pigs.

Sitting on the top rock, he opens the leather binocular case and pulls out the precious binoculars which he's stolen from Uncle Honk's room. Uncle Honk hasn't used them in a month of Sundays, but that won't stop him thrashing the hell out of Judd if he finds them missing. Whenever Honk does the thrashing, which is nearly always, he takes off his belt with a tight look on his face. Judd has been on the receiving end of that tight look and the leather that gives it tongue more than once. At such moments, Uncle Honk would kill him quick as look at him.

But it is worth a whipping or two to find the pig. And if he killed it he might escape a thrashing altogether.

He starts systematically, going over the territory in his mind as he surveys it through the lenses, searching for any likely signs. If he can keep the pig under observation for a while he may be able to set a trap for it. He could steal one of the possum traps from the barn. Covering every nook and cranny in the surrounding territory is painstaking work and after a time he takes a break, idly throwing stones to confuse Mut and trying to imagine where, if he were a pig, he would head for.

He props the binoculars up on a rock to keep them steady, kneels behind the instrument and begins examining the slopes of the upper Dog-leg, segment by segment. It would be easy to give up. The pig might be anywhere; it might still be down on Scrubby Flat.

He is just about to drop the heavy instrument when a hawk flies into the circle of his vision, blurring quickly out of focus. Avidly he tries to follow it, turning the binoculars slowly in the direction of its flight, finally catching the soaring image above the line of the upper Dog-leg, specked against the high, white blue behind. He finds the focus and watches the bird lift in an updraft before circling lazily down back towards the river bed. Then he lowers the eyepiece, seeing if he can spot it without glasses. The huge panorama of mountains jumps out at him; the magnified spot containing the hawk vanishes into the sweep of hills. Quickly he returns to the eyepiece; there is only a jumble of rubble and cliff. Next moment the hawk flies into the magnified circle and with two slow pumps of its wings floats further up. It is blurring again, flying closer. He can see the abrupt movements of its neck, turning its head to scan the territory below.

Across the river, the pointed head of Sister Peak stares at him. He has never seen her so clearly: the faint suggestion of eyes; the shiny, slate cleft of her chin as she fattens out, without any neck, into the bulk of the hill; the overhanging rock that makes her nose and creates the ambiguous shadow of her mouth; the precipitous forehead that merges back into the scaling rock. Below the chin there is a jumble of shadows and boulders and beneath that, like a vast napkin, a shingle fan spreads with beautiful precision down to the river. The shingle fan was formed in a slip that took nearly the whole side, face and all. This gives precariousness to the image of Sister Peak, her nebulous gaze looking something less than ancient and eternal.

As the hawk loses height again, dropping towards the river bed, there is a flash of movement. He focuses directly down on the slopes below and sees it. Pig. A heavy body, dense and solid, sliding into the shadow of a rock, dark enough in itself to be a shadow. This side of the river, on the upper Dog-leg just as he'd thought. The signs had not lied.

Another shadow passes over him, slipping across the rocks on which he is sitting. He jumps as if he's been touched on the shoulder. Mut, quivering with excitement, leaps up barking. The bird is right above them, limned against the blue. It is falling, neck tipped forward, angling across his line of vision. There is a thump and squeal from beyond the rocks and a moment later, as he jumps up, he sees the big bird hauling off, wings stretching, pulling deeply. Mut slides recklessly down the rock and vanishes. Judd follows. A moment later Mut reappears, carrying a rabbit, his hind quarters swinging in an ecstasy of self-congratulation. When Judd tries to take it from him, Mut shies away and Judd has to grab the collar the way he's seen Uncle Honk grab the sheepdogs.

Reluctantly, Mut releases his trembling burden. The rabbit is alive, stunned or in shock; a young one still delicate of bone. Nothing but a little life wrapped in fur.

Nodding to Mut who is watching expectantly, he wrings its neck, feeling, as the life passes out of it, a quiver through his buttocks and thighs.

High above, almost invisible to the eye, the hawk swings, a single slow-wheeling speck.

On his way down from the Dog-leg, the rabbit hanging from his hand, Judd comes to a small lake nestled in a shallow depression. It is utterly windless and, despite the apparent heat, covered with a thin coating of ice, except at the edges where the water lies still around the stony shore. The coating of ice makes the water look dark and full of frozen seams.

Mut, somewhat relieved at a sudden piece of flat, takes a random wander along the shore.

Judd picks up a small flat stone and throws it out across the lake, listening to the chirping sound it makes as it skates across to the other side. As if this were a signal, a light wind blows from the mountains into his face, and the ice sheet begins to move, riding gently up over the stones at his feet, snapping and cracking so all along the shore. He kneels, picks up a piece of fractured ice and sucks on it. The ice cries out on his tongue; he can taste the lake, bitter and dark.

The pig may be anywhere now. But it probably comes here to drink; it would be a safer place to come than the river. If he could wait here for long enough, with a gun maybe, he could make his kill. He'd have to steal Uncle Honk's .303 which would earn him the thrashing of his life if he failed.

Mut steps back and looks at the ice suspiciously.

Suddenly Judd thinks he sees somebody, a small boy like himself, moving on the other shore. When he stares hard the movement vanishes and is replaced by a bank of grey, unmoving stones. He picks up another stone and chucks it in that direction; it whistles across the ice and jumps into the water on the far side. As if this were another signal the ice at his feet stops moving and a great dome of silence comes down over the lake. The light wind has pushed the ice as far as it will go and the cracking and snapping stops immediately. The wind-driven ice lies still on the stones.

There is no movement from the other shore but the soft, dark ripple of water.

Judd approaches the house sideways, like a wary cat trying to look over its own back. He's seen Croak do that when the sheep dogs are loose. The house is quiet; yard and barn are still. The dogs chained in the shadow of the barn look up at him and Mut without interest or hope, as chained dogs do. He has approached from the river side, the north end, where he might slip into the kitchen without risking the yard.

He is about to make a break for it when a shadow detaches itself from the house and walks towards him.

It is Uncle Honk, walking slow and unhurried, as if he's going nowhere in particular. When he reaches Judd, the boy throws the rabbit down on the ground in front of him. Mut takes a quick sniff and jumps away to avoid Uncle Honk's boot.

- Where'd y' get it? Uncle Honk says in a neutral voice. It is a flat voice to come from such a meaty body.

- Dog-leg. Hawk dropped it.

Judd keeps his eyes on the rabbit in front of him.

- Where's the binoculars?

- I don't have im.

- Where'd y' put im?

- Nowhere.

Uncle Honk pauses to digest this. - It's only a baby, he says, pushing the rabbit with his toe.

- It'll taste th stew. Judd pulls his shoulders up around his ears. He aims for Aunty Pi's righteous tones and fails miserably, his voice emerging as a horrible whine. He is developing a bass croak that will give away his fear every time.

Around the corner comes Maverick, bearing the binocular case, a proud, important look on his face.

- Where'd y' get im? Uncle Honk asks Maverick in the same neutral voice.

The important look withers. Like Judd, Maverick knows the meaning of that neutral voice and a boy never knows which way justice might fall. He holds the binocular case to his chest.

- I found im in th grass by the corner post, he announces, braving Honk's stare. The very picture of sincerity.

Judd starts to move towards the house.

Uncle Honk signals Judd to stop with the flick of his wrist. Judd freezes.

- Y' took im. Uncle Honk says, hardly interested in the answer, it seems. Across the yard Uncle Owl and the other children have gathered to watch.

Judd nods. He wishes the other children would go away and stop watching. He'll get them later.

Uncle Honk clicks his tongue across his cheek. - What'ja want t' look at?

Judd doesn't answer. His story of the pig may not be believed, since pigs didn't often come east of the river, the Dog-leg wasn't natural pig country.

- Ws there somethin y' wanted t' see? Somethin y' wanted t' spy out?

- Rabbits, Judd says, hardly moving his mouth.

Uncle Honk affects a look of disbelief. - Since when've you been stealin m' glasses t' hunt rabbits? He laughs and pulls the case roughly out of Maverick's hands. - Are y' goin t' shoot im with these? He shakes the case under Judd's nose. Or jus' watch im dancin around?

Knowing the sudden fury a wrong answer might produce, Judd says nothing. There's nothing he can say; Honk will eat the rabbit and thrash Judd anyway. Judd will be lucky to get a taste of the stew.

- Pig, Judd said, deciding to play his only card.

- I beg y' pardon?

- I was lookin f' pig.

- What pig?

- The pig I seen.

- Y' seen pig?

- Yip.

Judd points. - Upper Dog-leg. I seen im with them binoculars.

Uncle Honk appears to think. His fingers stroke the leather on the binoculars as if it were his belt.

- What'd I tell y' when y' last took im? He says patiently. His voice is quiet but it can be heard right across the yard.

Judd says nothing.

- What'd I tell y'?

Judd says nothing.

- Do I have t' ask a third time?

Judd says nothing. Uncle Honk nods to himself. - Looks like y' already know the answer. What's the matter, cat got y' tongue? He grabs hold of the boy's collar. - What'd I tell y? Come on, you remember? What'd I tell y' last time y' took im?

- That y'd belt me. Judd tried for a sneer.

- When w'd I belt y'?

- When I took im again.

- Do y' think I should keep t'm' word?

- I dunno.

- What would you do, if you ws me?

- I dunno.

- You dunno much. You dunno nothin except how t' steal things. Lyin 'n stealin; stealin 'n lyin. Creepin around the place. What ws y' spyin out? I bet y' never saw no pig.

- I did so.

- I bet y' didn't. Yr lyin t' save y'self. First y' spyin rabbits, then y' spyin pigs. Whad're y' spyin?

- I dunno.

- You dunno much.

Judd says nothing. At that moment Mut appears, doing something a dog should never try to do, which is to run one way and look another. Only the most hare-brained beast. Uncle Honk, who is standing squarely on his two feet leaning forward, is hit squarely from behind, bowling him so neatly he drops onto his knees in the dust as if he's been hit by the hammer of God.

Mut panics and leaps away but in the wrong direction. Uncle Honk is back on his feet, his boot already swinging. The dog begins yelping before the boot lands, which it does, with a satisfying crunch of bone. Mut spins away, trying to keep his hindquarters under control.

- I'll kill that fucken dog.

When Uncle Honk turns to Judd his face is hot with blood. - Y'know very well, don't y'?

- No I don't, Judd says defiantly.

Uncle Honk points to the house.

The beatings always take place in the bathroom, being the most decent place for a beating, and it is usually Uncle Honk who administers justice. Mother will creep into the hallway to the bathroom door, sink her head in her hands and allow every blow to fall upon her own body. When the beating is over, she will move silently back to the kitchen where she will take up her post under the watchful eye of Aunty Pi. At such times she will shuffle, bent over like an old woman.

In the bathroom, it is Uncle Honk's belt, Seth, who rules, and Uncle Honk is its instrument. The smooth, brown leather writhes and twists in his hand, urging him on in a sharp, whistling voice to use the buckle end. Seth is saturated with the oil, sweat, piss and bile of Uncle Honk who it works with a will.

Being a girl confers no automatic immunity. As Aunty Pi has pointed out many times, that would hardly be fair on the boys, and the boys have to agree with her. Boy or girl, Seth's appetite is the same, except with a girl Aunty Pi may be the preferred instrument. At least, it is Aunty Pi's prerogative, a prerogative to which Uncle Honk, no matter how angry or bent upon speedy justice, defers.

Like the boys, the girls have to take down their pants, bend over the toilet seat and submit to the mercy of Seth. Pleading and whining merely angers Seth further. Neither is Maverick spared on the grounds of being Uncle Honk and Aunty Pi's child, that would not have been fair. Fairness, in fact, is the ruling ethic of the beatings. It is not fair on the children to allow them to go unpunished, since they would do the same again. It is not fair to punish one more than another, or the reverse, for the same offence, just as it is fair to strap every child involved in an offence no matter how big or small a part they may have played. By the same token, punishment increases according to the degree of resistance the child puts up to the processes of justice. Fair is as fair does, Aunty Pi would say.

This fairness stems from a logic dear to Seth, a line of reasoning that reaches right out into the universe, the whole of creation, and dictates the terms in no uncertain manner. It is this logic Aunty Pi is referring to when she says that something is as plain as the nose on y' face. Such plainness brooks no argument. The children remember a time when two dogs were put down for the killing of a sheep, although only one did the deed. Blackie was there at the time, Aunty Pi said severely to Uncle Honk when he hesitated over the loss of a second farm dog. This was conclusive. It was not so much that Blackie, having smelled blood, might be led into doing the same one day, although that was always on the cards, but by being there while his companion killed the sheep he took part in the crime, was equally culpable, and had probably, being an animal completely without pride, crept up after the deed for a lick at the guts of the kill. In this case the logic of Seth entered the rifle, Uncle Honk's World War I vintage .303, soon to speak sharply for the egalitarian nature of death.

Judd thinks about those dogs as he sprawls over the toilet seat, bum exposed. In fairness, Honk has to identify two crimes here, three in fact. First, Judd stole the binoculars. That is worth a couple of whacks. Then he tried to hide them in the grass. That is worse than the first, but let's say a couple of whacks. Then he tried to lie about having them, saying he hadn't had them. That is worth a couple of whacks at a conservative estimate.

Not to mention refusing to say why he'd taken them in the first place. Bloody kids and their secrets. So there's six whacks owing Seth, and Seth collects immediately unless the child is sick. That is only fair.

Judd isn't sick, is he?

Judd makes a last minute effort to implicate Maverick, still blustering as he goes over the toilet seat. Maverick knew where the binoculars were. Maverick put them there. Maverick helped him steal them. Maverick had put him up to it.

But he has to shut up when it is Seth's turn to speak, and on this point a common ethic binds the children. They will not scream. They will not let the sound out of their bodies. So they screw up their mouths and block up their throats and hold their screams inside their skin.

In front of Judd is the bathtub, still half full of dirty water from someone's bath. A light scum has settled on top of the water. This neglect is an offense to Aunty Pi. When the hiding is over, she sends Mother in to let out the water and scrub the bath down.

Judd hates dinner at the best of times; the coming on of evening makes him feel small and lonely, even when he's not nursing a thrashing.

He's expected to help Princess set the table, a precise and ritualistic art governed by rules that have evolved over long years of practice.

The right action, in the right order, as Aunty Pi has it.

Mother is the custodian of plates and napkins, tablecloths and cutlery, but it is Aunty Pi who is keeper of the faith and who schools Mother, who never quite seems to get it, on exact procedures and sequences. Aunty Pi's faith, being Godless, puts much store in the appearance of things, in order and routine and table manners. Table manners are something children have to be taught, for brats share the lawless, uncontrollable attributes of nature and are not born fit for human society. Mean, cruel, scheming and devious, and above all, grubby, you have to watch these bloody kids like a hawk, she maintains. If they weren't taught any better they would eat off the floor like animals. Once she made Nerida, who was one of the worst offenders, get down and eat out of the cat's plate on the floor just with her mouth, her hands clasped together behind her back in case she tried to touch the food, while the cat, Croak, watched, bored, from close by.

- How does it feel to be an animal? she'd asked the girl.

When God is gone only Cleanliness is left.

To begin with the table has to be scrupulously wiped down, scrubbed in fact, so that it might be a fitting vessel for the tablecloth which is always starched, fresh and neatly pressed. Nothing looks worse than stains coming up underneath the tablecloth. Once the tablecloth is laid, and smoothed down with a brisk movement of Mother's lovely fingers, the condiments follow, the silver salt and pepper set the children are not allowed to play with, the tomato sauce, vinegar, chutney, whatever else is on hand.

Then the cutlery, knives on the right, forks on the left, spoons across the top. Knives have to be facing inward; dessert spoons cannot double as soup spoons; soup spoons can't be used for stews though dessert spoons maybe if there is too much runny gravy and no bread or potato with which to soak it up.

These are the commandments, and where tradition does not provide Aunty Pi interprets. No, Uncle Owl cannot smoke after a meal at the table. Smoking is a filthy habit anyway. But coffee may be taken after dessert. If there is any coffee. And Mut is not allowed to lie under the table, waiting for scraps to be secretly fed to him by Uncle Owl. The dinner table is no place to feed dogs. Dogs are filthy creatures and bring fleas into the house. By the logic of fairness, the same rule applies to Croak, whose only officially approved activity is the hunting of rats and mice. A cat that sleeps too much is overfed. One that scavenges under the table at meal times is getting lazy.

After the cutlery, the placemats go into place, and the heat pads to protect the tablecloth from hot pots. Finally, the food itself arrives. First the vegetables in a black, cast iron pot. Potatoes, carrot, cabbage, then the meat, grilled lamb chops or a roast leg of mutton. The plates are brought out hot from the oven warmer. The dinner-set has blue pictures of hunting scenes in England; dogs that look a little like Mut chasing foxes followed by men in tight riding pants and closefitting jackets riding beautifully groomed horses, all porcelain-blue fired under the glaze and covered with the tiny hair-cracks of age.

Uncle Honk carves the meat while Aunty Pi serves up the vegetables. Then Aunty Pi gives the signal to eat by bending over her food, knife and fork at the ready, as if she were saying a quick prayer. As she takes the first bites, Judd can see the neat part in her hair which is pulled back tight into a bun revealing the narrow, severe lines of her skull. Nerida says that Aunty Pi's hair is long and thick, like Mother's, but the other children don't believe that. They know the bun is artificially thickened by a light mesh bunroll of hair taken from Aunty Pi when she was young; Princess told Judd she knew that because its hair was of a different hue. She saw it once on Aunty Pi's dresser where, uncharacteristically, Aunty Pi forgot she'd left it; such a personal item usually goes into the same drawer as her underwear, which Princess has also secretly inspected and duly reported back to the other children.

Everybody knows that Judd got a beating but nobody says anything. Aunty Pi never countenances any giggling or silly chatter about the punishments afterwards. The least said the soonest mended; y' put things behind y' and get on with what y' have t' get on with an' there is plenty t' be done God alone knows.

Certainly Judd himself is forbidden to mention it. Officially, the ban extends to the children talking among themselves yet they do, of course, at night in the hush of their room. How many did y' get? Did it hurt? Did y' cry? Did y' cry?

Aunty Pi eats with spare, precise movements and generally frowns on any kind of serious conversation at meal times. Serious conversation is bad for the digestion. Only Uncle Owl ever flouts this rule, openly provoking her with his Bolshevik comments.

- Bank foreclosed on Lester's place, he announces, after inspecting his mashed potatoes, and seeking a little butter to grace them. - Th poor sod couldn't meet his mortgage.

Aunty Pi snorts. This is old news, at least three weeks old, but Uncle Owl is obliged to discover it all over again every so often and bring it out for inspection. She says, - If we were as lazy as Bill Lester, our place'd be under the hammer too. Some people don't realize there's hard work involved runnin a farm. It's not all beer 'n skittles, runnin a farm.

There is a faint emphasis on the some people.

Aunty Grin murmurs in assent. She, for one, has worked her fingers to the bone for the sake of others.

The women know what hard work is all about.

Uncle Owl considers this as if the argument were new to him, to be chewed over with a mouthful of spud and peas laced with gravy, and to consider whether or not he falls into the same doomed category as Bill Lester. After a time he lifts his fork solemnly in the air. - Big farms buy up th littleins as th littleins go t' th wall. He draws his fork across his throat. - You cn only push rocks uphill f' so long. We're sittin pretty here because he, Uncle Owl points his fork up at the ceiling was cunnin enough t' get the place paid off while everybody else ws borrowin money.

- Cunnin ws he? And who did all th work? Who kept th place runnin? Mary, before she died of overwork, so th kids never got t' have a grandmother. I seen Mary at the tubs at night, tears of exhaustion runnin down her face. Oh he ws cunnin alright.

There is a vehemence and bitterness in her voice that shuts everyone else up, but Uncle Owl has taken off along his own line of thought.

- The Capitalist is a carrion bird, he says grandly. Feeds off th dead, and th livin too, it doesn't matter, it's all meat, y' see. It's all dead by the time it gets t' th stomach, y' see.

He waves his chop in the air.

Aunty Grin puts her fist delicately to her mouth and coughs.

- I seen Bill Lester shear a sheep once, Aunty Pi says. Y' never seen a bigger mess. The sheep ws bleedin all over. The legs ws runnin with blood. I says t' m'self at the time, if this man thinks he's goin t' run a farm he's got another think comin.

Uncle Honk nods and snorts. He's seen the same thing himself. - Bill has some fancy ideas. He done a fewa them too.

Aunty Pi nods grimly. She's seen a few fancy ideas come and go in her time. - There's none so blind as them that will not see, she says, remembering her own mother saying the same thing, and how true it turned out to be.

Uncle Owl wraps his well-eaten chop in a piece of old newspaper for Mut.

- It's a mortgagee sale, he says ominously, putting the chop in his shirt pocket. - The banks flexin their muscle, suckin out the cash. Bill ws goin t' join his brother on th Coast but his brother wrote an' said not t' bother comin. There's no jobs there an' it rains all th time, he said, all th time. It's so wet y' have t' have a fire in summer. If y' don't y' get mould growin outta yr ears. And other places. Y' get mushrooms jumpin outta yr nostrils.

The children don't dare giggle. Aunty Grin looks shocked. She sets her mouth in a thin line. Aunty Pi throws Uncle Owl a warning glance.

- They build their houses with prows and sterns, Uncle Honk says. He doesn't look at Judd; he just acts as if Judd isn't even there.

Uncle Owl is quick in - That's right. They've got kids out o' nappies who've niver seen th sun. He winks at Nerida who is staring at him with big eyes. - Kids who learn t' swim before they cn walk. Babies born with gills.

- And there's some wet enough behind the ears t' believe anything they hear, Aunty Pi says, bidding the conversational topic a dismissive goodbye. She knows too much of a good thing when she sees it. And she can smell whisky on a man's breath too, no matter what kind of fancy talk is coming out.

Mother says nothing but concentrates on her eating. She is squeezed in between Aunty Pi and Uncle Owl who speak to each other over her head. For one moment Uncle Owl puts his hand on her shoulder as if to hold himself up. Mother lifts her face up and stares straight at Judd and Princess. Her eyes are such a stunningly pure forget-me-not blue Judd can't face them and Princess wants to weep.

Father doesn't eat at the table with the adults and the brats who are being civilized, because Father is beyond the discipline of Aunty Pi, his gaze being tuned to another world, one which keeps blowing up every five minutes, giving him no rest nor table manners worth the teaching. The area around his plate being like a culinary war zone, he is banished to the kitchen where he sits and eats at the bench, his mess blending in with the cooking scraps, all of which mother will later be cleaning away.

He eats very little, and then with nervous haste, often sitting in front of his food, rocking back and forth, until the rest of the household has finished eating. Then he will bolt bits of his meal while Mother and Aunty Grin clear the table and the dishes pile up like fortifications around him. Mother finds opportunities to speak gently to him, offering him this and that, offerings he invariably refuses, pursing his lips and shaking his head like a child. What he doesn't want, Pito gets, and what Pito doesn't want, Princess gets, a perk for helping Mother clear the table. It is a small infraction of the rules to which Aunty Pi turns a blind eye.

Sometimes Princess, being self-possessed and of royal bearing, will stand by Father's chair while he eats. He eats as if it were a criminal activity, eyes roving for danger, and if the children speak to him he will give them a startled glance, sometimes answering and sometimes acting as if they weren't there. Pito especially, with his gentle, unobtrusive demeanour, puzzles Father, and he will track the boy's movements with a suspicious stare.

- The stars fell to the earth and exploded like forty-four gallon drums of petrol, he says, perhaps to Princess by his side, perhaps to no one. At that moment, the war is in the past and the sound of the explosion a mere echo, and not the terrible buzzing which comes out of the sky and penetrates the thickest of concrete bunkers. It is like the sound of a Stuka in dive; a great wail of death opening its mouth, spitting holes in the earth. Meal times are the worst, because that is when you are least prepared and the most exposed, the most vulnerable. And that is when the enemy most likes to strike, of course.

This time Judd joins Princess. He comes up behind her and stands silently by Father's chair, face mottled and pinched.

- Uncle Honk beat me, he says in a voice low enough not to be heard.

Princess looks sharply at him and Father jerks his head as if he's been slapped. His fork falls, handle first, into the gravy. His hand begins to shake. It shakes the way the ground shakes when bombs are falling and the earth is a red lava of faces. Something cold burns in the middle of his forehead, like a piece of stuck shrapnel. He knows there has to be a way through the maze of death to the living world, he can see its light, he can hear voices from the other side speaking in hushed tones. He can see the rich ripe wheat bend to an open wind. That is enough.

Beneath the chair his legs begin to walk. The irrevocable sound of men marching. He holds his elbow to his forehead to ward off blows, and cries out when he looks at Judd. The cry makes Judd go pale and step back, his mouth twisted with the pain he's still carrying from the beating.

Mother comes in from the kitchen and shoos the children away. Father is not well. Father has bad dreams about the war and has terrible noises in his head, Mother says. He even dreams in the day-time because he's sick.

Judd is the last to leave, dragging his feet and looking around. He hangs close to Father, whose feet are marching off to hell and who sees the heap of stones he's so patiently collected blown apart by a random shell. Judd understands, he thinks, why Father acts this way when the children come to him.

Father is terrified of them.

That night, after dinner, they hear it. A sound they have not heard for a long time. It is light and distant at first, little scribbled sounds across the window. They feel the house move, shifting to accommodate itself to a new set of conditions. The scribble on the window turns into a scratching.

Nobody says anything. One by one they realize what it is, and allow it to become familiar to their ears once more.

It takes Nerida, the youngest, the longest to understand. She sits on the couch, her teddy suspended over her knees, staring in wonder towards the window. She sees dozens of fingers with silver nails running down the window pane. Each one chooses a different course.

- We might get a garden, Uncle Honk says sourly.

There is a hard, brittle sound from the mountains.

Nerida puts her hands over her ears.

Judd hears it too, and thinks of the pig, his pig, somewhere up on the Dog-leg, huddling under rock for shelter.

The rain comes hard, filling the rusty guttering, filling the river bed with yellow, heavily-moving water and shifting rock. The children lie in their bunks and listen to the steady tintinnabulation on the iron roof and the thunder breaking over the mountains.

Nerida gets scared and hugs her knees with her teddy in between and Pito creeps into Princess's bed to snuggle up close, burying his head in her shoulder. She puts her arm protectively around him and runs her fingers through his scrubby hair. On the opposite bunk Judd snivels his beating into the pillow, trusting the rain to muffle the sounds. Maverick says nothing because he is the brave one.

Judd curses softly as he slips into sleep.

Princess and Pito go under the blankets to escape the thunder.

In his dream Judd is back at the lake up on the Dog-leg. The surface of the lake is black with ice. There is a boy standing opposite, across the dark expanse, too far away to make out. He wants to shout out but the sky is too huge to carry his voice. He is sure the boy is looking in his direction. The ice begins to wrinkle and slide as if it were alive. The boy vanishes and a hawk rises up into the air. A rabbit appears in Judd's arms. It is not a rabbit but a small child.

Tenderly he cradles it in his arms.

The morning is still grey and misty with rain when Judd goes with Mut to watch the river fall and listen to the rumble of stone and rock being dragged along the river bed. He looks up to the Dog-leg; the Knee is shrouded in dark rain. The welts on his bum have lost their heat but are still sore when he moves. It doesn't matter. The beatings never matter except at the time.

Mut stands back a respectful distance and looks quizzically at the moving water. Nothing in the dog's short memory equates with this blistering yellow tumult, nor the raw smell that accompanies it, a smell that comes up mineral-fresh from deep in the earth.

- Would y' like t' try and cross the water now, Mut? Judd uses the sneering, derisive tone he reserves for the dog and his two stupid sisters.

Mut cocks his head, looks interested, then puzzled and sad. His front legs go stiff and one back leg begins to quiver, a sure sign of impending cowardice. This is the same leg Uncle Owl once drove the tractor over as the dog lay quietly asleep in the sun. Shaken but miraculously unhurt, Mut has favoured the leg ever since just as if a real accident had happened; sometimes in sleep it will twitch and Uncle Owl says that the ghost of the tractor is passing over it once more.

Judd picks up a wet stone and rubs it aimlessly with his sleeve as if it were a piece of glass. He throws the stone out into the rumble of water. Mut looks with foolish expectancy towards the sound of its fall; for a moment he half looks as if he is going to run after it. Judd looks for a place nearby where he can sit down and watch the rush of water. There is nothing but stones and the white, stripped trunk of a beech tree tossed aside, but as soon as he goes to sit on it, he is reminded of his beating, and Uncle Honk's choked, livid face. It would be easy enough to kill Uncle Honk, stick his own pig-knife into his guts while he slept as he always slept, on his back, his mouth open, his gut sticking up, unpredictable noises coming from the back of his nose. Then to cut off his balls and feed them to Mut who would be sure to swallow them in one single joyful gulp. Girls' work.

He looks, yearning, towards the other side of the river. It would be good to climb Sister Peak to above the tree line, where the house looks no bigger than a pea and Uncle Honk no bigger than a speak of dust, if that. The misty rain makes the far bank look much further away than it is, but cannot soften the shattering rattle of the river; the sky hangs low, covering Old Snowy with a grey, wispy tea-cosy. The world stretches out up the riverbed into a stony nowhere. Judd walks in that direction, facing the tumult. It would be good to see Uncle Honk writhe in the dust, gored by some wild animal that secretly obeyed Judd's commands. A giant pig, perhaps. It would be good to hear Princess whine and beg for mercy after ordering everyone around. These things would be wonderfully good, and are satisfying to dwell upon, but they are not enough, not enough by half.

He moves his feet carefully over the slippery stones keeping as close to the muddy, foamy edge as he dares, accompanied by Mut who endeavours to do the same, or at least pretends to, but who has twice as many feet to think about. The fury of the river boils in Judd's blood; the grey of the rain, the grey of the slippery stones, the muddy grey of the river are lit by the quick, hot, bloody flashes of hatred and why shouldn't it be that way? Fair is as fair does; as Aunty Pi says, everybody gets what's coming to them. Justice goes all ways. Judd is coming to see how true that is; it is something bright, sharp and inconsolable.

Mut begins to look forlorn. Balancing on wet rocks is not his idea of fun, and soon his course begins to veer from Judd's towards solid ground. Imperiously, Judd calls him to heel. Where the river corners at the Dog-leg lie several huge boulders rolled into position by some massive flood. Perhaps he can get onto one and, ever accompanied by his loyal companion Mut, watch the torrent from closer quarters.

To get there it is quicker to shortcut across the bend in the river, through Scrubby Flat, where there is nothing but rock, broom and gorse. Mut is happy to leave the stones, and noses up into the broom and gorse with an overzealous rush. This heedlessness nearly kills him, death missing him by a few inches of boar tusk.

The tusker turns its fiendish face towards Judd, who is only a few feet behind. The dog leaps sideways as if he were trying to be a cat, the same leap that brought Uncle Honk to his knees.

Neither Judd nor the pig move a muscle.

The rain comes down hard.

Cleaning the guns, the old shotgun and the .303, is a sacred task as far as Uncle Honk is concerned, even though the tools are nothing more fancy than a piece of number eight wire with a rag on the end and a tin of kero. Mostly he doesn't mind the children watching as long as there are no interruptions or stupid questions. Sometimes the children may hold bits and pieces for him, other times they can't. Sometimes he lets them peer down the pristine spiral shaft of the barrel or wash the carbon soaked rag in kero. Other times they have to piss off.

There is no other task he performs with such care and concentration, such attention to detail. At these times he develops a fixed look, his tongue going into the corner of his mouth and he may appear, from a distance, to be one with the children who cluster around. Only at such times does Uncle Honk look like a boy. This shape-shifting doesn't fool Nerida and Princess, but it provokes in the boys an almost slavish trust in Uncle Honk, and they speak to him with an eager, confiding air while he, wholly absorbed in his task, ignores them or grunts in reply.

- How many pigs have y' shot Uncle Honk?

- Does th bullet fit in there?

- Tell us about th deer that you an' Uncle Owl shot.

- C'd y' shoot a hawk right out of th sky with this gun?

- How many guns do y' have, Uncle Honk?

- We found shells like this up the creek once. A whole pile of im.

Sometimes Uncle Honk stops and looks out over the yard and the river with an abstracted, brooding expression, the gun cradled forgotten in his arms. He may be recalling former victories, former trophies, the glories of the past, so the children leave him alone at such times.

On the day after Judd's beating, Uncle Honk is particularly serene. He sits on the back porch cleaning his gun, grunting almost affably to the chatter of Maverick, Pito and the girls. Princess and Nerida are not so interested in the gun; Nerida has a horror of it and will refuse to touch it as if it were something alive and repulsive. Princess doesn't like the clammy steel of the barrel yet loves the smooth oily wood of the butt, especially when she is allowed to hold it next to her cheek. She is touching it with the tips of her fingers, following the line of the grain, when Judd comes running up, Mut panting in triumph beside him.

- I seen the boar, he shouts. I seen im!

Mut nods and slobbers up to Nerida.

Uncle Honk is instantly alert but he doesn't look at Judd.

- Y' seen im? He takes the butt off Princess.

- Yeah, Scrubby Flat. He wants to say more but can only stutter. He hasn't stuttered since he was little kid.

- This side of th river? Honk is on his feet looking hard at Judd now, his hands working automatically at putting the .303 together.

- We haven't finished, Maverick complains. He's been holding the barrel still for Uncle Honk.

- In th scrub? Honk ignores Maverick. He's seen what the children are just beginning to notice, that Judd is scared.

- He coulda killed me. Judd's lower lip begins to tremble.

Uncle Honk vanishes inside and re-emerges with his hunting knife, slipping the blade into a sheath on Seth. Uncle Owl comes out of the house behind him. Mut goes to Uncle Owl, bungling past Uncle Honk who pushes the dog aside with the impatient end of his boot.

- We got the boar trapped this side of th river, Uncle Honk says to Uncle Owl.

- He'll be lookin t' head back up th southern side, Uncle Owl says, scratching Mut behind the ears. He is carrying a .22. - He'll be lookin to cross th river an' he'll end up round th back of Rocky Heads.

Uncle Owl sounds very sure.

- That peashooter isn't goin t' hurt no boar. Uncle Honk gestures to the .22 lying negligently in Owl's hands.

Uncle Owl grins - Sure's hell makes im mad.

Uncle Honk frowns. He doesn't approve of making wild hogs mad.

- I'll show y' where! I'll show y' where! Judd points. Realizing what is happening, Maverick is on his feet.

- Where? Uncle Honk works the bolt of his .303 and slips a live shell into the breech.

- I'll show y'. Judd doesn't whine or plead. He just tells them as if that is what is going to happen. For the first time since his beating, he meets Uncle Honk's eye. Uncle Honk nods briefly.

- I wan't' come too, Maverick says instantly.

Uncle Honk shakes his head.

- It's not fair! Maverick's face goes red. Uncle Owl laughs. He squats down and gives Mut a hug.

- A wild boar is a dangerous animal, Uncle Honk says, - We don't want more bloody kids than we bloody need.

- Judd's goin!

- Only t' show us th trail, if it's not already cold with all this yabberin. Uncle Honk is already moving. He unleashes two of his best pig dogs, Ran and Billy, who have been tied up with the rest of the dogs by the side of the barn; he isn't going t' stay and argue with bloody kids.

- We'll bring y' back a slice of bacon, Uncle Owl says to Maverick. And a piece 'f Grandfather too.

- He nearly killed Mut as well, Judd says to Uncle Honk.

- Pity he di'n't.

The dog in question goes as if to run on ahead, but ends up doing a tight circle back to Uncle Owl.

Uncle Honk, Uncle Owl and Judd set out towards the river, Judd running in front.

Maverick snivels because he's been left behind.

- Pito doesn't mind being left behind, Nerida says to him in an Aunty Grin voice.

Just as they are leaving, there is a voice from Grandfather's glass tower. It is thin and reedy and has a crackle in it.

- You bloody clowns cdn't hit th side of a house at twenty yards.

Uncle Honk does not deign to reply.

They walk in silence, Judd leading the way. The weather has closed in and they are walking through stringy grey mist. As they draw closer, they can feel the massive movement of boulders down the river bed through their feet. Mut casts more than one apprehensive glance towards the source of the noise, for once not ranging maniacally forward but keeping near Uncle Owl and walking almost delicately.

Uncle Honk walks tense, alert, pushing indifferently through the gorse, his head thrust forward, keeping a close eye on the behaviour of Ran and Billy. Their air of restrained excitement suggests that the boar is not far off. Uncle Owl saunters along in the rear, apparently enjoying the damp walk, swinging the light .22 in one arm, a dead roll-your-own hanging from his mouth.

Judd leads them to the shingle bank where Mut leapt bravely into the bush. Mut is not leaping bravely now, but hangs back head lowered.

- That dog's a born coward, Uncle Honk says. Mut looks back at him sadly.

Ran and Billy pick up the trail, blithely dashing past the scene of Mut's close encounter with death. Judiciously, Mut chooses another route.

- He'll go south, Uncle Owl moves the stick of ash to the other side of his mouth. - He'll follow the river up on the south side.

Ran and Billy trot purposefully into the bush. Uncle Honk hesitates.

- Y' never know with wild boar. Y' never bloody know.

With the thick gorse shoulder height, it isn't the best terrain for pig hunting. Motioning Judd back, he moves forward after the dogs, cursing the scratching gorse. Uncle Owl follows moving sideways, hip forward through the gorse, grinning at Judd who brings up the rear. Judd does the best he can to keep up, pushing back the spiny branches with two pieces of wood.

They come to a small clearing and Uncle Honk stops again. They can't move fast enough through this scrub to hunt anything. Even the pig dogs are slowed up, running back and forth along the gorse line sniffing. Uncle Honk turns back the way they came and looks north towards the river line. In the mist, there is nothing to see but densities and shadings. They might have been walking across an endless shingle flat.

The boar comes straight out of the scrub from that direction and stands stock still. Ran and Billy don't even see it they are so busy sniffing the scrub on the other side of the clearing. Uncle Honk swears softly and eases his rifle down off his shoulder. The boar swings its head in Uncle Owl and Judd's direction, taking them in in one swift, bitter glance. Mut sees the animal and panics. Uncle Honk is swinging the rifle in the boar's direction when Mut flings himself into the line of fire. Honk takes two steps forward and falls over the fear-crazed dog, his rifle clattering down on the hard ground. Mut yelps and leaps for the protection of Uncle Owl's legs. No one but Uncle Owl sees the boar move. One moment it is there, the next it is not. Uncle Owl is laughing so hard he almost doesn't get a shot away, but he does, triumphantly pumping a piece of lead into the boar's departing rump. The animal gives a squeal of outrage and Uncle Owl laughs even harder, having to double up through lack of breath. Belatedly, Ran and Billy give chase.

Uncle Honk recovers his rifle and gets to his feet. He is not laughing. His face is blotched red and purple. He swings the rifle up until he has Mut in its sights. Moving with great agility, Uncle Owl leaps forward and knocks the barrel aside. He is still laughing. A bullet screams uselessly off into the gorse. Judd crouches.

- Dumb fucken dog! Uncle Honk convulsively works the bolt of his rifle. - I cd of had th bastard. He ws starin right down th barrel at me.

Uncle Owl is trembling. His voice trembles too - It wasn't th dog's fault. Th boar came right at im. Any dog wd of jumped. That's one big side of bacon.

- With a twenty-two slug up its arse, Uncle Honk says sneeringly. - Now we've got a wounded animal on our hands.

Uncle Owl grins. - He won't be doin much sittin around, y' cn bet yr arse on that.

- Maybe I'll kill you. Uncle Honk's voice is ugly as he swings the gun around. Uncle Owl's face goes the colour of mist.

They hunt for the rest of the day and don't see any sign of Pig.

The pig is still there. Even standing off to one side with the children, watching the grocery truck arrive from the plains, Judd can feel it, can feel its abrupt piggy eyes staring into his. If he is sure of anything, it is that the pig is near the house. Uncle Honk seems to feel the same thing, for even while talking to the grocer, his eyes wander off towards Scrubby Flat.

The grocer is a big man with a florid face and a white apron. He huffs and puffs as he pulls out a sack of flour. - I tell y', he says between breaths, it got so cold down Arratown way that a bloke's hand froze, dropped off an' grew again.

Uncle Owl laughs unnaturally hard; he is peering into the boxes in the back of the truck. Judd's trying to do the same thing.

- But I'll tell y' somethin I did hear. Y' know on th Coast they've got these wasps jus' takin over whole areas? Places y' jus' can't go because there're so many of im. Me sister's family went there, up some river fr a picnic, and th wasps came, thousands of th bastards. They had t' sit in th car f' two hours with all th windas wound up because they cdn't even see t' drive.

Uncle Honk says nothing. He is picking up bags and weighing them in his hand as if his hands were scales. Uncle Owl looks as if he is about to climb into the back of the truck.

- We got wasps around here, Uncle Owl says, trying to smile, rubbing his hands on his trousers. Judd jumps onto the tailboard and peers into the boxes.

Uncle Honk gives Judd a dirty look.

Father comes up and stares curiously at the truck. He prods the bonnet as if it were living thing. Uncle Honk gives him a dirty look too. Father studies the catches that hold the bonnet.

- Everybody wants t' come here. The grocer pulls out a banana box and jumps it to the ground. It is made of wooden slats with a wooden partition dividing it in two. Both compartments are filled with tins. - Did y' hear about them spiders? Y' see, some tigermoth pilot seen these funny fluffy things in th air, blowin across Cook Strait fr'm north t' south, and y' know what they were? Bloody Spiders. Spiders on fluffy cushions they made themselves f'gettin around in th air. And y' know what they ws doin? He waits, unpacking several tins. - Comin down here on a fucken holiday.

Uncle Owl and Uncle Honk laugh obligingly. The grocer wipes his face with a handkerchief. - What about the bill? he says to Uncle Honk. Uncle Honk leans sideways and puts his hands in his pockets like a man searching for money. Uncle Owl gets preoccupied with the box.

- I got t' talk t' Pi, Uncle Honk says, and, quick as a skip, he's off for the kitchen. Uncle Owl immediately engages in a hurried, whispered conversation with the grocer. Father leans over the mudguard and pulls up the catches of the bonnet. He knows about engines, that's what the war is all about; fixing engines. Fixing them and blowing them up. Fixing them and blowing them up. Fixing them and blowing them up.

Judd is about to nip into the back of the truck when Aunty Pi approaches, Uncle Honk a few feet behind. Judd looks around quickly for a place to hide, but thinks the better of it and holds his ground. Aunty Pi looks disapprovingly at the children, who draw back a few feet. Judd pretends he's not standing on the tailboard and suffers Pi's stony scrutiny.

The grocer nods politely. - Good morning Mrs.

- Good mornin Mr Johnson. I hope Mrs Johnson is well. Aunty Pi's voice is all frosted sweetness.

- She cn still bake th best scones this side of th black stump.

- I'm sure she can. Aunty Pi hands the grocer an envelope. - This should just about cover last month. We're a bit short this month.

Mr Johnson sighs - Everybody's a bit short these days, Mrs. I got t' pay f' th stuff too.

- You'll get yr money next month. Aunty Pi uses her no non-sense, end of discussion voice and the grocer affects a shrug and a thoughtful silence.

There's a shout from the house; it's Grandfather in his glass-tower, shouting from one of the windows, the same witchy cackle. - Bob, y' old son of a gun. I see you're as fat as ever.

The grocer turns gratefully in the direction of the distraction. - Dunno how! I run on th smell of an oily rag, y' know. Never see th square end of a feed.

- It's all them scones, Bob. Bring some for me next time y' come. They're starvin me out up here.

Aunty Pi snorts with contempt. Judd sees what he's looking for at the back of the truck. Carving knives. Pig knives. Hunting knives. Knives made for slicing and sticking.

- Did y' bring any shells, Bob? .22s or .303s?

- I got a couple of extra boxes.

- Bring im over here.

The grocer walks with a fat man's waddle back to the truck. Aunty Pi looks sharply at Uncle Honk.

- He's got nothin t' pay f' them with, Uncle Honk calls out after the grocer. A rope snakes out of Grandfather's room with something attached. It hits the ground with a dull noise. The grocer tips something into his hands and they can all see the shining coins. Aunty Pi's face tightens. The grocer ties the boxes to the rope. - Y' goin t' be doin some huntin? he calls up.

Father lifts the bonnet and stares in at the engine. There are black things in there, shapes in sweating metal, and he doesn't have a clue what they signify. He stares broken hearted into the engine and begins to cry.

Judd slides across the tailboard into the back of the truck. The knives, he sees, are laid loosely in a roll of canvas.

- I cd blow th tail off a rabbit on Scrubby Flat from up here, Grandfather shouts. - I cd pick off a deer on the Dog-leg. The grocer laughs. Up at the window, Grandfather's head waggles. - I cd shoot aroun' corners an' still shoot straighter than these clowns. They went out after boar th other day. Honk tried t' shoot th dog an' Owl put a .22 slug up th pig's bum! They call that huntin! I thought I better get some shells up in case th boar comes wanderin inta th yard lookin f' someone t' finish th job.

The grocer laughs harder. Judd bends down and touches one of the long hunting knives. He knows what a blade like that will do; he's seen

Uncle Honk using his. A knife like that will go right through the belly of a boar. Even through that tough, hairy skin.

When he returns to the truck the grocer is still laughing. Judd hops out, empty handed. A knife is too big to steal any safe way. And Aunty Pi is around, she'd sniff out something like that in five seconds flat.

Aunty Pi's face is frozen in disapproval. - Next month is alright, the Grocer says to Aunty Pi. Her face does not change.

- What th hell, the grocer says. He's just seen Father, sitting up in the cab behind the wheel, staring mournfully out the windscreen towards the road and the river. He'd drive somewhere, if he remembered how to drive; he'd go somewhere if he knew where to go. Of course any movement could attract the attention of predatory eyes in the sky. He gets out of the cab when the sergeant opens the door. Bugger it, let the sarge drive then. Let him take the flak, the tracers that arced through the sky like live eyes.

As the truck pulls away, Uncle Owl leaps onto the sideboard and speaks fervently through the window. - I'll hold y't' that, they hear the grocer say. He hands a package over that goes straight into Uncle Owl's pocket.

Aunty Pi's voice is like chipped ice. Why can't y' stop this, Honk? Why can't y' put y' foot down. Owl's got a lot t' answer for.

Uncle Honk twists away, like a dog on a leash. - Owl's 'is own boss, he says in a low, growling voice.

Aunty Pi turns on her heel. The children get out of her way.

- I've had a gutsful of this, Aunty Pi says. - An absolute gutsful.

She sweeps through the children as if they weren't there.

Uncle Owl runs for the house, sideways like a crab.

Judd walks away, his hands full of the knife he couldn't steal. His eyes lift up to the Knee of the Dog-leg, and across to Scrubby Flat. One day he'll get it. He'll hold it in his hands and know what to do with it. He'll touch its blade and draw its blood.

There is only one way to do it. He will have to steal Uncle Honk's pig knife.

Sure as hell that'll be worth a thrashin.

Princess and Pito

DEEP POOL is not as deep as it once was, even after a flood, but deep enough for a Princess and her consort, Pito, to take off their clothes and frolic in the icy water that flows off the mountains. They are safely hidden from the house by the boulders that protect the pool. This shields them from Grandfather's prying eyes and from Aunty Pi, who would not approve of them wandering when there was a wounded boar loose. Or frolicking in any shape or form with their clothes off.

They splash each other frantically and leap about squealing with the cold, the spray creating t UNCLE HONK has just fed the dogs iny, temporary rainbows in the air about them. She uses their shared nakedness to draw close to him, and draw him close to her, entering his playfulness, pinching and rubbing him till he glows with joy. Then they lie on a rock like a couple of lizards drawing strength into their bodies from the sun. While they are lying there, Princess sees a red admiral butterfly swinging across the pool, its light, jagged, zig-zag movement in counterpoint to the deep, secretive swirl of the water.

She knows a sudden sense of expansion, as if she's just grown a couple of inches. The butterfly alights on a rock, igniting its grey with red, moves its wings in trembling slow motion a couple of times, like church windows opening and shutting, before taking off, quicker than the eye can follow, over the bunched stones of the river bed.

- Did you see't, Pito?

Pito nods but he has gone quiet. She hates his quiet mood for it opens a sad, empty space inside her, making the air around her sad and empty too. His moments of forgetfulness and joy are often followed by a sudden cooling inner reflection, as if they have brought him up sharp against some secret image in his mind that joy only makes more poignant, more unbearable. Not wanting to break the froth of the mood, Princess jumps to her feet. They dress quickly and race across the stones, Pito in the lead.

He seems to have lost all caution and is jumping recklessly from stone to stone, pretending to be crossing a frantic torrent.

- This one! This one! he shouts, pointing ahead.

- I can't jump that, Pito!

- I bet I can.

- Bet y' can't

- Bet I can.

- Bet y' can't.

But he can and does, landing on his own rock a swirling torrent away from her. His slight body pivots in the air.

- See!

It is not fair that he should dance away from her just when she's worked so hard to loosen him up. Not fair. Not fair that he won't tell her the great secret she is sure he is hiding from her. She won't tell anybody else. She has to know, doesn't he see that? She is the Princess and he her consort and magician; there can be no secrets between them. Doesn't he see that? He is not permitted to use his magic to escape from her. Not her, the Princess. She has the right of priority.

He gives no indication of seeing it, and shouts with laughter, turns his face to the sun which makes it luminous, sallow as a lily. He makes exaggerated jumping motions to make her laugh, leaping back in fear at imaginary torrents of water, pretending to slip. He is often like that when they are out of earshot and sight of Grandfather; a sudden gaiety hits him and he leaps about as if the air were full of angels and he was one of them. He shares, partakes, in that radiance.

Obligingly, she laughs.

- Tell me, Toetoe, why are y' afraid 'f Grandfather?

- I can't tell y'.

- Y' must. Y' just must. Y' got t'.

She makes the jump to his rock. They cling to each other as the torrent rages around them.

- Y' see, I'm a prince who's been banished here by an evil wizard. When th spell is broken, I'll take you t' my kingdom. His voice is serious but there is mischief in his eyes.

Nerida would believe him, and there was a time when Princess might have believed him too and built it into the game. Now she pulls a face. He is her consort and shouldn't make fun of her, nor hide behind his enchantment. Nor mock the game with make-believe. And he should tell her his great secret.

Pito is off to the next rock before she can go into a sulk.

Now they have to sneak back by the secret trail that hides their approach from Grandfather's tower, and Pito grows quiet, his movements becoming quick and sly.

Watching his slim, dark figure slipping through the tussock, Princess hopes fervently that she will die before he does.

At one time, there was a little girl with an ordinary name we're not going to tell yet, who, on the day old Wakefield's faithful mate Hattie died of wind in the stomach, climbed astride the still quivering neck and hacked a horn off with a hacksaw she'd found in the barn. While she hacked, she felt the great earth warmth of the beast seep up through her thighs and groin into her body. Dust went up in little spurts in front of the just dead animal's nostrils as if it were panting with her exertions. When the horn came free in her hand she held it up triumphantly to the rest of the watching children, renounced her ordinary name and declared,

- I am the Princess.

Even Judd couldn't have done that.

The game had begun, her kingdom founded. Her priority established.

When she got off Hattie and came over to them, she walked differently, held herself differently, spoke differently, sharply correcting Judd when he tried using her old, ordinary name. This was the Princess and they all had their assigned roles in the game.

Later, holding court with the cow's horn in her hand, she would recount how she had heard the great beast's vegetative thoughts winding down in a pasture of silence as she hacked; how its spirit came away in her hand when the horn was severed. She told them how sometimes Hattie's muscles would jerk, giving the girl a fright all through her body. How Hattie's head had shaken from side to side as she hacked, and how a thin line of red foam had bubbled from the cow's fat white lips as if she was trying to talk to them in the language of blood.

Nerida, the Princess's first devotee, covered her mouth with her hand when she heard this part of the story.

With this great deed of bravery, sitting astride death itself, the girl became the ruler of the kingdom, and her rule is absolute. It encompasses the house and the grounds around, particularly the barn which is freer than the house of the influence of adults. But it does not include Grandfather's tower, where other powers rule, nor the kingdom of the kitchen, where Aunty Pi reigns supreme and Mother is her slave.

Sometimes the game begins as soon as she wakes up in the morning — when she will call to Nerida in a special, imperial voice — until they go to bed at night, loftily commanding Judd to turn out the light; and sometimes, even when they are not directly playing it, it will be there in the background, hidden in an intonation, assumed in a gesture.

The game.

She is the Princess and Pito is her consort. Only reluctantly did the older boys accept Pito and his position, Nerida alone is adoring, and magicked by Pito's spells.

At the best of times, they will all play together. General Judd taking his right hand man, Maverick, to patrol the frontiers and fight wars, while Nerida plays lady-in-waiting, and the princess develops endless plans for her royal marriage to her consort. At the worst of times, Judd will rebel and stomp off with Maverick to play his own game, Nerida will sit listless with nothing to do, staring off into the distance like a bridesmaid who has no hope of catching the bouquet, and Pito is unreachable, caught in the chains of his own enchantment.

With the arrival of Princess, Pito came into his own and found a role for himself as chief magician as well as the Royal Bridegroom. The shy, dark-eyed boy who'd always been on the periphery became an important string to her bow; his quiet and his agelessness tended to subdue the others. Judd in particular could hardly meet his eye. Besides, he was more than just her consort, he was an important wizard, able to see the future, visit the dead in the underworld where Hattie lived, or hear Grandfather thinking. She leans on him more than she knows, and it makes her frightened, especially when he gets too quiet and a prey to his own spells. That was there from the beginning, from his emergence; he could always pull back again. He could always make himself invisible. And there is one spell stronger than his; he must never be spotted from Grandfather's tower.

She told them on one occasion, to bolster his image, that the Cow Goddess, Hattie, was Pito's real mother and that she'd given birth to him before Judd and Nerida were born.

- How come I don't remember that? said Maverick, the eldest and who could therefore remember everything.

- Because you ws sick, Princess said in her special, infallible voice.

Judd did not believe but he pretended to — all that's required. The game became ritual.

The princess too, she hinted, had had a special birth, but when pressed on the issue by Nerida, who was more than ready to believe, she fell silent and put on her never-you-mind face. If Pito could have secrets so could she.

Now, Judd and Maverick rarely play; only when Princess can cajole them into it. Judd is sick of being a General all the time, especially since his whole army consists of Maverick and Mut. And he is sick of having to report back to the princess all the time, sick of having to call her Princess and sick of having to defer to Pito.

Nerida keeps faith as lady-in-waiting from time to time, and the game goes on, but the magic horn has returned to being an ordinary, silly old cow's horn with nothing but its memories. Princess keeps her title even as her kingdom pales, though there are still nights when her mind is ablaze with the splendour of her eventual wedding, her union with her divine consort.

Pito won't go up to Grandfather's tower with the other children, even when they tease and cajole him as they will do, Princess especially, with all her snaky charm.

As the step-ladder comes out of the broom-cupboard and the boys fuss with its details, Princess and the sycophantic Nerida appear on either side of the boy like two suggestive spirits.

- Please, Toetoe, Princess says in shameless and craven appeal, making her eyes large and soft, pushing her lips out, a voice of tender innocence, - Princess won't love y' any more.

- Yes, please Toetoe, Nerida says in chorus. - He gives us wine biscuits, all soft an' sweet, and makes tea fr us.

Pito is shaken but remains silently adamant. Even Princess, who can lure him into anything, can't compel him up through the black hole in the ceiling to Grandfather's room.

- Grandfather doesn't keep rats, that's just a story Aunty Pi tells t' scare us, Princess says, doing a good job of hiding her own little worm of fear. She is after all the princess, sweet as sucked clover yet proud as the thorn; fear does not become a princess. - We are his friends. He calls us his little mice an' shows us his treasures.

- Yes, says Nerida, particularly pleased to have someone else's fears to smile about, - an' sometimes we fly with him over th mountains! She lifts her teddy and rushes him through the air to demonstrate. Teddy's fixed, amber stare passes right through Pito.

Then Pito draws a cloak of mystery about himself. His eyebrows draw together, his gaze becomes dark, fixed on things the girls cannot see. His great secret.

Firmly, he says, - Grandfather wd not like t' see me.

And when the ladder is up and the opaque square of mystery appears in the ceiling, a shadow crosses his face and his large, solemn eyes grow larger and more solemn, while his mouth, small and sensitive, is weakened by fear.

Devoted as she is to Pito, Princess will not forgo these visits to Grandfather. As she stands on the bottom rung of the ladder pulling at her brown curls, Judd and Maverick already clambering up through the trapdoor, a tense moment ensues in which love turns to pain. Half her body swings the other way as she climbs, wanting to return her to his side.

Pito watches as they all disappear to the upper world; Maverick first because he is the eldest and a boy, Judd next because he is also a boy, Princess and Nerida coming up behind, Nerida last since she is the youngest and a girl, all swallowed by the square mouth in the ceiling. For a few moments after they have gone he continues gazing upward as if he can see right up past Grandfather through to the heavens.

For the others, looking down from the dim world of rafters and musty distances, or already started upon the ladder up to the tower, Pito's face becomes a pale blotch in the cave of light below, swaying on top of a ridiculously foreshortened body, inviting somebody like Judd to lean forward and make the motions of spitting down, even sending a glob of real spit floating through the gloom towards the figure below, whose face is suddenly that of a baby.

For Princess, the ascent is like entering another medium. The gloom of the world of the rafters is like an aquatic kingdom for all its attic dryness. The air is different here, drier, cooler, with a faint acidic stench. The shadows oceanic and moving.

She turns one last time and whispers down to Pito. - I won't tell him 'bout you.

Above lies Grandfather's kingdom.

The journey to Grandfather's room is long and perilous; a still, dust-shot region lit by wisps of light. The ladder up which the children move has been made out of left-over pieces of framing and old scaffolding nailed into the studs and nogs. It looks like the sort of job Uncle Owl and Uncle Honk might do when there is no one around to see them, no one to complain but the old man and who gives a stuff about him? He will probably never come down anyway.

For Princess, leaving Pito behind and moving up the tower on these unsteady rungs is to move into a dark, creaky place that smells sharply of Grandfather's rats. Of course, they are not Grandfather's rats especially, but they live in the roof, along with Grandfather, and Aunty Pi herself calls them Grandfather's rats; they belong to him by association. At times during her ascent, Princess hears them scrabbling in the eaves and imagines them busy on Grandfather's business, scurrying to carry out his commands.

Then she pushes her face against the weatherboards and peers through the cracks to see the reassuring world outside, beyond the garden and Wakefield placidly browsing, to the cows beyond and the whole sweep of the dissolute river bed falling away from the hills.

Above her, Maverick and Judd are jollying each other along with jokes about Pito, hissing to one another like excited snakes, bolstering their courage with his fear, peering on up through the striped gloom. Below her, Nerida waits patiently, her teddy between her teeth, both hands held grimly to the rungs.

The next crisis is arriving at the trapdoor into Grandfather's room and knocking upon it as if it were an ordinary door, with taps as polite as ever so. Maverick admits no fear of Grandfather in his tower. Boldly, he will claim to be on close terms with Grandfather, his secret ally even, but he knocks timorously on the trapdoor as if he really were a mouse.

Jammed in under the floor with Judd pushing from below, banging his fists upward while holding his eyes against any descending dust, Maverick feels the full weight of being the eldest and a boy. With all the sloping dark behind, the tiny eye of the open trapdoor far below, there he is, fully discomforted and obliged to be unafraid.

The next moments are dramatic:

- WHO'S THERE? a voice booms, and feet walk over the sky.

- It's us, Grandfather, the fearless Maverick replies, - yr little mice come t' visit.

- MY LITTLE MICE! A banging from above. - AND WHAT WOULD LITTLE MICE BE WANTIN NIBBLIN AT M' FLOOR¬BOARDS? MISCHIEF? I'VE NOTHIN T' STEAL, NO CRUSTS SALTED AWAY. MY CRUSTS'VE ALREADY BEEN STOLEN.

- We don't want t' steal, Grandfather. We've jus' come t' visit.

Maverick issues these protestations and keeps his voice from wobbling while Judd pushes at him from below.

- WHAT? MICE WHO DO NOT WISH T' STEAL! WHO'S EVER HEARD OF MICE LIKE THAT? BUT TELL ME BEFORE Y' START TELLIN LIES AGAIN, IS MY LITTLE WHITE MOUSE THERE?

This is Princess's cue. - It's me, Grandfather, yr special little white mouse.

She has a special little white mouse voice with a special little white mouse quaver to go with it, much admired by Nerida.

- AND IS SNEAKY MOUSE THERE? SNEAKY MOUSE IS ALWAYS PLOTTIN AN' PLANNIN. HE HAS T' BE WATCHED.

- Sneaky Mouse is here too, Judd answers. Grandfather will never let him forget the time he took the last piece of cake off the plate when Grandfather, who happened to have designs on it himself, wasn't watching. It was the timing as much as anything that infuriated Grandfather on that occasion. On another occasion, he caught Judd peering under the bed where he keeps several rifles.

- AND MY CHURCHMOUSE?

Nerida has prepared for this moment by taking Teddy out of her mouth and calls with all her might, - Yr Churchmouse is here, Grandfather.

- AND WHERE DOES M' LITTLE CHURCHMOUSE LIVE?

- In a church, Grandfather.

- AND WHERE IS THE BEST PLACE IN THE CHURCH FR A LITTLE CHURCHMOUSE T' LIVE?

- Among the bells, Grandfather, the bells. Teddy nods.

- VERY GOOD. AND IS MY TRUSTY MOUSE STILL THERE?

- Your Trusty Mouse is still here, Grandfather, says Maverick, relieved that the ritual is coming to an end yet dreading the final twist of it.

- IZAT ALL? the voice demands suspiciously. - ARE Y' SURE Y' HAVEN'T BROUGHT ANY OTHER LITTLE MOUSE RIDIN ALONG WITH Y? SOME LITTLE SILENT ONE WHO'LL STEAL EVERYTHING FROM ME?

All of them think of Pito. His upturned face. His fear.

- There's no one else, Grandfather, Maverick says in his Trusty Mouse voice. - No one else.

The bravest of liars.

Up goes the trapdoor in a burst of light.

Grandfather rules from his glass tower. His windowed attic, perched on top of the house, gives him command of all four directions and their fractions. Before him, to the south, lies Dairy Flat and the swathe of white boulders Princess has already glimpsed. Behind him, to the north, the hills pull steeply back, eternally dry and bony, bulging towards the mountains that crowd close behind. Across the river bed, the huge cut of the valley sees Grandfather's kingdom stretch from the west to the north, following the line of the Southern Alps.

Behind the head of his bed, behind sheeted folds of hillside, rises Snowy Peak, remote and aloof, pristine in the sun, or looming and shrouded under cloud. Old Snowy, the adults like to call it, and the children do the same; phrases like *oh, he died two years ago up on Old Snowy or Old Snowy's cuttin the wind tonight* impress the children greatly.

Entry into Grandfather's room involves a strictly observed protocol. Princess goes first since it is more politic for the others to come in the wake of his favourite. She has to climb past the boys to do it. The Princess always smiles for Grandfather his favourite smile, a smile that would melt Old Snowy himself. Behind her comes Nerida, for what is less intimidating than a little Churchmouse, giggling and hiding her mouth behind Teddy's somewhat unravelled smile Then Maverick emerges, his Trusty Mouse with trusty smile to the ready, nodding and bowing in deference, not happy until he is joined by Judd, who doesn't pretend to smile at Grandfather and will not meet his eye. Sneaky Mouse lives up to his name.

As they come through, blinking in the hard light, Grandfather steps back past his bed as if he would step right out into the landscape; the room is small but seems vast. There is not much in it but a bed, half a dozen jerry-cans full of water, and a couple of chairs.

Once they are assembled, Grandfather becomes very jolly.

- All aboard! all aboard! m' little mice. Y've come t' see y' poor old Grandfather on his ship. Shall we go sailin, shall we go sailin over th mountains?

The boys say nothing. They are too old to go sailing over the mountains. Grandfather tends to forget that his little mice grow, and that Nerida is the only one young enough to really want to go sailing over the mountains. And when her main ally, Princess, claps her hands for joy, it is more to keep the old man sweet than to play their time honoured game. As Nerida scrambles for the privileged spot up on Grandfather's bed where she can see right around the horizon, the boys keep their silence; since Grandfather's tower is beyond the rule of the house, and so beyond the rule of Aunty Pi, they are not sure how to react. Since Grandfather shamelessly indulges the girls, while casting suspicious glances at the boys, it is their better wisdom to bide their time and to hold their eyes from moving too directly around the room.

Princess's main delight is Grandfather's box of treasures. Once he took from it a small stone he told them was a frozen kea's eye. It stayed frozen even when the ice went out of it. He has some small, perfectly round stones as neat as sheep's droppings that came from the stomach of a moa. He has a huge, shiny, polished ball-bearing he says came from the innards of an abandoned Ferguson tractor. He just found it there in among the grease, the rust and the exhaustion of iron.

Maverick and Judd are particularly envious of this possession, and Grandfather will not let them hold it.

He has two other strange dark stones he said fell to earth out of a shell of light. He saw it himself, the shell of light opening up into a necklace of sparks that jumped towards the ground. The next day he went out, climbed right over the Dog-leg and found them exactly where he thought they'd be, although he only found two.

He has a flower that blooms eternally inside a rock as clear as glass, and a piece of glass as dense and opaque as rock. He has a spiral shell crusted onto a piece of greywacke which, he says, proves that at one time the sea covered the mountains.

He even has a piece of gold no bigger than his fingernail shaped miraculously in the likeness of Old Snowy. All the features of the mountain can be traced in miniature; the knolls, the shingle-fans, the smooth steep upper reaches, the final lumpy summit. When he shows them this, Grandfather never lets it out of his sight.

Most of these objects carry with them, as part of their essential shape and mystery, a story, usually of their finding by Grandfather. Some of them, without these stories, might look very ordinary at first glance, hardly worthy of notice. One of these is a small fishhook worn curiously smooth and set beside an ordinary empty baked-beans can. The fishhook he found in the belly of a hawk he shot. He was preparing for breakfast out in the mountains one morning when he saw a hawk circling above him. Feeling uneasy at having the predator lazing around in the sky like that he took his rifle and downed it, as much for target practice as anything else, he said. Besides, a full grown hawk will kill a lamb. He knew that since he'd seen one lift a lamb right into the air.

He walked the few hundred yards to collect the bird, leaving his billy on the boil and an unopened can of baked beans beside the fire. When he found the bird, he slit it open to see what it had been feeding on and found the fishhook. Upon returning to his campfire, he discovered the tin of baked beans open, the contents vanished, and kea droppings all around. The remarkable thing is, he said, that the can had been neatly opened around the edge, as if a can-opener had done the work. He had the can to prove it, to prove that keas have beaks like can-openers.

Princess is fascinated by the way their histories hide inside these curiosities, invisible to the eye yet part of their fabric. It is like the way Pito holds his secret to himself. She likes to hold them, to feel their mute weight, to close her eyes and listen to their stories.

So Nerida and Teddy and Grandfather and Princess go sailing in his glass ship over the tussock-covered hills, over the mountains, over the snow, over the plain and city, with Princess pretending to go along and the boys looking the other way, Judd biding his time.

- High as a hawk, Grandfather says gleefully, as if he were riding over the mountains too, a little boy breaking out in his laugh. - A kea's beak'll open a can of baked beans but nothin but a hairyplane'll fly higher than a hawk.

Nerida squeals and their glass ship soars so high they look right over the peaks towards the West Coast where the rain boils against the mountains. There is a jungle there, Grandfather says, full of worms the size of snakes and spiders as big as plates. It's so wet the cows piss water into the milk cans and the feet of the sheep all rot if they stand in one place for too long. There are giant redback spiders as big as fists, and spiders that jump into the air and catch birds, and spiders with burrows as big as those of rabbits. And wetas as fat as your fist that could kill you with one bite.

They don't want to land in such an inhospitable place so they fly higher, high enough to see the brown, patchwork plains pushing east against the sea on one side, and the turbulent western coastline on the other. The glass ship goes so high that soon everything is lost in a great canopy of grey and green ocean, a tiny, uncertain slab of land beneath.

At this point Nerida holds on tight to the bed and closes her eyes. She doesn't entirely believe in the ocean; of all of Grandfather's stories it is this she finds hardest to credit. She laughs and giggles until she is giddy, and whenever Grandfather mentions the ocean she giggles more. Princess drives her further into giddiness and giggling by miming a hawk rider clinging to the hawk's neck, swaying this way and that in the abandon of winds, almost falling off the bed, causing Nerida to do the same, Teddy going into his own hectic orbit, while Grandfather laughs and describes the great ocean to them, how it is stretched from horizon to horizon and held across the curve of the world by its surface tension.

If she is prepared to fall herself, Princess can induce Nerida to fall also, have her plunge screaming towards the floor while the boys look on, disgusted. Grandfather however smiles and nods at the girls with a peculiar triumph, as if their foolery is his doing.

Then his gaze turns on the boys and his wiry body goes stiff, as if he were about to spring.

When the game is over, Princess proceeds to charm the old man, unabashedly praising his room and his view, his very person, smiling and blushing all the while, until he begins muttering and fishing about in his cupboard and finds a packet of wine biscuits or gingernuts, gone soft but still good for dunking into tea served weak in enamel camping mugs. Her flattery is smooth, so voluble and faultless, the boys and Nerida stare at her in amazement. Some sly devil has her tongue, extracting from Grandfather even some last, crumbling pieces of cake Mother would have sent up, slipping it past Aunty Pi's rigorous scrutiny.

- What a lovely room y' have, Grandfather, with so many windows all around, in every wall, so much light, it must be like livin in th sky. Y' cn talk t' Snowy Peak or fly as high as a hawk anytime y' want with nobody but yr little mice t' bother you, t' scratch at your door an' gobble up all yr food.

As she talks her body sways back and forth in a show of devotion, her hands inscribing graceful shapes upon the air. Judd sneers but Nerida nods in time to the chanting voice. She likes the idea of Grandfather talking to Old Snowy, telling it the stories of his treasures, or when to snow and when to be sunny, things like that. And if the mountain answers back, it will be in the voice of Grandfather too, only deeper, perhaps; she can't imagine the mountain having any other voice.

- Show us a treasure, Grandfather.

- If y' promise not t' steal it. Little mice have eyes only f' stealin.

- We promise.

- Cross y' heart an' swear t' die?

- Cross m' heart an' swear t' die.

Princess does it first and the others follow, Nerida fervently, the boys liturgically.

And he shows them. It is a gold coin he calls a sovereign. On one side it shows the head of a King of England, on the other a coat of heraldry. There was a battle, Grandfather says, between a lion and a unicorn. The children do not understand Grandfather's confused explanations but, held up in the sunlight, the coin speaks with its own polished voice.

Then Grandfather flicks it and it rises, turning over and over until it has reached its peak. At that moment, just before its descent begins, it hangs there, high in Grandfather's glass room, a tiny emissary of the sun, spreading its golden light around.

While the Dog-leg provides a better vantage point, it is the slender view of the plains afforded by Grandfather's room that draws Princess. She knows there are roads and towns out there; she has heard of the towns, places with empty names like Windwhistle, Hororata and Stony Gap. Places that are no more than a bare railway siding, a couple of unpainted state houses and a dirt road leading off to nowhere. It makes her feel funny about Pito, thinking of those places, and a further place, a city, where one day they might have to go to school. She can't imagine Pito out there, going to school in a city, and her heart aches fiercely just trying.

- I cn see a green smudge, she says, daring the world to grow bigger than her passion.

Grandfather nods. He is showing Nerida something. - It's called a Maori rubbing stone, he is saying. - See how it's hollowed here, that's where someone's thumb has been wearin away at it.

Nerida takes the stone and fits her thumb into it. - Why d' they do it?

- To give im somethin t' do with their hands. People need t' do things with their hands otherwise they start stealin fr'm their neighbours. I ws in Greece once. There th men have worry beads. They sit an' flick im through their fingers, around an' around. Grandfather demonstrates.

- Why?

- So they cn put their worries inta th beads. All their worries go out 'f their fingers and enters them beads. This stone's th same kind of thing. Th Maoris put all their rubs inta th stone.

He holds the stone up and looks at it critically. - This stone's collected plenty of rubs.

- Grandfather! Cn y' see th bridge from up here? I've never noticed it before.

Grandfather nods calmly to Princess and continues rubbing the stone.

- Y' cn, sometimes, in th right light, see a car cross over.

Nerida has taken the stone and is adding a few rubs to its collection. Princess, her hand daringly on Grandfather's arm, points to the gap in the hills where the river runs through onto the plains. He makes a face as if to spit and waves a scrawny arm. His arm is so scrawny Maverick often says it reminds him of the leg of an old rooster. He's even heard Uncle Owl referring to Grandfather as that old rooster. As further evidence, he cited the flap of red skin that hangs down under Grandfather's jaw behind his beard.

- I never thought y' cd see as far as th bridge.

- Y' may, Grandfather attests with a regal nod, as if Princess were somehow permitted to see the bridge by royal dispensation. - And in certain lights y' cn catch Old Snowy's beard, or see th woman's face in th granite hill ten miles north of here.

Princess's mind is bounding with his eyes over the plain.

- Y' cn see right across th plains, he says in a stern voice, as if Princess doubts the fact.

- Cn y' see th Port Hills? Princess asks, not knowing how far she can push it.

- Yes. Grandfather speaks with an air of finality, which is his favourite tone. - In special conditions y' cn see th Port Hills.

He waits.

- Cn y' see Christchurch?

All the children are still now, watching Grandfather.

- A little dirty gauze of smoke, sometimes, his bony arm outstretched - when th wind dies.

His voice dies with the wind. His finger points over foreshortened, shimmering stretches to man's fallen condition.

- Christchurch, he proclaims with perverse satisfaction.
Uncle Owl is watching them as they come out of the ceiling; he stands in the doorway to his room at the end of the hall, leaning against the door-jamb observing their hurried descent with a half smile.

- Silly as chooks! His slurred voice is rough and mocking but not unkind. - God knows what sort of silly ideas you've been lappin up. Did he tell y' 'bout th goat he shot whose heart wdn't stop beatin? Or th kea that opened a can of beans? Or the cat they cdn't drown?

Nerida runs to him. - Uncle Owl! Grandfather has a big glass ship, we cn go sailin over th mountains.

She likes Uncle Owl because he smiles and never locks her in the wardrobe, and seems to mean no harm by the strange things he says or the occasional swipe of his hand in her direction.

Uncle Owl tousles her hair. - And I'm th tooth fairy!

He doesn't look like the tooth fairy with his long drooping face and bony, drooping nose, everything drooping except his eyebrows which arch in a bushy, intimidating way, or sound like one, with his voice like a blunt rasp. His own teeth, certainly, have seen better days.

- Grandfather cn see all th way t' God, Nerida says in an awed voice.

- On the back of a white goose. Uncle Owl nods to himself and looks over their heads as if to an invisible adult. - I despair f' these kids sometimes, he says.

Nerida looks crestfallen.

Judd slips away, one hand thrust deep in his pocket. Princess wants to go also, and find Pito.

- Grandfather cn see all th way t' Christchurch, when there's no wind, she informs Uncle Owl.

- What about South America?

Princess looks uncertain. Nerida nods solemnly. South America sounds right. Uncle Owl sighs.

Maverick hastens to put the ladder away, driven to speed by the thought of discovery by Aunty Pi. Not that it is expressly forbidden to visit Grandfather in his tower, rather it is unwise to be caught doing so, for if they are, Aunty Pi will surely find something better for them to do. If the devil finds work for idle hands, then he must be kept awfully busy around this house.

Mut is standing behind Owl in his doorway, opening his mouth at the children in a dog's version of an enthusiastic grin, his tongue hanging at a sloppy angle in his mouth. Behind Mut, through the open doorway, they can see Uncle Owl's chaotic domain; one large room piled high with stacks of books, bottles and magazines. He has a deal with the children; if they bring him a cup of tea, they are allowed to stay in his room and poke about until he's finished it. Princess and Pito have spent time there flicking through copies of *The Monthly Review*, *The Internationalist* and *The Red Flag*, looking for pictures and cartoons to cut out. Once they found a cartoon of somebody who looked very much like Uncle Owl, being hanged from a tree called the Tree of Profits.

- Y'll get fleas in yr brain, if y' list'n t' that silly old bastard. He taps the side of his head with his forefinger.

- Don't be silly, Uncle Owl, y' can't have fleas in y' brain, Nerida says primly. She knows that Uncle Owl shouldn't swear around the children.

- Of course y' can. They hop around inside yr head. In through yr ear like this! Hop! Hop! Hop! He makes his fingers jump as if he were trying to catch a flea. - Flea brain! Flea brain!

- What wd they eat?

- All that superstitious nonsense.

- Uncle Owl!

Mut sniffs hopefully, but warily, at Uncle Owl's hand. Princess says nothing; she wants to remember everything that happened at Grandfather's so she can tell Pito.

- Y're tellin lies yrself, Uncle Owl, Nerida says in the outraged tones of Aunty Grin. She hugs Teddy to her chest; Teddy is something of a protection against lies.

Uncle Owl grins.

- I had two biscuits, Nerida confesses.

- Ah! Now we get closer to't. You young bandits go up there on raidin expeditions!

- Grandfather's nice t' us. A stubborn look has come over Nerida's face.

Uncle Owl nods indulgently. Then his face changes. - Did Aunty Pi know you ws goin up t' see old Moses? he asks severely. But not too severely. Nerida contrives to look offended and marches off down the stairs. Princess and Judd have melted away like ice-cream on a carpet, leaving Maverick, the eldest and most responsible, to brave out the questions.

Pito's signal is a triangular stone outside the old dunny behind the tractor shed. If the triangle is pointing up, he is there. No one else ever thinks of going there, not even Nerida, who knows all the other places they like to go and has an annoying habit of turning up just when Pito and Princess don't want her around.

Although it has not been used for years, the long-drop having been filled up, the dunny still has a smell about it, faint and loamy, in memory of its function. Pito said once that was the smell of graves. The dunny itself is made of corrugated iron with bits of what Uncle Honk and Uncle Owl call three b'two, and is hung about with grey, dusty cobwebs. Since there is nowhere else for them to sit, he waits for her on top of the seat where they both huddle. He holds her hand or just touches her lightly, resting his fingers on her palm or her wrist, and she tells him everything Grandfather has said and done.

She is not allowed to miss out a single detail.

He listens with great concentration, considering any treasures Grandfather might have shown them, giving equal weight to all her utterances. He is interested in the Maori rubbing stone that has collected countless rubs, but is just as interested in the gold sovereign. He listens to everything as if seeking some hidden pattern, some clue to a secret puzzle, and as she speaks he sometimes touches her face, the sensitive spots each side of her eyes, gently and tenderly, as if he were receiving direct transmission from her brain to his.

- What else did he say, Princess? Tell me! tell me!

She tells him everything, racking her memory in search of something she may have missed. She even acts out her dumb shows for him, as far as she is able in the cramped space of the dunny, showing him how she fell off the bed, pulling Nerida with her. Then, quite suddenly, he becomes merry and laughs and tickles her gently in the ribs and they share a close moment at Nerida's expense.

In repeating these dumb shows, she is able to refine and elaborate them, perfecting the expressions, even able to interrupt them with shows of Nerida's wide-eyed fright and Judd's poisonous glances, hamming it up for Pito's amusement.

It is particularly hot, and they have to leave the door ajar to let in air. In the distance, across the dusty yard, they see Uncle Honk driving his tractor, pulling a trailer behind. There is something satisfying about being able to see Uncle Honk without him seeing them, cuddling up on the old dunny seat, touching and sharing their sweat, her head on his chest, his palm touching her cheek. Any day now, the weather may switch to winter, and Princess luxuriates in her melting.

- Grandfather cn see all th way t' th bridge, she says lazily.

Pito is instantly alert. - What bridge?

- Y' know, on th plain, the one y' cn see from th Dog-leg.

Pito considers this weighty piece of information.

- An' there's a pine forest.

- Not th one where there's snakes 'n spiders? There's a tiny quiver in his voice.

- No. Can't y' see th pine forest from th Dog-leg?

Pito looks as if he hasn't made up his mind or can't remember. Princess wonders how much of the world he knows, and puts a protective arm around him. - The one with snakes 'n spiders is on the other side of the mountains, she says gently.

An awed, frightened look comes over his face.

The tractor is coming up towards the house. It stops by the lower gate where Father is working on the fence; Uncle Honk leans out to talk to him. He leans his head out as if he were going to spit on Father who is gesturing to something on the trailer.

- And Christchurch, sometimes he cn see smoke fr'm th city.

Pito sucks in his cheeks. He is darker and slimmer than the rest of the children, who tend to be fair and beefy; his complexion is sallow with a delicate, a refined aspect to the line of his cheek.

- That's at least a hundred miles, he says. - No one cn see that far.

Princess nods in the pleasure of heat and drowsiness. There is nothing but the intermittent sounds of animals, the distant huddle of water over rock from the river bed and the thump of Uncle Honk's tractor. She lies in Pito's lap, feeling his thighs beneath her cheek, not resenting their warmth, breathing in the faint musky smell coming off his skin. He brushes her hair from her eyes and runs it between his fingers.

- You're a real princess, he murmurs, touching her temples where he likes to make gentle, circular motions. When he does that she imagines all her thoughts unwinding before his eyes.

- I'm a princess with no kingdom, she says, thinking back to the time when she wore a crown, fine silks, and received many a bouquet of accolades from princes of distant lands. Once she was a real princess. She's seen her carriage where there should only have been yard, barn, and chained-up dogs. The horses must have had short halters because their heads were held back. Their tails were arched and they moved in a prancing fashion. The fine carriage stopped and a lady got out, a multi-coloured parasol in one hand.

She pulls her dress out from her body where it is prickling against the heat of her skin. It is not such a bad thing, she reflects, looking past the yard, past Uncle Honk on his tractor, past the faded yellow of the tussock fields and up, out over the hills to the washed blue of the sky beyond, not such a bad thing to be without a kingdom.

As long as Pito is there. Pito is her kingdom. She does not envy the woman in the carriage because although that woman was herself, and a real princess with everything a princess has, she did not have Pito.

Soon she sits up and gives him a turn, letting him put his head in her lap, taking pleasure in the weight of his head against her thighs. She leans against the back wall of the dunny. He drapes his arm over her knees and watches Uncle Honk talk to Father, letting his hand brush in a tickling way across her legs.

Since his hair isn't long enough to play with, she contents herself with tracing the outline of his head with her fingers, following the line of bone down the side of his cheek.

- Pito, what'll really happen t'y' if Grandfather finds out about y'?

- Somethin terrible. His voice is frighteningly calm. He speaks out of absolute conviction and she doesn't for a second disbelieve.

The tractor is moving again. The motor pounds. Uncle Honk jumps up and down as if riding an ungainly horse; two dogs with heads heavy trot behind. The corrugated iron burns against her back.

- What sort of terrible? Like a thrashin? You haven't done nothin.

- He'll bury me, he says sleepily, turning his head to breathe out the heat of his breath into the fabric of her skirt. Princess laughs softly to banish the dread in her heart. The dread is always there, with Pito.

- Why wd Grandfather want t'bury you?

- Because that's what he dreams about. In his dreams he has a huge long shovel an' digs an extra deep hole.

His voice has taken on a halting, singsong quality, his special magician's voice, and while, in the heyday of the game, this prophetic power of his thrilled her, now in the twilight of her kingdom it sounds like the very voice of dread itself.

- Why'd he dream that?

- Because he knows 'bout me. Who I am. The other grown-ups don't.

Cheerfully she says, - He'll never find out, y' know. We'll never tell im. Even Maverick 'n Judd are too scared. Maverick's th best liar y' ever seen.

Pito smiles.

- Even Nerida seems t' know. And y' know what a dilly she is.

The dogs tied up in the shadow of the barn erupt in earnest barking.

Uncle Honk leaps down off the tractor and runs to the trailer.

Princess feels herself melt down and spread out into the heat. Pito will never die; light as he is, the weight of him is solid in her lap. The dampness of his cheek soaks through onto her thigh.

- One of th children'll tell him. Pito's voice is quiet, barely audible over the racket of the barking dogs.

- Who?

- One of th children.

- But which one?

Pito is silent and she knows better than to press him further. They are delicate, these magician trances of his, and not subject to her sovereign will.

- Anyway, th grown-ups hardly ever go up there, she says, as if that puts an end to the conversation.

- Uncle Owl does, sometimes. He takes a bottle up t' Grandfather. An' even Uncle Honk goes up.

- Uncle Honk? What wd he want with Grandfather?

Pito's head shifts uneasily. He rolls back against her stomach and looks up into her face. - I dunno. Somethin t' do with th farm I think.

Uncle Honk gives a shout. Pito pulls himself up and peers through the crack in the door. There is something bulky on the trailer. The two exhausted dogs flop down in the shade.

Judd and Maverick come running out of the house, tripping over one another with shouts and curses.

- Ahoy! Ahoy! Uncle Honk shouts.

Mother, Aunty Grin and Aunty Pi come out of the house, Uncle Owl following at a distance. They crowd around looking down at the dead pig, now rolled off the trailer onto the ground by a sweating Uncle Owl and Uncle Honk. Pito and Princess push their way to the front. A fair-skinned pig lies on its side staring out with blank apathy; blood runs down its flank into the dust.

Uncle Honk holds up his hunting knife, long and bloody. The redness is smeared over his hands and wrists.

- When she got on th end of this, she wriggled an' squealed, he shouts hoarsely. - She bucked like a mare in heat. He surveys them all with wild, delirious eyes. Th dogs got 'er bailed up at Rocky Heads. I had t' come up underneath 'er, he flourishes the knife. - She fought like a boar so she mus' be in pup.

- There's a few meals in 'er, Aunty Pi says appreciatively. Already she is counting out the chops, rationing them. The heat from the spitting fat is already flaming on Mother's face.

- That's th sow, Uncle Honk says with authority. - Th boar's still out there somewhere with a slug up its arse, he gestures with the knife, - th big black bastard we seen th other day. He glances at Judd, whose face is full of envy and wild hope.

Nerida squeals and runs behind Mother. Judd looks at the knife and down at the sow. Princess notices he's fingering something in his pocket.

Uncle Honk kneels down beside his kill and wipes the knife on his trousers.

- I bet she's in pup. Grunting, he rolls her back a little so that he can get at her stomach, and, holding up her front legs, he inserts the knife at her breast bone and runs it down fast, slitting her open all the way to her arse. Red guts spill out, and more, a reddish-purple sack filled with pink creatures the length of a teaspoon, blind and groping.

- They're still alive, Nerida says in awe.

But they are not; it is the rush from their mother's gut to the dust that gives them this slithering illusion of animation. There are so many of them, dozens it seems, falling on top of one another, pushing out with still, dead limbs against the viscous cowls that cover them.

Father comes up and stares. There is nothing here but the dead giving birth to the dead. He's seen them before, along the sides of the streets and lying out in the dust without shame, women with their wombs ripped open giving birth to lumps of dark blood. Men running through fields of tall sunflowers with their heads on fire. He flings down the hammer he is carrying and marches off fixedly in the other direction, swinging his arms up to his shoulders. No one takes any notice. It is Uncle Honk's hour. He kneels over his shining prize, his red, beefy face suffused with joy. The chained dogs continue to go mad. Tonks and Peg lap at water with big dripping tongues. The children stand rock still, staring and staring, but it isn't long before Aunty Pi is organising Mother and Aunty Grin, consulting with Uncle Honk on the practicalities of dealing with the carcass.

- We're not goin t' eat those, she announces, pointing to the red blistered mass on the dirt. - Jack cn dig a hole for im.

Uncle Honk nods, but both he and Aunty Pi know that Father will not be digging any hole. Uncle Honk will feed them to the dogs.

- That boar'll be along soon, Uncle Honk says to Judd. There is a taunt in the voice. The knife he's still holding is one red, bloody curve. Judd looks up and Princess catches his eye. The voracity of his look forces her to look away.

It is Uncle Honk's hour; Aunty Pi says nothing when he and Uncle Owl break into the homebrew three days before it is due.

Aunty Pi's official explanation for Grandfather's exile in the tower is that

Grandfather is a stubborn old man who went into a sulk one day and has never come out of it. Too big for his boots, is Aunty Grin's supportive verdict.

None of these pronouncements satisfy Princess, who cannot bear a mystery unsolved. Like Pito's great secret. The day after the children's visit to the tower, she approaches Mother and asks her. Mother is hanging out the washing behind the kitchen, her movements slow and studied. A light, dry wind is coming from the east, lifting the clothes gently and turning the rotating washing line which groans in its metal socket with a long, ancient sound.

Princess approaches with care, taking her time, kneeling by the herb garden which is Mother's pride and joy and pretending an interest in sage, rosemary and devil's bit. She listens as Mother tells her that sage is an antiseptic, and that rosemary used to be given to people who had lost the power of speech. Devil's bit is effective against plagues, fevers and poisons. She listens, then phrases her question so that it trips lightly off her tongue with the most casual of sounds.

- Why doesn't Grandfather come down?

Mother pauses, her arms on the washing line holding a pair of Uncle Honk's dungarees upside down. Her body sways as if it too were hanging from the line. Beside the dungarees, one of her own nightdresses, so light it has already just about dried, fills out with air, softly occupied by an invisible body.

Slowly she drops her arms and turns to Princess. Her hair is a very pale brown and its delicate curls flicker in the wind.

- Because he is afraid.

There are some days when there is nothing better for Princess to do but follow Pito around the house, going wherever he goes, hiding wherever he hides, and thinking whatever he thinks.

She loves his thoughts. They have a darkness in them and a secret terror he doesn't disclose, yet they are pierced through with laughter, a catchy kind of laughter that makes her feel warm and safe.

And he is devious, the most brilliant liar of them all. He knows how to get rid of Nerida and where the best places are for spying on the grown-ups; he knows how to sneak out to the old dunny without anybody seeing and how to leave the yard without being spotted by Grandfather.

He knows things he isn't supposed to know, such as where Uncle Owl keeps his brandy and where the cartridges to Uncle Honk's .303 are stored. He knows what is in Father's dreams, and what happens at night when Uncle Honk goes to Aunty Grin's room. He seems to know all the secrets of the house.

There are spots, he says, special spots where, if you stand still enough, you become invisible. Standing in those spots, all the dealings of the house whisper around you as if you were at their centre. He says it is a 'sideways room' with one-way glass so that you can look out but nobody else can look in.

Over the years, these spots have migrated slowly from room to room. There is one, he says, moving down the hall towards the kitchen, and another one right in the corner of the kitchen. And there is one right in the doorway of Aunty Grin's room. There is another in transit from the kids' room to Father and Mother's room. He claims the only other creature in the house who knows of these spots is the cat, Croak, who uses them to outwit mice.

Challenged by Princess and Nerida to show them these spots, he takes them to the cellar where huge, ancient travelling trunks are stored, trunks which Aunty Pi said came over on the First Four Ships. He takes up position in an alley between four of these trunks, turns sideways and vanishes. Nerida stands back and puts her hands up to her eyes, peering between her fingers. Princess steps forward and tries to find Pito, convinced it is all a trick of the shadows.

- He's gone, Nerida says in a hushed voice.

Princess doesn't like it one little bit. It frightens her to think Pito can vanish at the snap of fingers just by standing on some magic spot. He may have locked himself in one of the trunks. That fear makes her aggressive.

- Stop being stupid, Pito, she shouts, her special princess voice muffled by the weighty trunks. He has to be hiding somewhere. Suddenly she notices a slim wooden case sitting on top of one of the trunks. She reaches up her hand.

- Gun trick, eh? Pito reappears beside her, close enough to reach out and touch her. - Would y' like t' try it?

Nerida refuses. Then says she'll try only if Princess does. Princess remains sceptical, but tries desperately to find the spot.

- Y' have t' stand just at the right angle, Pito explains to her as she shuffles back and forth, twisting this way and that.

- I cn still see y', Nerida keeps saying in a quavering voice until Princess tells her to shut up, thereafter shuffling about in silence, getting angrier and angrier.

- Show me again.

Pito obliges, stepping into the spot as if stepping into a pair of gumboots, and vanishes from the face of the earth. Nerida gives a short, sharp scream and puts her hand over her mouth. Princess gets even angrier. She is too conscious of the measured density of the trunks around her.

- Come back! she orders, staring around for a nook or cranny he may have slipped into. He doesn't come back and she grows frightened again. What if he never comes back? She fights against the smell of Nerida's fears. This is just Pito up to his tricks again. The trunks around her smell of dust, but the dust contains the memory of oceans. Again she sees the slim wooden case and reaches up for it.

- Easy-peasy, says Pito, stepping off the spot.

Princess declines, with dignity, a second try.

Pito doesn't mind Princess following him around, or if he does he never says anything. Princess is afraid he will use the magic spots to hide from her, but he never has, at least not that she knows of.

Mainly he uses them to spy on the adults because that is the most dangerous game they can play.

The night after their visit to Grandfather, with Maverick and Judd sulking in the kids' room, Pito comes creeping into the lounge where Princess is making shadow shows on the wall with her fingers. He takes hold of her hand and leads her down the corridor towards the kitchen. The house feels different, darker, creakier, larger, with longer corridors and higher ceilings. Vistas are dimmer and shadows blurrier. The storm and unexpected wet have warped the old house's sense of its internal spaces, racked its habitual quiet with dripping sounds.

Near the kitchen, Pito waves her into the shadow under the stairwell, steps lightly up near the wall, and vanishes. Two voices come loud and clear from the kitchen doorway.

- … t' eat. Aunty Pi is saying. An' Dot will ring again an' want t' know what's happening.

- That's half a sheep a week, Aunty Grin says. Hers are the wounded tones of outraged virtue.

Aunty Pi's voice comes back, quick and sharp. - Don't I know it. This place'll go under th hammer. We've got too many free loaders 'n no-hopers, boozers 'n losers, around here. Too many mouths an' not enough hands.

Aunty Grin is all sanctimony, - An' is Dot goin t' send money, then? Fr his upkeep? Since she's so concerned. She's got her stake in this too, I bet she'll want it when th time comes.

- She'll want it alright, but concerned? Not on yr nelly. All that concerns her is that stuff that runs through yr fingers like water.

- That's what I meant. Aunty Grin's tone has become peevish. - If only she an' Marl'd take some of the load…

Aunty Pi snorts. - Pigs might fly. There's a yob if ever I seen one. Sittin around pickin his nose an' saying, yes Dot, no Dot, Bob's yr Uncle Dot, how's y' father, I'll drive Dot…

- D' y' think she'll take im away? Look after im in Christchurch? Where he cn get proper lookin after, I mean.

- Not a hope in hell. She'll come 'n sit 'n hold his hand for a couple of days, make him feel hardly-done-by, and then be on her merry way, pattin th kids on th head as she goes. Nothin 'f them of course, no money f' their schoolin. Not even a kiss y' foot.

- Then there's Honey.

- Yes, there's Honey.

Both women fall silent.

There is a quiver in Aunty Grin's voice when she finally speaks, - We can't have that lot comin here, pokin their noses everywhere, tellin us how t' run things.

A moment later Aunty Pi's shadow appears in the kitchen doorway and hovers there. She is staring down the hall. Princess holds her breath and prays that Pito's invisible spot will work. Aunty Pi has eyes like a hawk and a nose to match. Croak the cat wanders out from the kitchen.

- The walls have ears, she says, turning away.

- The flap-flapping ears of children, Aunty Grin says with distaste.

Their voices vanish into the kitchen.

Afterwards, Pito and Princess have a whispered conference over who the adults were talking about. Dot and Marl they know to be Christchurch cousins. Pito maintains they were talking about Grandfather, but Princess gained an altogether different impression.

They were obviously talking about Father.

Her vision in Grandfather's room of the plains, and the strange places there, compels her to take Pito and go over the lower Dog-leg to the eastern side where the plains stretch from one horizon to the other. From here, she can see clearly the bridge, and the smudge of pine forest, and points them out to Pito.

Then Princess finds a red admiral butterfly. She is convinced that it is the same one they saw at Deep Pool, but Pito says they only live for one day.

It is sitting on a broom bush, looking like a fragment of exotic tapestry. Pito says the rain has brought it out, and Princess sees the red admiral, dehydrated, maybe even mixed up in the soil, magically combusting out of dust and rain to appear for them. They sit down by the broom bush to watch it obligingly lift its wings to reveal the fine, powdery colours beneath its slender black body. This body, in its form, is reminiscent of the caterpillar it has once been. She thinks of the slim delicacy of Pito's body and touches his cheek tenderly. Pito picks up her mood.

- D' y' want t' hear somethin spooky? he says. - Somethin I've just figured out.

- Tell me. She doesn't want to let her eyes leave the red admiral.

- Well, we think that seein an' hearin an' touchin are things that only go one way, but they don't. They go back th other way as well.

- What d' y' mean?

- Think about touchin. He taps a flat stone beside him. - We think it's just us touchin th stone, but it's not. The stone's touchin us! Feel f' yourself.

She touches the stone and feels its warm density touch her fingers, absorb her fleshiness. Pito laughs as she jerks her hand away.

- See! Now, it's th same with hearin. We think we just hear things, but if y' listen hard enough...

- Yes.

- Y' realize that y're bein listened to.

She tries it. She closes her eyes and listens hard. She listens until she can't hear anything anymore but a great silence listening back at her, hearing the sounds of the day, and the steady whisper of blood in her veins.

- You see! It goes both ways.

- Don't disturb th butterfly.

- Now this is th spooky bit. When we look we think it's just us lookin at somethin, but...

The world grows eyes. Everywhere she looks she is seen, beheld in a totality of vision that includes not only the mountains, plains, and sky of her day, but the vast night beyond the bubble of earth.

- Y' see, he whispers.

The red admiral turns its tiny head towards her and she knows it can sense her, and that it lives in a jewelled universe of utter transparency.

- That's not spooky, Pito, that's wonderful.

She pulls her eyes away from the butterfly and meets his. She can't communicate what she perceives, which is such a huge crisscross of seeing, listening, touching, tasting, smelling. The air tastes every piece of her skin; the earth touches her through its mineral surface; the sunlight inhales the fragrance of her body; the sky is an iris of blue in which she floats.

Her body fills up with a tender strength and trembles like the butterfly's wings. She sweats with heat and shivers with cold. Her head fills up with light. Amazed at her airy lightness, and the polish of the air, she reaches out her hand to touch Pito.

The red admiral leaps up and flies off, making jagged, scissor cuts in the air with its wings.

- Judd stole somethin fr'm Grandfather's room th other day, Pito says.

That night Pito wakes her up and takes her on one of his nocturnal hauntings. As they pass Nerida's bed, Princess sees two eyes staring at her and gets a fright before she realizes it is only Teddy, forever wakeful, his eyes glazed in the diffused light.

She moves as Pito has taught her, without creaking floorboards, listening at doors for sounds within. Croak, who pads their path out softly in front of them or sneaks along behind, is suddenly with them. At the beginning of the main hall they find her sitting motionless as glass, her uncanny yellow eyes turned in their direction.

There is nowhere in particular for them to go, they just drift around with the dust and moonlight, passing as quiet as a dream by the doors behind which the adults sleep, slipping up the stairs like the shadow of a cloud. Once they found Uncle Owl's door open and, with one accord, slipped inside, ghosting themselves around the piles of books and bottles to stand right by his bed. Mut was there, sleeping in his corner. He opened one eye and cocked one ear, the only acknowledgement, begrudgingly made, of their presence. They looked down at Uncle Owl's sleeping form, grinning at each other over his loud, abandoned snoring.

They have discovered that Father speaks in his sleep, more in his sleep than he does during the day, but they cannot decipher the sounds he makes. His shouted phrases and muffled cries of alarm seem to be in a foreign language, or, if it is English, the syllables are so mangled no meaning will attach to them. He can be heard from halfway along the upstairs hall, muttering and grumbling, mingling his complaints with Uncle Owl's snoring. Sometimes Mother wakes up and soothes him, her voice lilting him back into calmer regions of sleep.

Uncle Honk snores too, and sometimes he gets up and moves around the house. On this occasion, it is Croak who warns them. He runs on ahead down the hall as they tiptoe towards the bathroom and, when they hear her squeal, they stop dead still, easing the air in and out of their chests with as little sound as possible, flattened out against the shadow of the wall. Uncle Honk has just emerged from the room he shares with Aunty Pi and has stood on the cat. They hear him grunt and curse softly as he swings his foot at the disappearing Croak. He goes grumpily to the lavatory from where they hear unmistakable trickling sounds. They withdraw along the hall, past Aunty Grin's room, to the deep shadow of the far corner. Uncle Honk comes out of the bathroom and stands still; they sense rather than see his head swinging back and forth as he looks up and down the hall. Croak comes up and starts purring, rubbing along his legs.

Slowly he begins to walk towards them, placing one foot in front of the other with a deliberate tread. Princess looks questioningly at Pito who holds a finger up to his lips. When he gets to the door of Aunty Grin's room, Uncle Honk stops again. This time he goes very still, as one who is listening hard. There is only Croak, scrabbling at something along the wall. Then he opens the door and his shadow slips ahead of him into Aunty Grin's room.

Princess wants to get away fast, but Pito takes her wrist and places a finger over her mouth. She trembles. Something is going to happen and she wants to get out before it does. Whatever it is, she doesn't want to see it; yet the more determinedly she pulls away, the harder Pito holds her.

Uncle Honk has not closed the door completely and a thin wedge of light shows. From inside comes the sounds of hurried whispering, with Aunty Grin's voice raised in typical whining complaint. - Shut the door, they hear her say. Uncle Honk's voice comes, as gruff and blunt as ever, yet with an odd hoarseness Princess has not heard before. Aunty Grin's fussy voice comes again, but it is softer, more abject. A few moments later she begins to make a whinnying sound, eeeeeeeeeee, like air expelling from a balloon.

Edging her forward, Pito takes them back across the hall to where they can view the room obliquely through the crack in the door. A little light filters through from outside, making the room marginally brighter than the hall. It takes Princess a moment to understand what she is seeing, since she has to move her head back and forth to catch the full picture. Aunty Grin is standing bent at the waist, her arms out in front, holding onto the side of her dressing table, staring at herself in the mirror. Uncle Honk is standing behind her, lifting his hips up into her behind.

Aunty Grin continues to make the same sound, the same one long syllable of complaint, eeeeeeeeeeee, accompanied by agonized grimaces to herself in the glass. Uncle Honk begins to snort back through his nose like a snorer snatching at his breath.

- What are they doin? Princess whispers stupidly, for she knows, she's heard the same snorting noise from rams mounted upon ewes, she just wants to hear Pito say it.

- They're rootin, Pito says solemnly.

That night Princess dreams of red admiral butterflies. The air is full of them dancing about like demented autumn leaves. Princess is trying to tell Pito they must live a lot longer than a day, a week at least, but her voice keeps sticking in her throat. Judd is there somewhere with Uncle Honk's hunting knife. She hears Mother telling her to drink rosemary to help her find her voice again. By the time she is able to shape with words real human sounds, Pito has gone, lost in a carnival of red wings.

She wakes with a choked, stifled sensation in her throat.

After breakfast, Judd and Maverick take off for the barn, leaving Pito, Nerida and Princess in the lounge. The girls play with Croak whose vocal chords long ago degenerated and who can only scratch out a sound no better than the half-caw of a sick crow. This strangled sound makes Princess think of her dream and she glances involuntarily at Pito, expecting him to vanish before her eyes.

Instead Judd and Maverick walk in with smirks on their faces. Judd has his hand in his pocket.

- Y' stole somethin fr'm Grandfather, Pito says quietly. Judd stops still. He turns slowly towards Pito as Uncle Honk might. He takes his time in thinking out his response.

- Whaddiya' goin t' do about it? Go up an' tell im?

He laughs and Maverick joins in. The girls give each other a sick look and Nerida busies herself trying to interest Croak in Teddy's antics.

- I want t' know what it is, Pito says quietly.

- Do y' now.

- He might tell, says Maverick.

- Nah. I don't think he will. There is a horrible grin on Judd's face. Princess wants to say something but her throat is too caught up with muscles.

Judd pulls his hand from his pocket and holds it out, palm up, to Pito. A white slender thing lies in his hand. Everybody peers to look, even Croak, who's not that interested in Teddy anyway, and Maverick who's seen it before.

Pito looks at it longer than anyone. - Where'd y' get it?

- Found it on Scrubby Flat.

Instantly Princess says, - He's lyin.

Judd turns on her, red in the face and snarling, - How come y're so fucken smart that y' know everythin?

- He shouldn't swear, Nerida says primly to Teddy.

- It's jus' some old bone, Princess says, - it doesn't scare me.

- Nor me, Nerida says quickly.

Pito says nothing. He is staring hard at the small, ivory coloured object in Judd's hand.

Judd is all sneers. - Very smart, smarty. A bone! Any dumbhead cn see that. But what's it from?

- A bird, probably, Princess says with great carelessness, hardly deigning to glance down. She is more interested in stroking Croak's sleek body. Croak glances at the bone and glances away again, mirroring Princess's disdain.

- A bird, Nerida says, as if the idea has just occurred to her. A bird with wings like this. She stretches out her arms to demonstrate.

- It's not fr'm a bird, Pito says quickly. Princess looks again. It is a thin, delicate bone, with two joints. She is sure it's not off a sheep or a dog and she's seen enough chickens to know it wasn't from there.

- Where'd y' get it? she asks again.

- Wouldn't y' like t' know.

- Ask no questions y'll be told no lies, shut yr mouth an' y'll catch no flies, Maverick says in the sanctimonious voice of Aunty Grin.

- I reckon it's a finger, Pito says at last. - The finger off a little kid.

Judd grins.

- It's not a finger, Princess says, turning away from it. Croak turns back for another sniff.

- It's not a finger, Nerida says leaning closer, a look of morbid interest on her face.

Judd closes his fist.

- Why don't you get lost? Princess says to Nerida.

Croak sniffs casually at Judd's fist, turns and looks up at Princess, opening and closing his mouth soundlessly as if he were meowing in another dimension.

- It's a finger, Pito says with authority.

- It's got t' be, Judd said.

- Why? Princess really doesn't seem to care about the answer.

- Cos I got it fr'm Grandfather's treasure box while yous ws all gawkin out th window tryin t' see Christchurch. He wdn't keep some old bird's foot fr nothin, wd he?

- Y' know what a liar Judd is, Nerida says to Teddy.

- He wd, Princess says, stroking Croak under the chin, where he most likes it. - It probably got eaten by a dinosaur or somethin.

Croak suddenly leaps off Princess's lap onto the floor and stretches himself in one luxurious movement, as if he's just eaten.

- There's one way we cn prove it's a finger. Pito points upstairs. - Uncle Owl's encyclopedia.

- I'm not goin, Nerida says instantly.

- Y're not invited, Judd says.

- I'll go, Maverick says, the biggest and the oldest once more.

- So'll I, Pito says.

- So'll I, Judd says.

- So'll I, Nerida says.

Princess says nothing.

They decide to go right away, while the grownups are having some kind of conference in the dining room, taking the stairs as quietly as they can so they don't sound like a herd of elephants, which is what Aunty Pi says they sound like most of the time.

Uncle Owl's room is a great messy mystery as usual. They have to fossick around among the piles of magazines and bottles before they find the encyclopedia. The room has a heavy, boozy, papery smell. Croak accompanies them to the door but will not enter; rightly speaking, this is Mut's territory.

Mut is there, in his basket in the corner, watching them sleepily from between his paws. He flicks Croak a glance which Croak fails to return.

- Where'll we find it? Judd, puzzled, hauls some volumes out from under a stack of papers.

- Look under finger, Nerida suggests.

- Anatomy, Pito says, pulling the book from Judd's hands. - Human anatomy.

- You find it then.

Pito finds it, working through the book with quick, light fingers.

- Ooooo, Nerida makes a revolted face at the skeleton that grins up at her from the page. To one side there is an inset showing the bone shape of the human hand; the finger matches their specimen exactly.

Judd turns triumphantly to Princess, - Whadd'y' say now?

She says nothing, but wonders why Grandfather should have such a thing and what story might be attached to it.

Nerida is having similar thoughts. - Maybe a pig ate a baby so Grandfather kept it, she says half to herself.

- Pigs don't eat babies, Uncle Owl says from the door, - unless that's all y' feed im.

The kids all line up behind Maverick.

- We ws jus' lookin at yr encyclopedia, Maverick says. We diddin' touch anythin.

- That's alright, Uncle Owl says graciously, - that's what an encyclopedia's for.

The kids say nothing. Ignoring them, Uncle Owl reaches under a pile of papers and pulls out a bottle. With deliberate gestures he unscrews the lid and lifts the bottle to his lips.

- The fascists always suppress knowledge, it's th first thing they do.

His head lolls onto his shoulder and he gives them one of his drooping looks. Then he goes over to Mut and scratches his ears. The dog humbly lifts its head.

- There's some good pictures in these books, Maverick says in an eager voice.

- What ws y' lookin up?

Maverick looks puzzled.

- I mean, that's what an encyclopedia's for. T' look things up. He takes a casual swig at the bottle. Mut rolls over in an ecstasy of submission.

- The Great Fire a London, Maverick says.

- Skeletons, Nerida squeals a moment after.

- Right y'are, Uncle Owl says, coming forward and looking down at the book. - That Great Fire cleaned im out alright. All th shit 'n filth, crammed together like a bunch of pigs all shittin an' rootin an' fartin. He spits with disgust. - That's what they call late Feudalism. He lifts the book up onto his lap. - The barons've changed their names but it's still th same old bunch. The immortals, they reckon. So rich they don' even have t' die.

- What's a mortal? Nerida asks.

- An immortal is somebody like Grandfather, so full of shit they forget when t' die.

He grins at Nerida a mouthful of long, yellow teeth and droops one eye down in a nebulous wink.

- Y' shouldn't swear, Nerida says, sounding a little like Aunty Pi.

- I wish I could've been there t' see it, Judd says. - Everybody screamin 'n yellin. Flames leapin up 'n down. Smoke everywhere.

- Skeletons, eh? Uncle Owl says, reaching down into the book and, as if pulling it up from the pages, he produces the slender bone. He closes one eye and holds the bone up to the other. - Yes, indeed. He looks back at the picture, one eye still closed.

- Pito reckons it's a finger bone, Nerida says, giggling and putting her fist in her mouth. Judd gives her a quick I'll-get-you-later look.

- Does he now? Well Pito's smart, dead smart. Yes indeed. Where'd y' find it, Pito?

Princess holds her breath.

Pito shrugs, - Roundabout.

- Then I reckon it's yours.

Uncle Owl flicks it towards Pito who steps back as if it were a fiery brand or a sharp knife. Uncle Owl laughs. Snorting with disgust, Judd picks it up, giving Princess a hard look. She knows the thought of the cow horn has passed through his mind. Pito should have picked it up, she thinks.

Uncle Owl is still laughing as the children file out, Nerida first, Maverick last. As they run into the hall his laughing turns to coughing.

When they get back to the children's room, Judd turns on Nerida and begins knuckling her arm, pounding rapidly up and down on the same spot. Nerida screws her face up but will not cry out. Teddy jerks in her other hand.

- You're a silly bitch, he tells her. A stupid little stupid bitch.

Maverick comes up behind her and punches her in the ribs.

- That's one f' me, he says.

Princess digs her fingernails into the back of Maverick's neck. Maverick groans and shoves her back against the wall. Her head cracks against the plaster. - You'll get it too, he says, red-faced, his eyes bulging.

- Get what? Princess is white-faced, spitting contempt.

- This, Maverick replies, punching her hard in the breast. She goes down with a gasp, Maverick kicking her in the stomach on the way. After she's hit the floor, he goes around the other side and kicks her in the rectum.

- Give it t' her good, Judd says to him, still thumping Nerida's arm with vicious, mechanical strokes. Nerida hangs from his other arm as limply as Teddy hangs from hers.

Pito stands off to one side as he always does when they fight, watching them with big, round, dark eyes.

Nerida screams as Judd twists her arm, and goes down with Judd on top of her, punching her in the ribs. Then he puts his hands up her skirt and pinches her on the thighs and stomach. In the midst of her pain, Princess looks up at Pito. Her master magician. He does nothing but stare at her with some enormity in his eyes.

A few moments later, Mother comes into the room. She looks blankly at the children, dark circles under her eyes.

- What're yous kids doin? she says in the hostile, whining tones of Aunty Grin.

- Judd hurt me, Nerida says.

- *Tell tale tit*

Your tongue shall be split

And all the little puppy dogs

Will have a little bit, Judd sings, poking his tongue out at Nerida.

- I've heard quite enough, Mother says severely, more Aunty Pi than Aunty Grin now. - I'm exhausted. It's time yous kids went outside.

Nerida runs across the room and throws her arms around her mother. Mother strokes her head. Nerida closes her eyes and draws in the soft, carroty smell of Mother. - The boys're bein horrible, she sniffs.

- Poor little thingy, Judd sneers, but he's looking at Princess too.

Mother takes Princess and Nerida by the hand and leads them to her and Father's room. Father is sitting on the edge of the bed, his head down almost between his knees, his hands over his ears. They follow Mother to the wardrobe where she fumbles about for something.

Behind them Father unfolds and swings around. When he sees the children he leaps off the bed and backs away, holding his hands up over his eyes, peering through his fingers.

- Get away! Get away! His voice vanishes into a squeak.

This hospital is no place for children, for orphans; rather it is a home for the damned, a charnal house where the living and the dead walk together and talk in intimate whispers.

From the bottom of the wardrobe Mother produces an old belt of soft leather, thin and wide.

- Y' cn use this so y' don't stick out in front too much, she says, pushing the hair out of her tired face. - It's harder when y' develop early, especially if y're big in th front. It makes th boys very stupid. Take off yr top.

Princess takes off her top and mother fits the belt around, snugly under her arms and across her chest. Pulled gently tight, it covers her nipples and flattens her breasts.

Nerida stares at it, her eyes huge.

Princess puts her top back on and looks in the mirror. Her little protrusions are gone. The belt feels funny, but it doesn't hurt.

- This ws yr belt, wasn't it, Mother?

Mother nods.

As they go out, Father approaches them, his eyes wide and staring in the cage of his face.

- What're their names? he demands of Mother.

Mother salutes briskly. - Off duty, soldier.

Father's shoulders slump. Tears come into his eyes. He tries to look at Princess but a vast buzzing comes into his head making it hard to focus. He sees a little girl but her face is in pieces.

- Will I have one when I get older? Nerida asks Mother.

Later in the morning, Aunty Grin takes them for Correspondence School. They sit at the big table in the dining room, materials spread out, heads bowed over their work. Princess has to work on her arithmetic because that's what she is bad at; Judd has to work on his handwriting for the same reason; Maverick does a picture because he's finished all his other work, and believes that finishing before the others shows how much smarter he is.

Nerida enjoys colouring in, although she can't seem to keep the colours within the lines. She has a big book of drawings she is slowly filling up with patches of colour. Her favourite is Jacob's Ladder, a picture showing a man asleep with a staircase coming out of his head and angels flowing up and down. It is the angels she likes to colour in, with their yellow hair neatly waved the way she'd have liked hers to be; angels with little short nightdresses and chubby baby legs; adult angels with long flowing bodies and robes to match; all passing in and out of heaven, or meeting on the stairway to hug, their colours spilling over each other.

The sun she colours in yellow and hot, the way she knows it; into the empty circle, she places a face with a mouth that both smiles and sneers, eyes shaped like orange pips with tiny black centres. This face, her only addition to the picture provided, has already come under the disapproving scrutiny of Aunty Grin, who tells her that if the sun had a face it would have been put there, but she gives grudging praise to how neatly the angels' frilly frocks are coloured in. She ends by suggesting that Nerida not spend too long on that picture, that there are other pictures she's hardly touched, like the nice one over the page showing a field of spring flowers with some hills and butterflies in the background.

Maverick is allowed to draw anything connected with his Social Studies topics, so he chooses the Great Fire of London, laboriously drawing skyscraper-like buildings all leaning into one another since he isn't so good at drawing straight lines. Although these buildings are shot through with yellow and red lines, Maverick is dissatisfied with the result; the buildings don't look as if they are on fire, they just look like buildings with yellow and red lines through them. They end up looking silly and scribbled on, and, as Aunty Grin points out, they didn't have big tall buildings like that in those days anyway. Still he labours on, putting curtains in the windows (which is the only way he knows how to draw windows) and colouring the roofs green and brown. At the bottom of the picture, he draws some stick people who are supposed to be running away in terror. That hasn't worked out very well either, since the stick people don't look like they are running anywhere but are stuck in their big clumpy shoes, unable to escape, arms stuck out from their sides like gingerbread men.

It isn't fair that Pito may read a book while Princess struggles with her arithmetic, but then Pito can do arithmetic as easily as whistling. For her, the numbers stack up on top of one another like a house of cards and she can never resolve their meaning in the space provided at the bottom. Their values, while fixed in black pencil, seem to shift and change every time she does the sum, and the very idea that there is only one correct answer in the infinite jumble of possible numbers frightens her into paralysis.

And it isn't fair that Pito's not allowed to help her; she has to work them out herself, Aunty Grin says, for if she always relies on other people to do things for her, she will never learn to do them herself. Aunty Grin, for one, has no wish to raise a bunch of cripples who can't even tie their own shoelaces let alone put two and two together and get a straight answer. So she sits, rigid and blank, until Aunty Grin, with a martyred sigh, sits and works through them with her, keeping the little book of answers close but out of Princess's sight.

Sitting this way, half listening to Aunty Grin's litany of numbers, Princess becomes aware that there is somebody in the room watching her.

Raising her eyes, she encounters those of Uncle Honk who is standing just inside the door, staring at her. At the same time, Aunty Grin becomes aware of the silent figure and her voice runs out of numbers.

- Carry on, Uncle Honk says casually, moving towards the table as if he were a headmaster or something. Aunty Grin has lost her place and has to start the sum again.

Uncle Honk goes and stands behind Judd's chair, and Judd's pen creaks to a halt on the page. He tries to cover his work with his arm so that Uncle Honk won't see how some of the letters face the wrong way and tend to get clustered together on the page. If I've told him once I've told him a thousand times, Aunty Grin has often said.

- Jus' carry on, Uncle Honk says in a kindly voice, smiling at Nerida.

Judd tries to carry on. He is doing a line of small b's and is halfway through the downwards slope but has forgotten which way the loop goes. When the loop faces the wrong way, Aunty Grin gets angry.

- By th way, Uncle Owl sez y' found some kind've bone yesterday. Or ws it Pito?

Judd goes crimson and twists his pencil around in his fingers. So Uncle Owl has blabbed. - Yeah.

- Cn I have a look at it? Judd covers his book with his left hand and puts his right hand into his pocket. A moment later Uncle Honk is studying the slender bone.

- Where'd y' get it?

- Scrubby Flat. Storm must've washed it down.

- Izat so?

Aunty Grin sits stiffly, staring at Judd.

- What ws y' doin on Scrubby Flat? Collectin gorse?

- Jus' pokin around.

- Izat so.

- Lookin f' pig.

Aunty Grin lets out a long, disbelieving breath.

Uncle Honk wanders disinterestedly around the table, pausing behind Nerida to look down at her colouring-in.

- Whereabouts on th flat? He bends over and removes Nerida's hand from her page. The yellow sun looks back at him, the corners of its mouth drooping.

- At th water line. Where th willa's down. Judd is looking straight down at his book. His hand is ready by the top corner of the page, ready to turn it over and hide his lettering the moment he gets a chance.

- Where th willa's down, Uncle Honk says quietly, turning the syllables over in his mouth. He makes it sound like something nasty. He wanders back down the other side of the table and stands behind Princess's, his hands resting on the back of her chair.

- Y' know what's goin t' happen if it turns out y're lyin.

- I'll get a thrashin.

- Yous all'll get a thrashin. Every man Jack of y' will get it. He heads casually for the door.

- Cn I have it back?

Uncle Honk stops. He turns and looks inquiringly at Judd.

- Cn I have th piece of bone back?

A profound silence enters the room. The children can hear the distant sound of sheep and the rattle of Father's fence-mending machine; inside, the firm signature of Aunty Pi's footfall on the stairs.

By the barn, a dog barks, one sharp syllable.

Somehow without disturbing the suspended quiet, Uncle Honk goes back to the table and lays the bone beside Judd's book.

- That's not b, that's a d, he says, locating the spot on Judd's book with his finger. - The b goes th other way round.

- If I've told im once I've told im a thousand times, Aunty Grin says.

In the afternoon, rain comes and the children run. Up the stairs and along the hall to Uncle Owl's room; down the stairs and along the hall to the kitchen. They play hide and seek until they get sick of that; they can never find Pito, and Nerida keeps giving herself away by giggling and squealing and, as Aunty Pi puts it, acting like a ninny. It is the giggling and squealing that leads to the chasing, and the chasing that leads to hiding once more, until Aunty Pi ominously suggests they go and play in the barn and not be seen again until dinnertime.

Princess sticks close to Pito and nobody says anything about the finger.

A hard, early-winter southerly locks them in, wrapping the house with cold sleety pellets. The dash across to the barn is an occasion for oilskins and gumboots, and much pushing and shoving and squealing. The sharp wind stings their faces. The cold creeps into their scalps. Judd tries to push Nerida over and almost succeeds. Everybody has to laugh at the way her skinny legs, encased in oversized gumboots, go skidding and flying. Nerida screams, a thin, high-pitched sound, shredded immediately by the wind. She closes her eyes and is back in the wardrobe. The soft mud swallows her up.

Princess suddenly feels vulnerable to the eyes of Grandfather. He may be watching them now, lining them up in his little beady eyes, asking himself what his little mice are up to, asking himself which one of them stole his finger bone. She comes to the rescue of Nerida and tries to trip Judd up. Judd promises to get her back later, he is saving up all his get-you-backs for one grand revenge, he lets her know, as Maverick grabs hold of her oilskin and swings her around. By the time they get to the barn they are screaming and laughing. Judd sticks his finger into Nerida's ribs and wiggles it about to make her laugh harder. Nerida laughs the way a dog breathes when it has run too far.

In grey light, the barn is huge and full of gloomy corners. Rusted farm implements hang from the walls, and in one section there is an ancient car from another era, caught in a moment of disrepair. In front of it sits the old Bedford, leaky with straw, which Uncle Honk uses for his occasional trips to the plains. Last time he tried to use it, the motor wouldn't start. There are a few bales of spiky hay and some sacks of chook mash strewn around it. The whole place smells of dust and rats and animals, and there isn't much to do but play tag and have straw fights or crush prickly straw down someone's back. Or play the princess game.

They play the giggling game instead. To do this, everyone has to stay utterly silent and pull faces at the next person in the circle. The first person to laugh is suitably punished. In this case the punishment, set by Judd, is five seconds of tickling, more if the punishment is resisted. Surprisingly, Nerida is able to bring herself under control and watch with solemn calm as Maverick, who being the eldest gets to start, pulls a hideous, demon face at her. Then she turns to Pito, pausing for an embarrassed moment when she can't think of a silly face and a giggle is not far away. Suddenly her eyes widen, her upper lip arches, her face springs into a mask of loathing and terror, her mouth opens as if twisted by a terrible scream.

Pito does not laugh; he is the best of all at holding a neutral mask face. He turns to Princess and makes a sad, stupid, clown's face, waggling his hands behind his ears. Princess can feel the giggle ballooning in her stomach but she is determined to suppress it at all costs, to keep it inside and well away from the muscles of her face. As if holding something in her mouth, she turns to Judd and assumes her best drongo face; it is one she can do really well, lower lip hung, slack muscles, vacuous eyes. For a moment, her face is not her own but belongs to a vast emptiness, a great deadness that sucks everything into it. Such a face never fails to produce a nervous laugh.

Judd however regards her zombie face with nothing but contempt, sneering away all hint of laughter. He carries this contempt in his face as he turns to Maverick. Suddenly his face drops into the exact shape of Uncle Honk's when he is preparing Seth for the administration of justice. He lifts his arm back over his shoulder, his face bloated out, his eyes bulged, his mouth thin and mean. Maverick has to chew back a laugh which springs like vomit into his mouth and his face goes red. Now everybody is fighting it, a hard corkscrew of laughter twisting in their gullets. Maverick is holding it as he turns to Nerida. The sight of her stupid, Nerida-face trying to look natural is enough to make him want to spew his laughter. Instead, he grows stern and reprimanding, wagging his finger at Nerida in admonition, hardening his face into what he hopes is a good imitation of Aunty Pi on the rampage.

Nerida doesn't turn a hair, her dignity and composure are untouched by his silent telling off. She turns to Pito and performs her great trick which is to arch her tongue out until it connects with her nose and go cross-eyed trying to look at her tongue. Pito has seen it all before and is unimpressed. Princess wants to laugh, not because Nerida's face is funny, but because Nerida's serious efforts to be funny are funny in themselves. She is holding that laugh in when Pito goes into his Aunty Grin act.

While Princess prides herself on her dumb shows, it is Pito who, with great carelessness, seems to have the real talent. His Aunty Grin getting sloshed with the gin bottle is perfect. At first his posture is upright, stiff and Grin-ish, but soon begins to lean, his eyes grow dazed, then the famous grin appears, at first slight and sly but soon open and corrupt.

Princess can contain herself no longer. She opens her mouth and dogs bark laughter in her throat. Pito turns the same debased, fraudulent grin on Nerida who spews her laughter after Princess. Judd wastes no time. Without a sound, he is on top of Princess, forcing her down and digging his fingers into her ribs.

- Wait! she screams, trying to push him off, feeling herself weaken as the air is pushed out of her by his weight and her own laughter. Soon she is fighting for breath.

Judd methodically pins her arms beneath his knees and begins to tickle her waist at his leisure, getting his fingers into the soft skin between her ribcage and hip. She screams and thrashes about. Maverick joins the fun, sitting on her legs so she won't struggle as much and tickles her feet.

Princess flails around in failing breath. Her face and lips go purple. She can't breathe in, can no longer even call out. She feels her body drift away from her into a huge starry silence. Suddenly Nerida is screaming and Maverick is looking at her with a shocked face. She can hear them and see them on the other side of a great divide.

The other children are shouting and pulling at him now but still Judd will not stop.

He goes on tickling her until she loses consciousness.

Coming out of her faint, Princess dreams of Pito. She is in her bridal gown and is holding out her arms to him as he jumps away from her across a huge river bed, from stepping stone to stepping stone, getting forever further away. It feels as if this has happened many times before, only this is the last time, the very final time of all. The great arch of the sky, the falling plains, the vistas of rock, all conspire to make him smaller and smaller, more and more distant. As he recedes, her bridal gown slips from her and she is dressed in the rags of her old self; her old ordinary name comes back to her, a single hard syllable she cannot utter. Something has happened to her throat and no words emerge.

When she wakes up the breath is back in her chest.

During the dark, overcast hours of that afternoon, Princess decides what she'll have to do. It will take a lot of thought and careful planning. Nerida has to be involved but not until the last minute, when she will have no time to get scared.

Pito mustn't know, and this makes her sad. She remembers how he leapt away from her across the rocks as if across an ocean, from ice floe to ice floe, getting further and further away. She remembers how close she felt to him on the hillside watching the red admiral, how sure she was that they would be together forever.

That night she has Croak in her bed to keep her awake. After she has taken off her breast belt, carefully concealing it from the boys, Croak puts his head there and purrs. He is still purring when she wakes later. The house has that utterly still feeling of the dead of night.

She slips out of bed, into her clothes, and wakes Nerida. Nerida's eyes are wide and glassy, like Teddy's. She looks very calm, almost old. As Nerida pulls on her dressing gown, Princess approaches Judd's bed, kneels down not inches from him and eases her hand under his pillow. The boy turns a little and moves his mouth around.

When the girls leave the room, Princess has the finger in her hand. As she goes through the door, she glances back and sees Pito, his eyes wide, watching her from his bunk. It's true, she thinks with a shiver. He never sleeps.

At the last minute, she modifies her plan and ghosts her way down to the kitchen. Inside the tin with the Macintosh lolly lid, she finds what she wants, a slice of pork pie which she puts in her jacket pocket. Aunty Pi will probably think Uncle Owl took it and, with a bit of luck, Uncle Owl will do the same.

Nerida watches. She's brought Teddy along too, maybe just as witness. She holds him up so that the theft enters the compass of his stoical gaze.

- I'll need y't' help with th ladder, Princess whispers as they climb the stairs. Nerida tries to look brave.

- Judd'll belt y' when he finds out.

Princess doesn't answer; all of that will come afterwards, after she's returned the finger to Grandfather. After she's heard its story.

Judd meets them at the top of the stairs, by Uncle Owl's room. He is sleepy-eyed but alert. They talk in fierce whispers.

- Where d' y' think yr goin?

- To Grandfather.

- Not with me bone y' not.

- It's not yr bone.

- Tis now.

- Y' stole it.

- Give it back.

Judd moves forward, his hand out. Suddenly Pito appears beside Princess. His face is drawn, as if he has a fever, and his eyes are big and luminous.

- Let 'er pass.

Judd tries to laugh quietly. - And who's goin t' make me?

- I am.

- You an' who else?

But there is a pale edge of fear in Judd's voice. You never know with Pito; you never quite know what he's capable of. There is a magic about him that lingers from the days of the Game, when Princess and her magician consort ruled the known world.

He shakes his hand more insistently at Princess. - Jus' give me the fucken finger.

When Princess draws away he leans forward, momentarily unbalanced on the top of the stairs. Pito approaches him, holding his hands out in front as if he were about to push him. At that moment Judd overreaches himself and slips, tumbling past the girls down the stairs.

The children listen into the silence that follows, straining their ears for adult sounds. From Uncle Owl's room comes a reassuring blast of snoring.

Princess and Nerida flee down the hall towards the ladder cupboard.

In a moment the ladder is up and Princess is through the trapdoor, which she carefully replaces, blocking out the framed picture of Nerida's anxious face staring up at her. She turns and begins the long ascent.

Around her the house leans and sways, rubbing its timbers along the edge of her bones and multiplying its spaces among the shadows. There are scuffling, shuffling sounds and she thinks of rats. Uncle Honk put Croak up here once and shut the trapdoor; there was a terrible screeching and screaming and thumping as if the cat were doing battle with a legion of devils.

To see a little more light, she peers through one of the cracks in the wall boards and looks out on a segment of the river; the rocks are dense and bunched, the colour of bones in the moonlight. She can see across the river to the beech forest, spread as thick and dark as oil across the lower slopes.

When she reaches Grandfather's trapdoor, she knocks timorously, befitting Grandfather's little white mouse, and huddles beneath the timbers waiting for an answer. Then she taps again, louder, imagining the sound reverberating through the whole house, imagining Aunty Pi waking up and shaking Uncle Honk. Nerida running but finding no place to hide.

The trapdoor opens an inch or two.

- It's yr little white mouse, Grandfather, come t' bring y' some pie.

The trapdoor goes up and moonlight floods down on Princess. Grandfather's room is awash with pale silver, looking bigger than it really is, the sharp, iron lines of the bedhead looming against the mountains behind. She thinks the room is empty until she sees him, flat against the east wall, severed by the shadow of the window sill.

She stays crouched by the trapdoor and pulls the pie out of her pocket. - Pork pie, she says in her best white mouse voice.

- Put it down, Grandfather commands. Princess obeys, placing it on the floor in front of her.

- Now. Why sneak up here in th middle of th night? Is Pi puttin her foot down, is she? Has she issued her orders? She's good at orders, is Pi.

- It ws my idea, Grandfather, Princess says humbly, casting her glance down from the shadowed face with its moon-hollowed eyes. - And Nerida, yr little Churchmouse, she helped me too.

- M'little Churchmouse, Grandfather says thoughtfully, - and where's she now?

- She's keepin watch below, Grandfather.

- Y' stole th food frm th kitchen?

Princess nods.

Grandfather laughs. She feels him come out of the shadow and approach. A moment later, a hand touches her hair. Fingers scrape gently along her left temple and enter the thick mass of her hair, feeling their way across her scalp.

- An' tell me, me brave little white mouse, is there an extra child in th house? A little boy?

Princess raises her head up and looks at Grandfather. She sees the valleys and crevices of his cheeks outlined by the moon and feels the crablike strength of his hand in her hair. What she cannot see are his eyes, hidden by shadows.

- That's a strange question, Grandfather.

- Strange it may be, but I want y't' answer it.

- There's only us, Grandfather.

Grandfather grunts, picks up the pie and moves back onto the bed.

- Come on up, he says in a friendly voice. - There's no need t' crouch on th floor. Come 'n tell me what they're doin down there. How're they goin t' murder me, eh? Come on and tell me? Will Honk do it? Or Owl? Surely not Owl, he might fall over on the job. He did last time. Grandfather gives a short, bitter laugh. - Or one of th women? Pi herself, or m'be Grin. Or even one of th children. Yes, one of th children perhaps.

He takes a bite out of his pie.

- No one wants t' kill y, Grandfather, Princess says, standing up and taking a pace closer to the bed.

That's what you think. They're goin t' kill me or send me t' some home in Christchurch, which'll kill me anyway.

- I've heard nothin about that, Grandfather, Princess says, thinking of the conversation she and Pito had overheard.

- You wouldn't.

- Judd got beaten.

- Serves im right. He's a rotten one, that one. Funny thing, though, y' cn belt th rotten ones an' it don't make a skerrick of difference. It's like they ws born with somethin missin. The belt cn never put it inta them.

- Don't y' get lonely up here alone all the time, Grandfather?

- I wouldn't give y' kiss m' foot fr that crowd down below, I'll tell y' that. They'll rob me blind as quick as look at me, then murder me. But this is my house, see. Th whole shebang, lock, stock and barrel. I've got papers. Signed papers. Sometimes that pirate Honk comes up here with some booze an' tries t' get me t' sign th place over t' him 'n Pi. He tries t' get the papers off me. Or find out where I've put im. But I've got lawyiz in Christchurch.

He pats the bed beside him. - Come an' sit by an abandoned old man.

Princess doesn't move. - I can't stay. I'd like to though, t' stay and have a talk.

- Pi'll skin y' alive if she finds y' here, eh?

- She might. Princess fingers the bone in her pocket. Now that the time to bring it out has arrived, she is   too scared.

- How many children are there? Grandfather rubs his head as if age had erased the proper count of his grandchildren.

Princess counts on her fingers. - There's me 'n Nerida, that's two, an' Judd 'n Maverick, that's four.

- Only four? Honk 'n Owl haven't killed that boar yet, have they? I heard im shootin over on Scrubby Flat. Grandfather shakes his head, - They cdn't hit the side of a house if it fell on im, those clowns.

- Why d' y' stay here all th time, Grandfather?

- Because I like it up here. I cn see all around. He gestures to the valley with its flanking mountains all laid out in front of them on a silver platter.

- They can't fool me. Frm up here I cn see everyone comin an' goin. Every sparra.

Princess is not fooled either. - But Grandfather, y' must want t' come down. Sometimes.

The old man smacks his lips. - That's a nice pie. Yr mother hasn't lost th art of cookin I see; they take care of their own down there alright. He pats the space on the bed beside him once more. - Come an' tell me how they're goin t' kill me. You must know. You kids get t' hear everythin. O' course they're fools. I cd come down any night of th week an' slit their throats an' they'd be none th wiser.

Princess takes a step back towards the trapdoor.

Grandfather's old hand lies on the bed beside him like a claw, ridged with veins. It is possessed of that spiderlike intensity of stillness which precedes sudden movement. She looks at the dark, knotted fingers and remembers them moving sensitively across her scalp, feeling their way by the lightest touch. There is a ripple and quiver across her skin, and a sudden weakness, as if her blood were draining away.

To break the spell, she looks out the window towards Sister Peak. After the rain, with the air washed clean, the Milky Way is slung out before her with a glittering, silent ferocity. They're all inside my body, she thinks. In the space of my breath.

She doesn't hear Grandfather get up and come over to her. One minute there are the Three Sisters with their hoops of stars and the dark wind of the river below, the next Grandfather is in front of her.

- Hold still, child.

When Grandfather's fingers alight on her face, she closes her eyes. She can still see the stars there, behind her eyes, and the shapes of the Three Sisters, but even as she watches they begin to blur and merge. An undulation goes through the stars. The pressure on her skin is light and steady, not a tickly light but soft; so soft and sure it could have been Pito's.

She sees herself standing in the middle of the mountains, the dark, gnarled claw moving across her face.

Like a blind creature learning to see, it touches every part of her face, lingering around the inside of her eye sockets, feeling through her lips to her teeth and running along their moist, smooth edge, whispering along the line of her cheek bone, searching for something in the contours of her face.

Pito.

The fingers are searching for Pito in the cartography of mouth and eyes, and Princess is suddenly terrified. To lie with your voice is one thing, words are great distracters, but to lie with your face is another.

She opens her eyes and sees the soft, touching creature up close, the crinkled, knotted fingers and the coarse, spiky, silver hair that grows from the joints; the rutted and wrinkled landscape of the back of his hand. Across the knuckles the skin is stretched tight, showing the shifting of bones beneath.

- And there's no other child in th house, m' brave one? His voice too is soft and slippery; his fingers touch on her eyelids, then slide down to her throat, thumb and forefinger resting gently each side of her windpipe.

- Not a one, Grandfather, she says in her most pure voice, feeling the flutter of her skin between his fingers.

Grandfather sighs and his hands drop from her. - That's one thing, at least, he says, turning away. - Goodbye m' little white mouse.

He stands with his back to her, his shoulders hunched up, his hands by his side, slowly opening and closing like a sea creature.

Princess quickly pulls the bone out of her pocket. - Judd stole this, she says in a rapid voice. - I brought it back cos Judd shouldn't've taken it.

Grandfather turns around. - M' Sneaky Mouse, he says with some glee, taking the bone in those same, careful fingers. He holds the bone up to the moonlight where it looks like a sharp-jawed, starving creature.

- He's turnin inta a horrible mouse.

- An' y' sneaked it back off him?

- Yip.

- Why?

- T' return it t' you.

- An' bring me a piece of pork pie?

- Yip.

- Why?

- Judd's gettin too big fr his boots.

Grandfather pulls the bone out of the moonlight and thinks this over, - An' what do I have t' do in return. I don't have no biscuits. No biscuits comin up here now.

The bone disappears into his pocket.

- I just want t' know th story of th bone.

- Do y' now.

Princess holds her ground. She has not come this far to surrender to cowardice.

- What makes y' think it has a story?

- Cos th other adults seem t' know about it.

- Like who?

- Uncle Honk.

Grandfather walks about for a time without talking. It's a peculiar slow walk, as if he's not living the moments through consecutively, but one prolonged moment against which he must stretch his legs. During that moment, he stops at the window and stares out, the light from the mountains full on his face. One hand gropes in the pocket that holds the bone.

- Yeah, he says, as if talking to someone just outside the window. - Honk'd know alright.

The way he says it, so bitter and quiet, warns her off speaking again too soon. She waits, and lets Grandfather catch up with the moving moment once more. He does that by sighing and turning away from the window. She gropes forward, blind, into the conversation.

- Well, he wdn't tell us, wd he? He jus comes in when Aunty Grin's doin our lessons an' starts questionin Judd, who lied through his teeth.

- I bet he did.

- Well, what is't?

- What is what?

She catches a spark of cunning in the old man's sideways glance. She daren't look at his moon-baked hands, now moving restlessly against his legs. To look at them would remind her too strongly of how they moved through her hair and across her face, searching for what she would conceal.

- The story of the bone.

- It don't have a story.

- Y'jus said it did.

- Izat so?

- Y'said Uncle Honk'd know it.

- Izat so?

- So tell me.

All the while she has been standing by the trapdoor, as if ready for a quick escape, but now she moves forward, towards the bed. It is like pulling teeth, getting the story out of the old man, but he's going to tell her.

She'll make him tell her.

But Grandfather has moved away from her, to the top end of his bed. When he speaks it's as if he's talking about something else altogether. - That's th funny thing about bones. When they get restless they start comin up out of th ground. Then y've got t' bury im a second time. There ws this cemetery, y' see, and, since the people of that place didn't do right by th bones because of fightin an' sqwabblin, th bones started resurrectin onta th surface like they ws strugglin up out of their graves, and so th people had t' rebury them.

He isn't making sense. His voice keeps catching on something the way gorse pulls at a shirt, tearing little holes in it.

- Izat what happened t' this bone?

- Y' cd say that. Bones need their sleep too.

He is drifting off again into some world of his own, memories that make his hands jump around like hooked trout. Perhaps she can lull it out of him.

- Y' know who that finger belongs to, don't y?

She makes her voice very light, very easy to agree with.

- M'be.

He stands at the head of the bed, the half-eaten pie on the window sill in front of him.

She keeps her voice very soft, as if it comes from way off out in the stars somewhere. - Whe'd y' find it?

But Grandfather is not fooled. He knows the voice is not coming from the stars; trying to trick it out of him is just making him more stubborn. At the same time, if she lets up, she might lose the moment for good.

- An' y' think this bone might need reburyin, she says, as much to cut off his retreat as anything else.

Something breaks loose in Grandfather's throat.

- A proper burial, on decent ground. He turns on her ferociously - An' whe're we goin t' find that around here, eh? There's no place t' bury im, he says, the voice backing up against tears. If he has to cry she will bear it; she'd bear anything now to hear the story. She's seen Maverick cry like that, just to get pity, just to get himself off the hook.

- Bury who? she says, voice soft as Croak's midnight padding in the hall.

- Bury im, Grandfather says, deliberately this time, looking at her, daring her to speak out the name. There's a dare in the look, and mockery too. The mockery of someone who knows a lie when he hears one; his look and tone suggest that she knows as well as he who they are talking about.

The name doesn't get as far as her throat.

- How'd he die?

- He ws just a baby.

Grandfather leaves the window and sits on the bed beside her. Now it's Princess's turn to take refuge in the view. The moonlight makes everything smooth and pale. Even the beech and fir trees look soft and shrubby. Only the mountains above, and Old Snowy, show a sharp edge. Grandfather sits quietly, the moon behind him, his face in the shadow.

- But how'd he die, Grandfather?

- He ws butchered, Grandfather's voice says. She sees his profile, gaunt and worn, like a rock face. She sits at the other end of the bed and holds onto the sides as if she were sailing. I've got to get to the trapdoor, she thinks suddenly.

- Who butchered im?

- A butcher.

His eyes, like the shells of black, glaucous insects, fasten onto the side of her face. There's a cunning, stubborn sound in his voice, the way Judd gets when he thinks he's being smart.

- Who ...?

- They hated im.

- Why?

- Jus' like some animals, they eat their young.

- What animals?

- Gruntin an' piggin. Y' know.

Princess doesn't know, but she nods anyway.

- Ws they all in on it?

Grandfather nods. - Cept me an' Mary, he says quickly. - Mary, she stood up t' Pi, she did. Pi didn' cut no ice with Mary.

- An' what about Mother?

But Grandfather has been quizzed for long enough by his little white mouse, who, of course, has lied to him. Lied in a voice as pure as spring honey.

- There is another, isn't there?

There's a cruel softness in his voice. She nods. She can no longer cover for Pito, because Grandfather already knows. He has the bone to prove it.

- A little dark one, like a shadow?

She nods again. She needs to get to the trapdoor but has lost the power of movement.

He brings the finger out of his pocket and lies it on her knee. For a moment his hand lingers and she sees the finger bones of the old and the young, one separated from death by only the most translucent shell of flesh, the other, long dead. She is about to pick it up when the finger moves. To watch it, as she is doing, is to see something like a shifting alignment of bones, as if there were several shadow bones coming into focus as one. What she feels is a faint clawing, as if there were a kitten on her lap. It comes again and she sees a twitching movement.

The finger is trying to pull itself up her thigh.

A sound comes from her throat, high-pitched, like a child trying to scream. She leaps up and jumps away. The finger bone bounces onto the floor and rolls over. She jumps across the room towards the trapdoor.

- Pito! is the sound that comes from her throat. Hardly a sound, more like a brief, hoarse rush of air.

- He never had no name, Grandfather says. He bends over and quickly picks up the finger, sits it on his knee and begins to stroke it. Standing by the trapdoor she watches, wondering how she can lift it up without him noticing.

- That ws always his name, she says, kneeling down and gently lifting the trapdoor. There is nothing below but a deathless opacity. She speaks, but every word is a countdown. She only has a certain number of words left, and when they run out, there won't be any more.

Grandfather sits bent over the bone, his silver hair flaming cold in the moonlight, the gnarled fingers caressing the bone. Princess thinks of how one day she saw Judd stroking a frog to get it to jump. - Y'jus stroke their tails, he'd said. - Down th tailbone.

Suddenly the finger springs off Grandfather's lap and he is on his feet. She is halfway through the trapdoor when he arrives and kneels beside her. The bone bounces across the floor towards her.

- Don't you worry, he says intensely, - I'll get im. The bastard butcher. I'll spill his guts.

Tears are coming onto his face now, breaking out like sweat.

As her feet connect with a lower rung, Princess slides a little further down. Looking up at him, for only her head and shoulders are above floor level, he looks, despite his halo of silver and his ancient hands, like a boy, a little boy with an old face.

- Let me tell y' now, he says speaking in a desperately adult, oracular tone, - let me promise y' one thing. I'll get im back. If it's th last thing I do. I promise y'. I'll get im back fr Mary. An' you 'n th boy. I'll make im sweat!

But Princess, her body half in the lower world, half in the upper, doesn't believe him. It sounds like something he's said to himself often, in the aloneness of his room.

- I'll make im sweat, he repeats, and the edge of enthusiasm that comes into his voice makes him sound like Judd when he's planning some atrocity, or Pito when he's trying to cover up his big secret. He holds out his arms in a curious gesture that might be supplication, a beggar's supplication, his arms are so skinny; so scrawny he is, just a little malice wrapped around some bones.

- They're no children of mine, he says gravely. - No children of mine'd go on that way.

Then he grins. It is an ugly, mad grin, full of false reassurance.

- I spit in their mouths, he says.

Princess slips down through the trap door. As she goes past the level of the floor, she sees the finger bone lying nearby, playing dead.

The journey down is swift, her feet blindly finding the next rung, and the next. She doesn't feel her body. She doesn't believe she can fall. She doesn't think about the words she's wrenched from Grandfather's mouth, just Pito and how hard it will be to lie to him. She has never tried to lie to Pito before. He can put his fingers to her forehead and her thoughts just flow between, straight to him. Harder still to lie to herself, to not face that she will lose him, has already lost him. And that without Pito there can be no Princess. Hard to know the truth and go on as if you don't.

Can she lie to herself and pretend to be a princess when she has no kingdom and no royal consort? And if she is not the princess then who is she, and who will mourn for Pito?

Who will mourn for Princess?

Light as a cat, she steps on the rafters, listens for a moment to the silence beneath, and pulls up the trapdoor. Another trapdoor. A passage to the world.

Aunty Pi is standing directly below, looking up at her.

- Come on down, Aunty Pi says.

- I'll need th ladder.

Soon she will have no words left, even sullen ones. Her meagre store will be gone.

Aunty Pi goes to the cupboard and opens it. Nerida comes out, holding Teddy over her face. Aunty Pi puts up the ladder and Clare climbs carefully down, limbs shaking.

- Y' stole food. Aunty Pi says. It is not a question.

Clare nods. They don't seem to notice that she is no longer the Princess.

- I diddin do nothing, Nerida whines. It is her craven, Aunty Grin voice.

Aunty Pi puts the ladder back in the cupboard and closes its door.

- Are we goin t' get a hidin? Clare asks.

Aunty Pi frowns. - We'll see in th mornin.

- What're we goin t' do now? Nerida says, bewildered.

- Go t'bed, Aunty Pi says, heading off down the hall.

Princess lies in bed waiting for Nerida's sobbing to die down. Nerida is afraid of the wardrobe, but that's nothing as far as Princess is concerned, because the princess is in line for a beating.

The wardrobe's nothing.

But, lying there listening to the sounds of the other kids breathing and Nerida sobbing, she feels squeezed by the dark and the narrowness of the room, as if she were in a wardrobe herself. Once, with Uncle Owl, she walked to the Lesters' place and they passed an old cottage that had burned down. She'd stood in one of the phantom rooms and marvelled at how small the floor looked without the walls to give it body, and how even smaller the rooms looked.

As if, perhaps, to compensate, her body begins to grow, to inflate, her limbs to bloat out to impossible size. She tries to cry, using Nerida's sobs to get her going, but no tears come. Where there should be tears there is only a mute darkness, and she is just a tiny head floating on a vast body. Yet, it is then, lying quietly in the night, with numbness and the sounds of breathing, that the princess dies. The little girl who climbed off the dead cow, brandishing the horn and declaring herself to be the princess, must now step back through time to that moment and assume once more her old name, her ordinary name.

The little girl with the ordinary name is cold and lonely and shivering. Her name is not full of soft, gentle sibilants, as is the sound of Princess, with its rustle of silk, but a single, flat, hard vowel, like the edge of a saw, or the nasal bleat of a sheep. Less of a name than a hook to lodge in her flesh and pull her up out of childhood.

She is no longer Princess.

Her name is Clare.

In the morning, Aunty Pi lines the kids up in the kitchen. All of them, from Maverick, the biggest, to Nerida, the smallest. Mother stands with her back to them at the kitchen sink, her body outlined in the morning sun. Aunty Grin sits at the kitchen table cutting pieces of meat into thin strips. The early sun falls bright and hard across the table, illuminating the knife, the meat, and Aunty Grin's hands.

The children stand stiff and straight and say nothing.

Many searching questions are asked.

- How often have ys taken food up t' Grandfather?

- How often have ys visited Grandfather?

- And why?

- What's he told ys?

- What d' ys do when yr up there?

- Do ys know that he's a foolish old man with foolish ideas in his head?

- Do ys know he'll fill ys up with all kinds of lies?

- Why go up at night?

Questions are interspersed with asides to Aunty Grin on the calibre of the children's grandfather, what kind of influence he might be on them, and what sort of nonsense he would spout. Her voice is as stretched as an overwound spring.

At the same time, Aunty Grin looks very serious and shakes her head and nods where required, reinforcing Aunty Pi's comments with observations of her own. - The kids shd know better, is her conclusion, and Aunty Pi concurs one hundred percent.

- They've been told a thousand times, Aunty Grin says. - They'll take the best years of yr life and leave y' nothin.

- They knew they shdn't be goin up there, why else sneak around at night? This is Aunty Pi's logic and it is impervious. Clare has no answer.

Nerida sobs. Judd smirks. Maverick looks innocent. Pito says nothing. He is pale and shocked and doesn't look at Clare; he alone knows that Princess is gone, and that her kingdom has turned into a body of grief. He can see the woman in her face and his slight form rocks with fear. There is no magic for what he now must face.

- They stole, Aunty Grin points out in a prim voice, her lips forming into the pucker of a prim smile. - They knew what they ws up to.

- I want t' make it very clear, Aunty Pi goes on, - that Grandfather's room is out of bounds. He's not fit company fr human bein's.

- Uncle Owl reckons that Grandfather is sulkin, Nerida says, - and when he stops sulkin he'll come down.

- Does he now? Aunty Pi's face grows dark with anger, - Well, yr Uncle Owl wdn't know th time a day. He wdn't know if he ws comin or goin, yr Uncle Owl. He wdn't know a day's work if 't jumped up 'n hit him in th face. He's full of wild talk. He thinks he knows how t' run th world. It's a pity he doesn't work as hard as he talks.

- It's disgusting, Aunty Grin says.

Aunty Pi says, - These children have t' be brought up short on this. We have t' nip this sort of thing right in th bud. This galavantin aroun' at night stealin stuff fr'm th kitchen.

At the sink, there is a rattling of plates. Mother's body stiffens. The space around her head darkens, shutting out the blue behind.

Aunty Grin slices the meat with thin, hard strokes. - That's the best policy. You've got t' come down like a ton of bricks. Stop it before it starts. That's what I say.

Aunty Pi looks thoughtful. She glances across at Mother and back to the children. Finally, she makes up her mind. The boys are to go immediately and help Uncle Honk and Uncle Owl move the sheep from the lower paddock, except they have to tell Uncle Honk to come back to the house for a minute. She turns to the girls. Nerida is obviously an accomplice, a willing accomplice, and her punishment will be three hours in the wardrobe where she can sort the potatoes, the big ones from the little ones, the rotten ones from the sound ones. She can feel out the rotting bits with her fingers. There are three sacks to do, so that will keep her busy. She's not allowed out until she's finished them, even if the three hours are up. For Clare, instigator, the one who stole the pie, there is only one punishment possible.

A whipping.

She will go out to the old willow tree by the river and pick a willow whip so long and so thick ...

Mother turns. Her face is dark and sallow, like Pito's. Her voice too is wan. - In their eyes th kids've done nothin wrong.

- They've got t' learn that if they lie 'n sneak 'n steal they cn expect th worst, Aunty Pi says firmly.

Mother shrugs helplessly. There is defeat in her voice.

- The kid's too young, she says, her voice thick. Too young t' be locked up in th dark fr three hours.

She doesn't try to fight the battle over Clare's whipping. Her hands wring themselves on her apron. - Too young.

Clare holds her breath. The children stand silent as stones. Nerida looks up at Mother, a light in her face. The noises of the morning flood into the room. A magpie is cawing. The barking of dogs in the lower paddock comes faintly on the wind. Nearby they can hear the ratchet moving on Father's fence-mending gear, clattering its iron teeth. Croak comes in and jumps on the stool by the table. He appears not to notice the meat, lying in strips where Aunty Grin has cut it, and left it. She is on her feet, moving towards Mother. Aunty Pi is coming in at Mother from the other side. Mother looks at both women and turns back to the sink, dunking her hands into the foamy water.

- Too young t' steal binoculars, steal food, steal God knows what else, Aunty Pi says in a low, furious voice in Mother's right ear.

- Too young t' sneak about th house spyin 'n whisperin in corners, Aunty Grin says in Mother's left ear, her voice as thin and bright as wire.

- Too young, of course, t' lie t' yr face, t' tell y' black's white and white's black...

Mother blocks out their voices and looks down. The sun has come up over the Dog-leg and is shining into the sink. A few soap bubbles float quietly on the water, rocking gently around her wrists as if her hands have just drowned. The bubbles gleam with colour, like distant cities.

Aunty Pi and Aunty Grin turn back to the children. Aunty Pi's verdict is incisive. The punishments will begin immediately. Aunty Grin will escort Nerida to the wardrobe. As a concession to Mother, she will be allowed to take Teddy. Clare is presented with the small, serrated kitchen knife mother uses for the potatoes to cut a willow stick for her own whipping.

Croak nabs a piece of meat and jumps under the table, just as Aunty Grin is turning in his direction.

Clare goes out to the willow. Each step, diminishing in length from the previous one, passes through a long terrain of numbness, and she cannot bear to think of Pito at the line-up this morning, as pale as ever, trying to look firm and brave and avoid her eye at the same time. Each step becomes a pilgrimage of love and renunciation, surrender and reflection; the willow a distant, forbidding shrine. Pito, her divine magician and consort, who was to be with her in love, in the body of feeling, forever. Pito, who grew up in the shadow of his own grave.

How long has he known? she wonders. Or does he still not really know. And how can I tell him?

From a distance the long, whip-like stems growing out of a fallen log look light and feathery, but the springy growth, each branch hugging small hard buds to itself, makes for a vicious switch. Carefully she cuts a stick that is very young with plenty of bend, and takes it back to Aunty Pi, re-traversing her steps of pain. On her way back across the yard, the dogs, Tonks and Peg, tied up by the barn, run out to the ends of their chains and look up expectantly at her. Peg sniffs the air as if there were something strange about Clare's smell.

Aunty Pi inspects the stick critically. It is too skinny. She suggests a shorter, whippier piece, not quite so bendy. A good willow whip will have a certain whistle as it goes through the air. This time Tonks barks as she crosses the yard and silly Peg follows suit. She can hear the pumping of Uncle Honk's tractor in the distance, coming across the paddocks. Pito, Pito, Pito, her footsteps say as they hit the ground. Pito, Pito, Pito, the tractor says, the seat bouncing up and down. Clare has a great space inside her as empty as a bare hillside, as lonely as the sound of a distant kea. She knows what is required of her. She must retrieve Pito's finger and return it to the earth, some special place where she can put it in the ground with Princess's old cow-horn; she would never have to be separated from his love. Princess and Pito would be buried together.

Choosing the right whip is an agony of decision making. Aunty Pi might increase the punishment if she thinks Clare is trying to fool her, and she has a fine nose for deceitful children. Clare has no choice but to pick a good whippy stick and suffer for her choice. As she chooses, she feels a movement down inside, very deep and unfamiliar. Somewhere at the base of her spine, a tingling, a tearing. She felt it last night with Grandfather, some new shape growing out of the bones.

After a close inspection of the whip and a little testing in the air, Clare is sent to the bathroom to await Uncle Honk's arrival. This is not long delayed. She hears the tractor pull up and stop. Clare hates the bathroom. The strong antiseptic smell makes her think of illness. Outside the bathroom, the world is big and empty. Full of bare, open hillsides with scraps of gorse and broom in the gullies. A picture comes into her mind of a hillside and a broom bush lit by the single bloom of a butterfly. -That's where I'll bury him, she says to the bathroom.

Aunty Pi comes in followed by Uncle Honk. The two adults seem to crowd out the small room with their bulk. Uncle Honk has a belly nurtured on homebrew that bulges out in front of him as if he were pregnant, and his arms are big and meaty. Aunty Pi doesn't have to be big to fill up the room; her voice can do that for her.

- These kids've gone too far this time, she says to Uncle Honk. Uncle Honk tests the whip on his hand and nods with satisfaction.

Aunty Pi's voice is tight, her eyes narrow and cold. - Y' know why we're doin this?

Clare nods.

- Then tell us.

- Because I stole.

- That's th main thing. What'd y' steal?

- A piece of pie.

- Y' know that Judd got a hidin f' stealin th binoculars.

- Yes.

- D' y' think that ws fair?

Clare bites her lip.

- Y' said at the time it was fair. People heard you. Are y' goin t' lie t' me about that now?

- No.

- I'm glad a that. So if Judd got fairly punished why shdn't you?

As expected, Clare has no answers. Uncle Honk shifts impatiently on his feet, but Aunty Pi carries on.

- What else? I mean what else've y' done?

- I went up t' Grandfather's room.

- Y' what?

- I went up...

- Y' what?

- I...

- You sneaked up t' Grandfather's room, that's what y' done, in th middle of th night when no one ws around, you thought. When y' thought y' cd run riot. She turns to Honk. - These bloody kids think they rule th roost.

Clare says nothing.

- What have y' got t' say?

- Nothin.

Uncle Honk snorts with contempt.

- That's bloody typical, Aunty Pi says to him, her voice shaking with fury, her thin lips pulled tight across her teeth. - Y' cn work yr fingers t' th bone, y' cn stew yr guts out worryin about these bloody kids, and y' don't get so much as a kiss y' foot.

Her eyes have gone a brittle blue, like glass that has already shattered. - Come over here.

Clare stands by the bowl. Aunty Pi kneels down lifts Clare's dress and in one brisk, no-nonsense movement, pulls down her pants.

- Bend over the bowl, she commands. Clare feels the bowl hard against her knees and mother's breast-strap tight against her chest. Blood runs into her head. Aunty Pi is still kneeling beside her. She feels an insect like tickling on her thighs and knows that it is Uncle Honk stroking her with the switch, getting his range. The blood in her ears is pumping out the same word over and over, Pito, Pito, Pito ... It is a soft sound, low and whispery.

- Get on with it, Aunty Pi says.

Clare thinks of Pito, standing by the door on one of his invisible spots listening to this, and an unbearable love fills her up. I love you, Pito!

The whip gives a shrill whoop of anticipation but, like Judd before her, she clamps the scream inside her mouth just as she's clamped her love for Pito inside her body, closes her eyes and lets the pain go up in lights behind them.

- Another one, Aunty Pi commands. - Hoe inta her.

A second path of pain opens up, lower down this time, across her upper thighs. Her throat tightens further.

- Another one.

- Shit, she's bleedin like a stuck pig.

- A good switch doesn't draw blood.

Aunty Pi looks down. The two welts are red and proud but there is no blood.

She's bleedin from below.

Aunty Pi looks.

- How long has this been goin on, y' filthy little beast? Her voice is shrill. - Tell me or I'll whip y't' rags myself. She is taken by such a frenzy of rage she can hardly keep her hands still. They thresh against her own thighs like newly-caged animals. Then one hand breaks free and leaps up, landing on the side of Clare's head, knocking her off the toilet seat. She lands awkwardly on her back, Aunty Pi beside her, raining blows down on the girl's shoulders.

- It's th first time, Clare tries to say but her voice comes out as a gargle, as if she has blood in her throat as well. Her legs fall open to Uncle Honk's piggy stare.

Aunty Pi takes her by the shoulders and shakes her until her teeth rattle in her head. - You filthy little pig. Why didn't y' tell me! Walkin aroun' bleedin like an animal?

Before Clare can answer, Aunty Pi hauls her back up and makes her stand, bent over the bowl. The whip lands again, very deliberately, directly between her legs, undercut from below.

- She's a filthy beast, Aunty Pi says between clenched teeth. - Filthy, filthy, filthy.

When the next blow lands, in the same place, Clare's throat loosens, she opens her mouth and Pito shrieks, using her body to make a human sound, the only human sound he can make. All his agony moves through her. She makes the same sound when the whip lands once more, with all the power of Uncle Honk's muscle behind it. This one is so viciously undercut it slices right up to her navel, and she feels Pito go from the world, finally severed. She sees him losing grip of the shadows he's been holding onto so hard, and float backwards out of the house.

Red grief runs over her.

When she wakes before dawn the next morning, the first thing Princess sees is the finger bone. It is on the edge of the bed, just a few inches away, thin end towards her. From her vantage point, with one eye open, it looks like the fossil remains of some prehistoric monster. If she closes one eye and opens the other, it appears to jump, to leap closer to her.

It doesn't matter if Grandfather brought it down and placed it by her pillow, or if the thing found its own way down, she thinks. What matters is that it is there, in front of her, and she has a job to do.

One last royal duty as the Princess.

Instinctively she glances over to Pito's bed. It is empty, but she can feel him in the room. Hanging around her. Around the finger bone. His finger bone.

Working slowly against the pain between her legs, and a heavy, clotted feeling down below, she slips out of bed and into her warm outdoor clothes. It is not yet light and the room is possessed by a stillness that takes hold of the world just before dawn. She thinks she sees Pito standing by the door looking her way with huge, dark eyes, his slight body swaying.

She finds Hattie's old horn amid a pile of childhood stuff, and slips out the door; the last thing she wants to do is waken Judd or Maverick, or the restless Nerida shut inside her dreams of closed spaces. Before she leaves, she picks up the finger itself, handling it gingerly, as she might a pet mouse, placing it carefully in the ample pocket of her overcoat.

Out of the house and around the corner of the barn she goes allowing the tears to run hot on her chilled cheeks and her breath to come in ragged gasps. The dogs watch her with lowered heads and shadowed eyes. They give the air a desultory sniff as she passes them. Peg makes a yearning sound in her throat.

A thin light is trickling in from the plains by the time she has laboured up the slope of the lower Dog-leg and reached the ridge. From here she can look out to the plains and incipient dawn on one side, or back the river and valley, still sunk deep in night, on the other. Her wounds chaff and the rags she has used to catch her first blood rub blindly against her raw, tender flesh. She turns and faces the huge splendour of the alps and the great blade of snow that is Old Snowy. Even as she looks, the upper reaches of that mountain begin to redden, faintly, against the night stars behind in the west.

Pito is there, around her, somewhere, although she can't see him. This is his last dawn, and he hardly has body enough to feel the chill of it, or listen into its spaces for the great emptiness that is listening back; although at moments she thinks she catches a glimpse of him, sombre, hollow, moving at her side. If she spoke to him, perhaps he would hear her, perhaps take on a more corporeal form, but she has very few words left now and every step exhausts her.

Slowly, she makes her way to the broom bush where, at least for a little time, the magic of the world opened to them in the cathedral wings of a red admiral. There opened too, a partial glimpse of the great living universe that holds everything in the net of its own senses; if Princess and Pito have any kind of shrine this is it, facing east into the dawn.

She sits under the broom bush and stubbornly unpacks the earth, stone by stone, until she has a hole big enough to hold the cow-horn and the bone. It is not easy work since the ground is hard and rips at her fingers. Pito is very near. She can feel his agitation. Now that the moment has come, he doesn't want to go. In her mind she talks to him quite severely, telling him that he has to go, at least from her. She must never see him again.

When the hole is ready she places horn and bone in it, and begins to pack the stones and hard earth back on top. As she does this, her last duty as Princess, she uses her last store of sounds to chant a prayer over Pito's new grave. She makes it out of broken syllables and passing fragments of words, an ululation as much as a prayer.

The most ancient sound grief can make in the human throat.

Siege

UNCLE HONK has just fed the dogs and is returning from the barn to the house when the boar trots purposefully into the yard. Along the shadow side of the barn, Tonks and Peg, Ran and Billy, go mad, choking themselves hoarse on their collars. Mother looks up from her post at the sink-bench and squints against the sun.

With nothing more lethal than a spoon in his hand, Uncle Honk does all he can do; he freezes motionless as his shadow. Only the clouds keep moving, low and fast across the sun. The faintest breeze stirs tiny eddies of dust.

The boar stops and swings his head from the house to the barn and back to the house again; he has his head in the air and is sniffing like a dog. Uncle Honk stands still as a post. The sheepdogs choke on their barks. Uncle Owl ambles out the back door, cursing at the dogs. Having made its decision, the boar heads towards Uncle Honk who makes a break for the house. At that moment Mut appears out of nowhere, also racing for the back door. He runs right under Uncle Honk's feet, squealing as Uncle Honk goes down on top of him.

The man has hardly hit the ground and the boar is on him, goring his leg to blood before swinging away towards the barn. With one inspired leap Mut is in the house. Blood soaks through Uncle Honk's dungarees. He stares stupidly at the spoon in his hand. The pig gallops over to the barn and rips the guts out of the yapping Peg. The others slam themselves up against the corrugated iron of the barn wall in an effort to get away.

Uncle Honk pulls himself across the yard using his arms. Staring at him with wide eyes, Uncle Owl turns and vanishes inside; the pig turns once more towards the house, as if considering another pass at Uncle Honk, who's wriggling forward on his elbows like a lizard, hauling himself up onto the back step. Mut, racing ahead of the returning Uncle Owl, almost runs straight into Uncle Honk's face; Honk takes a snarling bite at the animal.

Behind him, the boar veers away towards the gap between the barn and the house, moving faster than you'd think a pig could move. Mut runs with a barking bravado into the middle of the yard, one eye on the steaming innards of the dead Peg. Uncle Honk, lying propped up on the back step, rips the rifle out of Uncle Owl's hand. Before he can get it lined up, there is a sharp sound from above and the boar falls over, asleep in midstride.

- My kill! Grandfather shouts from his glass tower.

- Y' diddin finish th job, Uncle Honk says in a dull voice, firing twice. Mut leaps in the air, blood squirting out of his mouth. He lands heavily on his back; the sound of his spine breaking reverberates through the whole house.

At the back door, Uncle Owl begins to cry.

The children have come out to inspect the dead boar. It is almost as long as a man and its curved tusks, four or five inches long, are covered with blood. Its dark, almost black skin seems to be quivering.

Nerida is frightened of it and hides behind Teddy, but Judd is boastful. This is the same boar he met on Scrubby Flat, with the fool dog, Mut. The boar nearly killed him that time. One day he will kill his own boar with a real pig knife. Anybody can shoot a pig. Even old Grandfather in his glass tower. It's another thing to stick a pig properly with a knife. That's the only real way to kill a pig. Having met such a lethal animal in the flesh, and having survived, confers on Judd absolute authority in such matters. The pig is all but his.

Grandfather's voice crackles out across the yard, - I'll have th meat off this one m'self, by God. I'll winch it up here with m' bare hands.

Aunty Pi comes out into the yard from the kitchen door. She faces Grandfather's window. - You'll do nothin of th sort. We got a wounded man in here. We have t' tend t' him. Then we got t' get that pig out of the sun an' cut im up.

Her voice is curiously flat in the open yard.

- You're a thief an' a liar, Pi. That pig's mine! Mine! Mine t' cut 'n cure. D' y' think I don't know how t' cure a bit of pig meat? Now get a rope on that hog!

- Get a rope on it y'self, Aunty Pi says, going back into the house. A moment later she reappears, her face bloodless with anger. - You might try askin y'self how we're goin t' manage here with th only able-bodied man in th place on his back.

She doesn't wait for a reply.

The children go and look at Mut. He has been shot twice, once through the hindquarters and once through the stomach. He lies at an unnatural angle in a puddle of blood. His legs stick out as if he is still trying to run. Looking at him, the children fall quiet.

Uncle Owl approaches on wobbly legs. His hands shake as he holds a sack open. A dirty yellow rolly, soaked in spittle, hangs from the corner of his mouth. He runs the back of his shaking hand across the rasp of his chin. There is a heavy, sick smell in the air about him.

- The bastard ws jus' waitin f' th opportunity, he says to the kids in a broken voice. Mut goes into the sack. His legs are all stiff and seem to resist, just like he would have in life. A final indignity.

Uncle Owl, sack in hand, staggers down towards the macrocarpa where Father is repairing the fence.

Father has heard the snipers at work, and has taken refuge behind the macrocarpa. He's watching for the first sign of enemy soldiers. Any walking, crouching death. Instead he sees Uncle Owl coming, carrying a spade and a sack that is turning red at the bottom, followed at a distance by a straggle of orphans. Uncle Owl stares at Father but doesn't recognise him. Father has seen that look many times. It's the look of a dead man. A dead man who must bury another dead man. They all did it. Armies of the dead burying each other as fast as they could, but the bones floated up from the bottom of the world and tossed about on empty fields for everyone to see. Sometimes there wasn't much to bury, just a limb or two, a memory, not much more than you could shove into an old sack, like the one the dead man was carrying. And always, of course, a straggle of orphans. Children whose faces would be familiar if you looked at them for long enough.

Father makes hectic sounds in his throat and looks at his innocent hands; his hands have killed no soul, so why should they bring him such bloody offerings? There must be a sniper nearby if the dead have come looking for graves.

Snipers are the worst for you never know where or when.

The children watch Uncle Owl bury Mut. It takes him quite a long time because the ground is so stony, but he persists, sweating grimly at the spade. When he has done, and erected a small heap of stones to mark the place, the children turn back for the house.

At the spot where Mut was shot there is a spatter of drying blood. Maverick kicks some dust over it - Someone'll have t' bury Peg, he says. He sounds worried. Since Uncle Honk is sick, Maverick, who is the eldest, will have more to do. Already the chores will be piling up on Aunty Pi's list.

- It's high time s'me people round here started pullin their weight, he can hear her saying.

At first Mother won't touch Uncle Honk, not even to cut away his shredded dungarees. She sits at the kitchen table until Aunty Pi comes in from shouting at Grandfather. Aunty Pi is in no mood to stand for any nonsense from Mother.

- I won't touch im, Mother says, her voice full of quiet violence. She clasps her hands together before her on the table. Croak comes running in under the table and rubs up against her legs.

Aunty Pi whirls around the kitchen, picking things up and slamming them down, opening cupboard doors and throwing them shut. - Y' won't touch him. That's nice. That's bloody nice. Coming fr'm you. His sister 'n all.

The first aid box appears from one of the cupboards.

- You're in no position t' start layin down th law around this house, m' girl. Aunty Pi leans down close to Mother. - Just snap t' it, or there'll be hell t' pay around here. Hell t' pay!

Mother makes a half strangled movement to rise. She looks across at the door and sees Nerida staring at her, Teddy clutched in her hand.

Watched by Aunty Pi and Aunty Grin, Mother dresses Uncle Honk's wound. For a start, the leg of the dungarees is cut away and Mother cleans the area with hot water made purple with Condy's crystals. Uncle Honk winces, grins and winces, but does not cry out as Mother does her work, dipping her cloth into the hot water which turns a muddy, bloody brown.

There is a set look on Mother's face. She could be standing at her old post at the sink, doing the dishes, not seeing the dirty plates and pots in front of her.

- It mustn't turn septic, Aunty Pi says, handing Mother a pair of scissors. Mother puts them to one side.

- We might have t' get in th doctor, Aunty Grin says.

- Only if it turns septic.

- That tusk cut right t' th bone. Aunty Grin's voice is a thin, insistent whine.

- It'll heal, Aunty Pi declares.

When the wound is cleaned, Mother covers it with honey and binds it firmly. - Sage, she says quietly. - Sage t' protect fr'm infections.

- Maybe it will, maybe it won't, Aunty Grin says, taking no notice of Mother.

- I should of nailed th bastard t' th barn, Uncle Honk says, voice thick with phlegm. - That dog diddin' deserve a quick death.

- These dungarees've had it, Aunty Grin observes. She holds them up for inspection. The thigh is ripped out on one side and the crutch is soaked with blood. Mother won't look at them. Aunty Grin insists on showing her but Mother turns away, her lips curling.

- For the rag bag, Aunty Grin says with some satisfaction, rolling the dungarees up in a tight ball.

- I should of done it a long time ago, Uncle Honk says, turning restlessly against the pain.

Aunty Pi decides he should stay in the living room on the couch rather than try to move him. The living room, with the shades pulled, will become his sick room.

- We'll have t' keep th kids out of here, she says to Mother.

- Somebody's going t' have t' go outside and cut that hog up before th flies get it, Aunty Pi says. - Where's Owl?

- With Jack gettin drunk, Aunty Grin says, quick as a flash.

- What a fine bloody pair they are, Aunty Pi says bitterly. - I'm goin t' smash every bloody bottle in th place.

- Jack doesn't drink, Mother says. She speaks in her usual half tone, as if she is not talking to anybody but herself.

But Aunty Pi doesn't let it go past. - That's cold comfort. But I suppose we have t' be thankful f' small mercies.

- One thing f' sure, we'll all be dead 'n gone before that fence is mended, Aunty Grin says, but nobody takes the bait. Mother just looks tired.

- I'll just have t' do it m'self, Aunty Pi says in her Little Red Hen voice, taking the carving knife from the drawer.

She gets to the door just in time to see a hawk circle with apparent laziness and land on top of the dead animal.

There is a sharp sound from Grandfather's room and the hawk flies to pieces.

Aunty Pi approaches the boar with the carving knife in one hand and an empty sugar sack in the other. The body is wreathed with bloody feathers, giving it a ritual, totemic aspect, but that does not bother her. Her strategy is clear cut; she will take it in bits and pieces. A leg here, a rib there. She will send up the liver, the kidneys, maybe the heart, to

Grandfather, as delicacies, keep the old bastard sweet. Salt the rest quietly away. There will be enough pork in the house to keep them all going for a month of Sundays.

The children watch from the protection of the side of the house. Judd sucks his cheeks in, pushing his hands into his pockets. Nerida moves closer to Clare. She was the first to notice Clare's silence, and finds in it something she takes for strength.

There's a quick, flat sound from Grandfather's room and dust flicks up a few feet ahead of Aunty Pi who stops, turns around and faces the house.

She has to scream to be heard across the yard. - How cn we get im t' y' if we can't cut im up?

- Just get a rope on it, Pi. I cn do th rest frm up here. I'll pull it up m'self.

- You'll do y'self an injury. That's just what we need. I'm not haulin y' out on a stretcher.

- Just get a rope around it.

Pi hesitates. The old loon is not about to shoot her in the back, no matter how much he hates her guts. What would he do with her dead? Who else has held this place together for all these years, Jack away at the war, coming back with his marbles rolling around in his head, Owl turning into a right no-hoper, on the booze all the time? Who took it all on, and did the work of two men around the place with never so much as a kiss y' foot in return? She should be able to carve that beast up calm as you please, she has every right, every right in the world.

She takes a step forward and there is another shot. There is a spurt of dust in front of the pig's head, as if it suddenly exhaled.

Aunty Pi turns for the house, her face set in a thin line. - It'll be a blowflies' picnic, she says, loud enough to carry across the yard.

The children scatter.

Clare is waiting for Judd to take revenge on her for stealing the bone and taking it up to Grandfather. For all she knows, Judd believes Grandfather still has it. Judd has had other things on his mind however. As the children climb into the bunks, he paces around the room; the excitement of all the shooting and the rich spectacle of the dead pig, the gutted Peg and the stiff, still incompetent Mut, has made his blood hot and his memory sharp. He sees himself on top of the Dog-leg, binoculars in his hand, sweeping the hillside for the very beast that now lies in the yard, fresh in death; he remembers meeting the animal face to face on Scrubby Flat, and Mut flipping around like a cat. He laughs out loud just like Uncle Honk does after a few beers. Stupid dog! Dead dog! He remembers, too, the look of intent on Uncle Honk's face as he took a bead on Mut.

Behind that, there's a memory, or maybe the memory of a dream, of standing beside a frozen lake when the ice sheet starts moving towards him, tinkling against the rocks like fairy bells, while on the opposite shore a boy slips away.

Then he remembers the confrontation at the top of the stairs. His bitch of a sister and her sorceror. He walks around for a while thinking about that, laughing and snarling to himself. Finally, he wanders over to Clare's bunk and makes an ugly face at her.

- Let's see im, he says, curling his lip.

Clare looks puzzled.

- I mean them welts. Them welts Uncle Honk gave y' with th switch.

- Yr not allowed t' ask that, Nerida says. - I'll tell Aunty Pi an' y'll get another beatin.

- Izat right? Judd says, looking with mock surprise at Maverick. - Y' won't be sayin anythin t' anybody when I've finished with y'. He turns back to Clare, - Let's see them welts.

- Yeah, Maverick says, matching Judd's tone. - Let's see im.

Clare shakes her head, and makes the motions of attending to her bed.

- I'll tell, Nerida says.

- What's wrong with 'er? Can't she speak fr h'self? To Clare he says, - Not talkin, eh? Cat got y' tongue?

Clare shrugs.

- I mean why aren't y' talkin?

Clare settles down in the blankets and pulls them around her.

- Look't this Mav, she's dumber than a post.

- Yeah, maybe she needs a little proddin.

- Maybe she does. Judd pokes Clare sharply in the ribs with two stiff fingers. - Come on, talk, tell us what Uncle Honk did t' y'.

Clare turns her back on them.

- Uncle Honk's not goin t' like this, Judd says to Maverick.

- He'll probably give her another switchin.

- No he won't, Nerida says to Teddy. – 'Cos he's laid up in th lounge.

Judd pauses to consider this; when it sinks in he feels as if a huge burden has been lifted from his shoulders. He feels exultant, giddy, as if he were standing once more on the Dog-leg, the dead rabbit hanging between his hands, a tingle in his groin.

To Nerida he says, - Then it's not much use yr runnin off tellin tales, is't?

- Aunty Pi'll do't herself, Nerida says quickly.

- There y' go, Judd says to the back of Clare's head. Pi h'self'll take y' in hand. He prods her, harder this time, and nods with satisfaction when she gasps and pulls away. - Y' see, he says to Maverick and Nerida. - I wonder what'd happen if y' stuck a pin in her? D' y' think she'd squeal?

- She would, said Maverick. - It wd get her yellin fr grown ups.

- Go get a pin, Judd says to Maverick, keeping his eyes on the back of Clare's head. - There's one stickin in th wood above m'bed.

Clare doesn't move, and continues to stare at the wall as if she can't hear him.

Maverick hesitates.

- Do it, Mav.

Maverick whines, - I don't want t' get a beatin.

- Remember in th barn, Mav. What happened in th barn.

- You mean with th finger? There's a quiver in Maverick's voice.

- Jus' tell me.

- Y' made th finger move.

- It moved, didn't it, Mav? It moved by itself.

- Yeah. But y' can't make it move again because y' don't have it.

- I don't have it Mav, but look around. Where's Pito? I used it t' make Pito go away. You'll never see Pito again.

Clare turns over violently and sits up, fixing on Judd a hugely contemptuous stare.

Judd returns it with arrogance.

- Well where is he? Why don't y' call out fr im?

He jabs her again with his fist, on the thigh, close to one of the welts and she jerks away. Maverick arrives by his side with the pin.

- Are y' ready t' stick it in 'er? Judd says, looking gloatingly at Clare.

All fear seems to have left Maverick who, sensing victory perhaps, looks flushed and eager. - Yeah, he sneers, where d' y' want it, Juddy?

- In her leg'll do.

Clare's face goes blank. With slow, dignified movements, she slips her pants and pad off under the blankets, pulls the covers back and rolls over, revealing her bum and her welts. Judd sucks air into his cheeks with satisfaction and Maverick just stares. Nerida cuddles Teddy as hard as she can.

Casually, Judd says, - Y' know what th grownups say, don't y'.

- What's that, Juddy, Maverick says, the pin still poised in his hand.

- I heard Aunty Pi 'n Grin talkin. They sez that Pito ws an *imaginary playmate*. Kids often have im if they don't have many friends t' play with. He puts on a baby voice for the last two words.

Maverick comes in on cue with a nasty laugh. - Imaginary playmate, Juddy.

Clare grabs the blanket to cover herself again.

- Don't move, Judd says commandingly. - We want t' count im, don't we Mav.

- Yeah. There's one, two, three, four ...

- Nice 'n red. Standin up proud.

Her face flaming, Clare pulls the bedclothes around her and turns to face them, her mouth working in mute speech. Judd takes the pin from Maverick and jabs it into his own hand; not a flicker of pain crosses his face.

- D' y' know what she's sayin, he says to Nerida. Clare goes red in the face and shakes her head violently. Her hands fly around like demented birds.

Nerida doesn't look at Clare but consults with Teddy.

- Pito ws a ghost, she says with an air of complete finality.

In the course of her usual inspection in the morning, Aunty Grin discovers what she expected to discover, that Nerida has wet the bed again, and this fact she reports immediately to Aunty Pi. Bed-wetting is an offence in a category of its own, and does not merit a thrashing. Instead Nerida is locked in the wardrobe for two or three hours, to go without breakfast in the dark, in order that she may, as Aunty Pi puts it, think about what she has done, and what a filthy thing it is.

Beforehand, her nose is rubbed vigorously in the offending patch, Aunty Pi doing the rubbing while Aunty Grin holds the offender steady, because Aunty Pi says that that's how you train an animal, and children learn just the same way. Aunty Pi knows because she's dealt with children before and knows their ways even better than they do. As she points out to Nerida, while rubbing her nose in it, not even an animal soils its own bed.

- As if we didn' have enough t' deal with, she says to Aunty Grin, ripping the blasphemous sheets off the bed and hurling them at the blubbering girl's feet.

Before they leave the room, bundling Nerida between them, Aunty Pi stops for an imperious look around.

- And you wipe that smirk off yr face, she says sternly to Judd.

Judd doesn't know he has one. He has woken after a deep, refreshing sleep, his mind crowded with ideas. He doesn't need the silly bone, not with Pito out of the way. He gets up and goes over to Clare's bunk. It is useless for her to pretend to be asleep. He speaks in a pleasant voice.

- How're th welts this mornin?

Clare stares rigidly at the ceiling where a stain has made a magpie shape.

- Still mum. Well listen t' this 'n listen good. Since Pito's gone an' taken yr voice with im, y' can't be th Princess anymore. Right?

Clare thinks of Pito and tries to bring his image back into her mind.

She sees a pile of stones under a broom bush and a wisp of dark hair.

- So y' got t' have a new name, an' I just thought of one. D'y' want t' hear it? I guess y' do. Sickface. Can y' say it? I guess y' can't. Well Sickface will do anythin we want 'er t' do, won't y' Sickface? Just say nothin if you agree. I got th idea lookin at y' face, y' see. Yr sick face 'n yr sick mouth.

Clare shakes her head hard, making the magpie twist its wings.

- She agrees, right Mav?

Maverick, who has trouble waking up in the mornings, croaks out his support. Judd takes a deep breath. The air is clear and hard in his lungs. The world has split open before him like a ripe peach, and he sees right into the juicy flesh of it. He can see it, as ripe and proud as the welts between Sickface's legs.

And he knows just where to sink his teeth.

Judd's first task is an innocent approach to Aunty Pi in the kitchen. - I thought I had t' tell y', he says, looking serious and concerned, - that Clare's gone dumb on us. She's not sayin a word.

Aunty Pi gives a deep, martyred sigh and wonders why she carries on, carries the whole damned load for all of them. At the stove where she's stirring porridge, Mother frowns but does not turn around.

Judd races back to the bedroom before Clare can escape and informs her that Aunty Pi wants to speak with her, putting the emphasis on speak. He moves in behind her as they trail into the kitchen.

Mother is sitting at the table, her eyes on Clare as soon as she walks in. Clare looks for strength there but finds none. She knows immediately that Mother has just lost another battle over Nerida going into the wardrobe. Mother is listless, her pretty white skin puffy, as if bruised from beneath, and her impeccable hands lie helpless at her side.

- What's all this nonsense then? Aunty Pi says.

Clare points to her mouth, makes movements with her lips and shakes her head.

- Is there somethin wrong with y', girl? Are y' sick?

Judd smirks.

- She don't look sick t' me, Aunty Grin says, carrying some plates in behind the children.

- She's just clammed up.

- She needs a short sharp shock t' knock it out of her. Aunty Grin bangs the plates on the table in front of Mother. - His Lordship is requirin room service.

- Snap out of it! Aunty Pi snarls. Jus' snap out of it right now.

Clare shakes her head helplessly. Behind her, Judd looks serious and sad.

- It's just sulkin, Aunty Grin says.

Without warning, Aunty Pi steps forward and slaps Clare across the face, leaving red marks. A gasp comes out of Clare, nothing more. Mother stares down at Uncle Honk's plates. They are covered in gravy-streaked fat.

- Maybe she needs stiffer medicine, Aunty Grin says. - A regular beatin.

- M'be.

- If y' beat that girl again I'll scream th house down, Mother says quietly.

- Scream away, Aunty Pi says.

- She'll be hidin somethin, Aunty Grin says. - A daily beatin until she talks is th answer.

- There's a lot t' be said fr it.

But for the first time in many years, Aunty Pi does not know what to do. She is convinced thrashing will not work, and would thus violate the principle of fairness; on the other hand, she is tormented by the fact that as long as Clare remains silent she is getting away with her disobedience. It is as if Judd had stolen the binoculars, say, and refused to return them, keeping them in open defiance.

- Let's see how't goes, she says, heading Grin off. - She won't be able t' keep it goin.

- Wouldn't bet on that, Grin is quick to put in. - Anymore than I'd bet on that old crab in th tower.

Every morning a small ritual is enacted in which Grandfather throws a rope to the ground. Any food for the day is placed in a billy and attached to the rope for Grandfather to haul up to his room.

This morning however, when Grandfather throws the billy back, food spills out of it into the dust. There are two turnips and some oats. Croak, keeping a wary eye out for dogs, makes a rush for the can but, after a brief sniff, turns away disappointed.

- It's animal tucker, that's what it is, Grandfather screams from his window. - It's pig slop.

Aunty Pi goes to the kitchen window and opens it. She looks at the billy and the spilled food. - Y' had pork yesterday, she snaps.

- A few skinny chops. Soup bones. That's what they ws.

Aunty Pi slams the window shut.

- I've had a gutsful of this, she says. - An absolute gutsful.

Aunty Grin, who's decided to try and mend Uncle Honk's dungarees after all and is fussing with the sewing kit on the kitchen table, assumes a sanctimonious look. - He's getting too big fr his boots, she says, taking the words right out of Aunty Pi's mouth.

- He's got a bee in his bonnet, Aunty Pi says.

- Let im stew in his own juice fr a while, Aunty Grin says.

The wardrobe has a thick heavy door that does not admit even a chink of light. It is quite tall and airy, big enough for her to stand upright if she doesn't mind standing among the clothes that hang there, shirts, pants and dresses belonging to Aunty Pi and Uncle Honk. She can't see the clothes but can smell them, and feel them whispering and touching her body. Standing gets boring after a while, and tiring too, so she ends up spending most of her time crouched on the floor among the shoes confiding in Teddy. Being allowed to have Teddy in the wardrobe is Aunty Pi's single mercy, an indulgence Aunty Grin never ceases to comment upon.

Sometimes she gets frightened and says the words Jesus Jesus Jesus Jesus over and over again until the fear goes away. That usually takes a long time because she has to pass through the memory of when she was first put in the cupboard for talking about Uncle Honk's penis and how she'd seen it.

She'd blundered into the bathroom while Uncle Honk was in the bath and he just up and faced her, soap and water running down his slithery penis. Then Uncle Honk did an extraordinary thing. He grabbed hold of his penis in one hand and wagged it at her as if it were a puppet, screwing up his eyes and making a silly face at the same time.

So great was Aunty Pi's wrath when she heard Nerida describe this that she punched her in the mouth and flung the screaming girl into the wardrobe for twenty-four hours where she had nothing to do but think about her foul mouth. In the middle of the night Uncle Honk had come, but not to let her out, rather to fumble around with her and hurt her between the legs with his fingers.

When she was let out she had a strange, frail quality to her that made the other children shy away, until later when they got used to it.

A dark shadow touched under her eyes, like a bruise, and never went away.

The boys and Clare are standing in the shadow of the barn with Uncle Owl watching the drama unfolding in the yard. Judd stands behind Clare, his fingers occasionally squeezing her elbow.

- Ol Moses is chuckin his food aroun', Uncle Owl says. His eyes are alight with a febrile excitement. - He's got everybody hoppin. Look! Here come th battleships, Pi, an' Grin in 'er wake, and is Pi steamin! She's built up a head a steam like y'd never believe.

Aunty Pi walks over to the billy and looks up at Grandfather's window, screwing up her eyes against the hard blue behind.

- There'll be no more food unless y' come down 'n get it y'self, she announces in a flat voice. - Don't think f' one minute I'm goin t' stand by an' watch good food get chucked inta th dust.

They can see Grandfather's snowy head bobbing around at the window. - Who are you, Pi t' stand aroun' out there waggin y' jaw at me? Jus' get a rope hooked t' that boar.

Judd can't help but smirk. As if she knows it, Aunty Pi turns and peers into the shadows of the barn. Uncle Owl gestures to the children to stay out of sight, giving them significant looks. Children are not welcome at scenes like this.

- Rope it y'self.

- You'd feed me shit a pig wdn't eat. You've a lot t' answer for, Pi. I saw meat come inta th house th other day. A sow in feed condition. What'd I get out of that? A few bones good fr th dogs. Gristle 'n marra.

Aunty Grin has joined Aunty Pi. She looks with disgust at the spilled billy. - What're y' talkin about? she shouts in a shrill voice. It's not even cured yet.

- Cured? Cured, y' say? Chopped up in th fryin pan with plenty of butter'll soon cure it.

- Close yr mouth y' silly old goat, Aunty Grin retorts with false bravery.

- Yr greedy father only married y' into our family t' get y' hands on th land, Pi, y' know that. Well, y've made yr bed and by God y' cn lie in't.

Aunty Pi laughs. - Then he ws a fool, and I ws an even bigger fool. Mary 'n I, we ws both fools.

- Mary ws a good woman. She ws one of th best. I seen 'er up all night with a cow in calf an' feed a team of shearers th next day without turnin a hair. I seen 'er birth some hulkin children that never thanked 'er fr't. I seen 'er by th graveside of 'er own mum, back as straight as a tree trunk. I seen 'er stand up t' the lot a ys when that other business came roun'. There's a woman! And y' have t' hound her t' death with yr butchery. Y' as good as murdered 'er y'self.

Aunty Pi shades her eyes. She and Aunty Grin have gone as still as dead trees in the quiet dust of the yard. Squatting beside the children, Uncle Owl is breathing heavily. He takes out his tobacco and peels off two white papers with large, trembling fingers. One he puts on his tongue, closing his mouth over it as if it were the most delicate of morsels, or a communion wafer. Then he curls the remaining paper around a few shreds of tobacco, his face devout with concentration. Clare removes herself a few steps from him.

Aunty Pi rocks slightly on her heels as she looks up. - It ws you that killed Mary, *Dad*. Y' killed 'er with overwork. Work cn kill a woman, y' know.

Grandfather comes back as quick as a whiplash. - Y' tell Honey that. Don't think I don't know what goes on down there. Yr murderin her now.

Clare looks towards the kitchen and sees Mother's face, pale at the window. Aunty Pi turns and looks at the children. It is the fearful look adults give children when they are witnessing things they should not be witnessing and hearing things they should not be hearing.

Uncle Owl bends down low to the children, who, from long practice, lean away from his breath. - You kids'd better scoot. The cigarette goes into the side of the mouth; a couple of threads of tobacco smear across his lower lip.

Aunty Pi turns back to the window and looks up, her hawk face hooded in shadow. Her voice goes hard and tight. - We'll see y' starve before we lift a finger for y'. Let's see how big y' talk with an empty gut.

Having put Grandfather in his place, Aunty Pi walks stiffly back to the kitchen. She looks at the children as she turns but her face is closed to them.

Aunty Grin, however, has the bit between her teeth. She remains in the yard to shout up a few more insults. Tall and skinny, flushed at her own boldness, here she is, giving lip to Grandfather as if she were Grand Duchess herself.

- Don't worry Grin, horseshit'll be repaid with horseshit. Y' won't get a penny, not even six square feet. An' don't think you'll get anything frm Pi when I've gone. Once she's got her share she'll cut y' off like a piece a rotten wood. Grandfather's voice is hoarse from shouting. - She'll wipe y' like a dirty rag.

Uncle Owl giggles. - He's right, he's right! The old bastard.

He pulls out a box of matches. His fingers, large, awkward and yellow-stained, tremble as he pushes open the box. Clare looks uncertainly towards the house. Aunty Pi is at the kitchen window where Mother was, looking out at them. She appears to be looking straight at Clare.

Aunty Grin stages a grand walk off, swaggering a little. Grandfather's window bangs shut. Silence comes down over the yard. Uncle Owl strikes a match but the head breaks off and flies into the dust like a tiny flaming comet.

Nerida discovers a blue world hidden in the recesses of the wardrobe. She talks to Teddy about light, and that's how it starts. She doesn't care what sort of light, any old light will do. First she becomes enamoured of moths, the way they flutter down over her eyelids, making a soft, pattering sound, and she can't bear to kill them so she pushes them aside and tries to see the light. She gets all sorts of colours which, she tells Teddy, are not really there, just patterns on the insides of her eyelids, so she pushes those aside and tries to see the light. Then she gets the usual pictures of Uncle Honk and his penis and his probing fingers; she knows these are coming from her memory so, after telling Teddy, she pushes them aside and tries to see the light. Then there is nothing. No light, nothing at all, just a kind of rushing, as if she were travelling through space at great speed. Then she sees the light. It is blue. It pierces the darkness but she cannot tell if it is near or far away. It is a little splinter of sky. A secret cave of light in the dark. As soon as she sees it, she stops shivering and holds it in her gaze.

It is her light, she tells Teddy, and it will always be there.

In the kitchen Aunty Pi talks, and her words build up an edifice of unshakeable and relentless logic. The issue is one of fairness. The boar was shot in the precincts of the house. It belongs to the house, with Grandfather getting the share that belongs to him, no more. But, just like a spoilt child, Grandfather wants it all to himself, won't share it with the rest. Honk killed the sow, but he didn't want to eat it all, did he? It never occurred to him to keep it all to himself, even if he did want the choicest cuts, which is only natural.

Just like a spoilt child. And, as the children well know, there is no room in the house for spoiled children. If he gets away with this, there'll be no end to his demands. - He's just in a paddy, she says. While she talks, she keeps one eye on Mother, as if daring her to contradict, but Mother says nothing. Clare, who is much more successful than Princess in making herself invisible, and without the use of any wizardry, hides herself in Mother's shadow and listens. She remembers the look on Grandfather's face when he told her he would make them sweat. Remembers the vulnerable curve of his back as he hunched over, stroking the bone, and wonders if Aunty Pi understands the source of Grandfather's rage, or is pretending not to.

Aunty Grin concurs one hundred percent with Aunty Pi and daringly goes a step further. If Grandfather is going to act like a brat, he should be treated like one, and punished accordingly.

Aunty Pi has to agree with that. But what kind of punishment? Certainly he isn't going to get any more food. - We're not goin through this rigmarole ev'ry mornin, she says.

- A thrashin, is Aunty Grin's answer. - Strip th shirt off 'is back an' thrash im. It's good enough f' th kids, she says.

At this point Aunty Pi grows thoughtful. While she is thinking, she takes some potatoes up to Nerida to sort.

Later in the morning, Grandfather issues an ultimatum. He's not going to stand by and watch his pig reduced to a pile of wriggling maggots. If they don't have a rope around it by twelve noon, he'll shoot one of the dogs, Tonks or Billy. He'll shoot it right where it lies in the shadow of the barn.

Aunty Pi takes the ultimatum quietly. There is no way, of course, that they can bend to this sort of threat; if they give in this time, the old man will rule the place from his tower, shouting out his orders and snapping off shots right left and centre. On the other hand, the waste of both the pig meat and a farm dog cuts her cruelly; after all a good farm dog is worth a lot of money, as is a couple of months supply of pork, and Peg is already lost.

- Mad as a bloody meat axe, Aunty Grin says, leaving the kitchen to check on Uncle Honk.

Aunty Pi notices that Clare is in the kitchen and decides to give the girl something useful to do. Brusquely, she says, - And what d' y' think, little miss. There ws a time y' had a lot t' say f' y'self.

Clare looks somewhere over Aunty Pi's left shoulder and moves a little closer to Mother, wondering how much Mother knows about Pito.

- Cat still got yr tongue? Aunty Pi's voice is a shade sharper than she would like it to be, for the red marks are still visible on Clare's face and Pi finds herself regretting the hasty blow, disturbed by some niggling intuition that kindness might do as much as punishment in this case.

Tucked under her mother's wing, Clare nods and gives Aunty Pi a silly smile. Sweat, she thinks, go on, sweat.

Aunty Grin returns with the news that Uncle Honk has gone into fever.

Nerida and Teddy are sorting potatoes in the dark. She shows Teddy how to probe around the potato for rotten spots. With practice you can cover the whole potato in a few seconds. When she finds one, her fingers go in with a squelchy feeling. She wipes it on her dress, not daring to get any on the clothes around her. Teddy doesn't manage to do too many potatoes but it doesn't matter. She reminds Teddy, who tends to get afraid, that Uncle Honk can't come and hurt them because the pig came and ripped his leg open with tusks as sharp as a razor blade, but Teddy is hard to reassure; he nods and agrees but in his heart he doesn't believe that Uncle Honk's leg will stay ripped open for long. Blood clots; flesh knits.

After a while she becomes afraid too, not of Uncle Honk but of everything. The silent clothes smelling of Sunlight soap and hanging down around her like the husks of people. Then there are the shoes and boots with their feet-stink, and the musty walls that sometimes tick with the clicking of strange insects, like tiny clocks winding up and down. The cold floor whose rough planks pinch her bottom and which deposit a coating of dust and fluff burrs all over Teddy, an insult to his dignity he bears with some stoicism. And, of course the potatoes, lumpy and stupid and suffocating.

Her worst fear is that she will go crazy and beat her hands to a pulp on the door. Then it's like the floor is falling away beneath her, tipping her at such a steep angle she does not know up from down, top from bottom, and her head hurts as if it's taking the weight of her body. Then her blood rushes around inside her with no rhyme or reason, making one part of her burn, another prickle with cold.

- There's plenty of air in here, she says to Teddy, sucking the thick air back into her lungs. Once Judd told her that if she were kept in the wardrobe too long she would die because there wouldn't be enough air for her to breathe, and though she didn't believe him exactly, there are times when she gulps air down hard, expecting it to run out at any moment. To banish this fear properly she has to try to bend right down to the floor and suck the air from under the door until her knees cramp.

- We cn find th blue light, she reassures Teddy, yet panics at the thought that they might not. She squints her eyes in a special way, and peers into the darkness as she did when she first discovered the light, discounting false darknesses and lights, until it appears, small and steady.

As she draws nearer to it, she fancies it to be the light from another world. If she can get closer to the light, she might see into the world, which must be blue. Everything blue, even the sun. She thinks of blue wraith creatures which leave soft, dissolving patterns of colour in the air when they move. They would be her friends and teach her their secrets, such as how to see light in the dark, and how to heat the body from within, from the bones.

Patiently she courts the light until it grows as big and as round as a window. Peering through this opening, she sees an ice world, the ice licked by the wind into tall, curved shapes that lean into, and away from, each other, creating sinuous valleys between. The creatures of this world can only take partial shape in her eye, as if they are constantly being moulded by the wind. What she knows for sure is that they have black eyes and blue fur which shines, and they are her friends.

Teddy is more certain in his judgement however. The blue creatures are undoubtedly teddies, for they are in possession of a certain rotundity, as he explains to her, and their fur is blue only because of all the ice. They are not toys, but teddies of great wisdom and power. Possessors of secrets. Beings who can change their shape to accord with the shape of the eye that captures them.

Using Teddy as their intermediary, the blue beings tell her not to despair, that light seeps in through the cracks of any sky. It is true she can pin her eye to the floor where it meets the door, and discern the faintest glimmer of light, but the posture is difficult to hold without pain and the little light is like a tiny drop of water to a thirsty person. The keyhole, which might have been a major source of light, has been blocked up by Aunty Pi.

Luckily the blue beings have a light, a tiny far off sun that flares up and gives off blue leaves. Nerida is grateful for their intervention, but they fail to save her completely from the panic. She knows it is wrong to dwell on the fact that she can't get out, no matter what, that she can kick and scream and soil herself and no one will come. If that knowledge takes hold, she will go crazy with suffocation, screaming and beating the door until she does herself damage.

She did this once, during her first punishment, and it left her battered and exhausted. Now she pulls back from it at the last minute, hugging Teddy close and staying with the blue beings, who have plenty of space to move even if it is all mountains and ice. They let her see through their eyes and look out at their blue, frozen world. She can laugh at all the crazy shapes in the ice. Every now and again she allows her hands, which still live in the old world, to pick up a potato and test it; the blue beings don't mind that at all.

A little later she cries, and marvels at how hot tears can be. There must be, inside, some very hot place.

Teddy, who's out of his depth when it comes to tears, lies face down on the floor and gets dust in his eyes.

The lounge is inhabited by a brooding, festering presence the children do their best to avoid. He sits motionless by the window as the minutes tighten towards noon, rifle in hand, looking towards the barn where the dogs are lying peacefully in the narrowing shadow. Every now and again one of them rises, stretches, and takes a desultory lick at a water bowl.

Uncle Honk has his own views on what to do about Grandfather, and they aren't as refined as Aunty Grin's. He didn't say anything when Grandfather delivered his ultimatum. He just listened and felt the flame growing in his face, a surety of darkness in his bones. The women went into a fluster, of course, but Uncle Honk knows, and knows that Grandfather knows, that if he harms so much as a single hair on one of those dogs' heads, Honk will come gunning for him. It is as simple as that.

Ran, Billy and Tonks. Already he's lost Peg. These are farm dogs, working dogs, and Ran and Billy are pig dogs in their own right. More than that, they are Honk's dogs. They work for him, they know the tone of his whistle and how to keep out of the way of his boot.

Kill a dog, and the old bastard will be dead meat himself, make no mistake. Wounded or not, half in and half out of fever, it wouldn't matter.

Despite Aunty Pi's explicit orders, putting the barn out of bounds at least until after the midday deadline, Clare sneaks in past the dogs, grateful for the musty shadows. She has a great need for silence and there is a place here by the straw bales, known only to her and Croak, where she can take off her painful underwear and cry. She calls it her crying place, falls onto it as if it were a soft bed and lets her tears nurse her eyelids. It is a silent crying in which tears do all the work, pouring out onto her face from somewhere deep inside her head.

Is this what happened to the other princess, she wonders, the real one with the carriage and the dresses who, like Cinderella, seemed to have found a life that fitted her exactly. One day she woke up to find that the fairy godmother had taken everything away, just as Hattie had finally reclaimed her horn.

She opens her eyes through the last of her tears and sees Judd squatting beside her, looking at her with curiosity as much as anything else.

- He's gone f' good, hasn't he, Judd says softly.

Clare nods

- I killed im, didn' I?

She shakes her head.

- Then what happened t' im? I know I killed im.

Clare does a sad little mime, lifting aside something heavy, digging with her fingers, and placing something carefully in the hole. She makes shaping motions with her hands back over the hole and ends with a little palms-together prayer.

- Y' buried im? Y' really done't?

She nods. There is a sense of triumph about him, a hidden frenzy just waiting for a chance to show itself.

- Whe'd y' do it?

She makes vague motions with her hands.

- It don't matter, he's gone an' yr name is Sickface. 'Cos y' still have a sickface.

He's gloating, openly gloating, and it's something more than Pito. He is visibly trembling with excitement, as if he is on the verge of doing something terribly clever.

She shakes her head.

Judd puts his hand behind him and produces Uncle Honk's hunting knife.

- I don't think Uncle Honk'll be needin this, he says, a big smirk on his face.

Even in the dull light of the barn, the edge of the knife gleams like a crescent moon. Judd leans casually forward and slices off a piece of her hair.

- You'll be Sickface, 'n Sickface does what she's told, alright? Otherwise I tell th grown-ups that y' stole th knife, an' I'm returnin it 'cos I've learned m' lesson. And I'll tell im about Pito and how y' ws goin t' do horrible things with th knife, but I won't say exactly what. Maybe that you ws goin t' kill Honk. Or I'll cut m'self an' say you tried t' kill me. Pi'll have yr scalp f' that. Grin'll make sure of it. They'll make a meal out of y'.

He has it all worked out. How he can get Clare in his power, turn her into his slave.

Clare goes to move away but is locked in the vice of his words. He could do all those things, he's capable of it; Pi would thrash her and lock her away somewhere. Clare reaches the bare, rope-end of her thought. She remembers how Pito left, all in a rush out of her body as the switch landed, taking her voice with him. What does it matter what Pi or Judd or anybody does to her now? What difference does it make? Even if Judd were to cut her to pieces she would feel the same.

Judd's voice follows her. - And I'll do more. I'll take that stupid teddy of Nerida's and I'll cut its head off. First I'll cut its eyes out, then its head off. I'll cut it up into little pieces.

As he waves the knife around in the dark air, the glint of the cutting edge seems to follow the rest of the blade in its flight.

- But I won't do nothin t' the teddy if y' do what I say.

Clare sits upright and meets Judd's stare head on. Judd's face is like a mask. Behind the mask, she sees the torture of Teddy, which would be like the torture of Pito's ghost, the desecration of his bones, the steady dismembering of his hereafter. It would be like that because Teddy lives for Nerida as Pito lived for her. She realizes, as Judd already knows, that she cannot allow that to happen, nor even take a chance that he might be lying.

Hearing his sneering voice, already thick with triumph, Clare perceives the weak position her silence puts her in, her total vulnerability, and struggles against the iron bars in her throat.

Following her line of thought, Judd nods and smiles. - Now, Sickface, I jus want t' touch them welts. I want t' feel im. Between m' fingers.

He lays the knife down beside him in a deliberate gesture and stares openly at her knickers and pad.

Clare begins to shake her head and stops; short of taking the knife and killing Judd now, where is there for her to go? It won't be me he's touching, she thinks as she opens her legs, but my wound. My body, my wound. Yet the first touch of him, soft as it is, is as hard to bear as the lash of the switch. Involuntarily, she pulls away. Judd raises a warning eyebrow and she tries to relax, just as she'd have to do if a spider were crawling across her thigh and she didn't want to kill it. Judd feels the welts gently, with genuine reverence and sensitivity, or at least admiration, running his thumb and forefinger along one line, finding the place, right in the join of the leg and the pelvis, where the wound, chaffed by the pad and knickers, is the most raw.

- Now, Sickface, you'll do anythin I tell you. I want y't' nod yr head t' show you agree.

Clare refuses, her mouth pulling up into a sneer.

Taking her wound firmly between thumb and forefinger, Judd squeezes. He squeezes so hard that his bones tremble with pressure. A stab of pain slices up inside her. Tears squirt into her eyes.

- Just nod y' head.

Clare nods. Her legs are trembling, shaking as if she were cold.

Judd gives the welts a final stroke and rises, satisfied. Sickface won't give him any more trouble. Now he can do some real planning.

A few moments after Judd has left, Clare gets to her feet and half walks, half staggers to the door. The bright, grey light blinds her eyes and she runs headlong into Father.

Father jumps backwards and holds his hands out warily.

- Don't shoot, he says.

At twelve noon Clare is with the women in the kitchen, the one place Judd can't use to torture her. Aunty Pi has fallen silent. She sits upright in the kitchen chair, staring through the wall towards the barn. Aunty Grin stands behind the chair, her back straight. Mother sits at the other end of the table, her head in her arms.

One second sweeps into the next. Nothing happens. Tonks gets up and laps indifferently at the tepid water in her bowl, then turns to face the dull afternoon.

Mother reminds Aunty Pi that it is time to let Nerida out and gets a dirty look from Aunty Grin.

Mother goes to leave the room and Aunty Pi gets up. Her body is as stiff as if she'd been sitting there a week. - I'll go, she says.

At five past midday, everybody in the kitchen breathes a sigh of relief. Clare decides to eat. Aunty Pi remembers there is work to do. Nerida stands blinking in the hall, her eyes still huge with darkness. Life is just resuming its normal course when the shot is heard.

Tonks lies down quietly and rolls over in the dust.

There is a howl from the living room. Uncle Honk appears at the kitchen door, his face grey as a dirty sheet. He is supporting himself on the doorjamb with one hand while in the other he holds his .303.

- Get me up th fucken stairs, he says to Uncle Owl, who is coming up behind him.

- What's th use, Hoppy? Y'll never get up th tower.

Honk levels the gun at Owl's chest. - Upstairs, he repeats. His voice is thick with pain.

Uncle Owl looks scared. - I'm on yr side, Hoppy.

Between them, Aunty Pi and Uncle Owl pulling from the front and supporting from the side, with Aunty Grin brought in to push from the rear, they manoeuvre Uncle Honk up the stairs. He keeps his back stiff and straight as a board, and he stares up and ahead as if no other direction in the universe existed.

- Where's Jack? he asks at one point.

- Under th macrocarpa, waiting f' th fence t' get fixed, says Uncle Owl.

- He's prob'ly got his head in th pisspot, Uncle Honk says.

- It's alright for some, Aunty Grin says from behind.

- I don't trust Jack, Honk says, trying to use his best leg to help them.

- Why not?

- I dunno.

When he gets to the top of the stairs, Uncle Honk orders them to take him to the spot in the hall beneath the trapdoor to Grandfather's room. Uncle Owl gets out the ladder and wobbles up it, puffing and blowing with concentration. The effort of pushing the trapdoor open is too much for him and he and the ladder tumble together, legs flying. He almost knocks over Uncle Honk, who hardly pauses to curse before stepping forward on his one good leg and firing rapidly up through the hole in the ceiling. Bullets zing up into the dark like hungry bees; shells flip in bronze somersaults from the bolt. Above, there is the sound of splintering wood and scrabbling rats.

- Y're not goin t' shoot through that floor, Hoppy, Uncle Owl says, pulling himself upright. - We built that floor solid with eight-inch macrocarpa bearers.

Ignoring him and still firing, Uncle Honk takes another step forward until he is directly beneath the hole. The bullets crack against Grandfather's trapdoor, knocking for entry with steel knuckles.

- He's not about t' stick 'is noggin over th edge f' you, Uncle Owl says. - I'd think again, Hoppy. He'll be sittin on his bed laughin up his sleeve.

- Brandy, Uncle Honk replies, working convulsively at the bolt. - Bring brandy.

Quick to obey, Uncle Owl scampers. He returns lightning fast with a bottle half-filled. Uncle Honk takes it and holds it up to his mouth. Uncle Owl snatches it back and does the same. In his enthusiasm, some of the liquid spills and rolls down his unshaven chin.

- We have t' go up there an' flush im out, Uncle Honk says with ponderous logic, fingering a fresh shell.

- Sure, sure. And make ourselves sittin ducks for ol' Sittin Bull up there who cn shoot th eyebrows off a fly at fifty yards.

- The old bastard's half blind.

- Not when he's lookin down th barrel of a gun he isn't. He don't have t' be standin right next to a dog t' shoot it.

Uncle Honk looks carefully at Uncle Owl. - He won't even hear y' comin, Owl, if y' do it properly. He won't know yr there until yr on top of im.

- I'll follow you, sarge. We'll send Jack up with a grenade. Uncle Owl laughs and takes another plug at the bottle.

- Tonight, Aunty Pi says quietly, - when he's asleep. We'll give im th boar, he'll fry some up an' stuff himself with pig. Then…

- … then nothin. Uncle Honk is shaking his head violently. Over my dead body we give im the boar. Stuff you with pig! He kills a dog an' you want t' give im a nice feed of pork! Give im nothin, let im sleep with his ribs clankin on his backbone.

He fires a few more rounds up through the hole.

- What makes y' think he sleeps? Uncle Owl says to Aunty Pi.

- He has t' sleep sometime, Aunty Pi says. - It stands t' reason.

- Not ol' Sittin Bull. He sleeps with one eye open. Only half of im sleeps.

- Then th pig'll rot under our very eyes, Aunty Pi says. - Th flies 'n maggots'll get th lot.

- Shut up. Jus' shut yr blather up! Uncle Honk sways. - I cn stay awake as long as he can, he says to Uncle Owl, passing into unconsciousness.

Uncle Owl tries to catch him, and misses.

Father treads warily down the hall. There has been more shooting, and the smell of death creeping over everything like a fungus.

His creeping takes him to the edge of the door to his bedroom. Very slowly, he moves his head into the light. Honey has her back to him and is on her knees in front of the dressing table. She stares into the mirror, a hairbrush in one hand. It is a three-piece mirror, with one large central panel and two swinging side panels which she has adjusted to give a double profile, and she is staring at herself, turning her head slowly from side to side, her hair fanning across her shoulders. Then, after pulling it back through her hair once, she puts down the brush, lifts her hands to her face, covers her mouth with them and stares at herself through the bars of her fingers. Another woman stares back at her through the cage.

She remains that way for a long time.

Finally, the fingers begin to glisten and the cage to shake. She moves to one side and Father sees her clearly. Tears are squeezing out between her fingers and rolling down her wrists.

Then she sees him.

The look on her face reminds him of why he might be afraid of such rooms.

Now her hands have fallen from her face and her tears have no bars to hold them.

Father nods very gravely, like a servant in the presence of royalty.

Nerida lies with Teddy. She has one of his eyes between her fingers and is staring at it intently. Inside the amber globe, there is a brown, frozen sun. It is an eye as well as a sun and it looks out over a landscape of standing waves and frozen valleys. It is the world as Teddy sees it, motionless and crystalline.

- I'd be happy if I cd speak t' him, she whispers into his ear. - He knows plenty of secrets. Even more than Pito.

- That's true, Teddy agrees. - But he prefers t' speak t' you through me. It's easier fr him because I don't have as many thoughts crowdin through m' brain as you do.

Nerida thinks this over. What Teddy is saying is probably true, and then again he might be just protecting his role. You can never tell with Teddy, for the landscape with the brown sun and amber sky never changes.

- Tell me where he comes fr'm.

- Y' know that already.

- I don't.

- He comes fr'm th blue place. The one y' saw. They've lots of ice but he's never cold.

- How come?

Teddy thinks for a minute, - Because he's got warm bones. An' things carved in ice.

- What kind of things?

Teddy pauses. Questions tend to confuse him. - Angels carryin children. Staircases with angels 'n saints going up 'n down. Angels with four faces carryin torches of blue flame. An' leafy suns on their heads.

- Does he have any message f' me?

- What sort of message?

It is frustrating sometimes, talking to Teddy. You need a special kind of patience.

- Any message. Something f' me. He knows I like t' get messages.

- Wait a minute.

Teddy falls silent. He lies stiffly on the pillow looking up at the ceiling. - Yes, he does have a message fr you.

- Well what is it? She picks him up and shakes him.

- Don't be rough. I'll tell y'.

- You're so slow sometimes.

- That's because I'm a teddy. Teddies can't go fast; that's just what being a teddy is like.

- Alright, alright. She can see that Teddy is going to cry and she doesn't want that. What'd he say?

- I've forgotten, Teddy says, definitely crying now although the amber sky remains unstained.

- But y' must remember. He's jus' told you.

Teddy puts his paws up to his eyes, - I can't. Wait! Now I remember. There is a note of triumph in his voice. Of course I remember.

This time she waits, making allowances for Teddy.

- He said you will escape, Teddy says sententiously.

Nerida thinks this over. On one hand, she is thrilled at the thought of the being from the blue world giving her such a message, on the other hand, there is a certain hollow sound in Teddy's voice that makes her wonder if he isn't just making it up for her benefit. Making it up because he's forgotten the real message.

- Where will I go? she asks, but Teddy has fallen silent. Even shaking him doesn't help.

That afternoon, as Uncle Honk moves deeper into his fever and the sound of his muttering voice gathers in the lounge, Judd, with Maverick and Nerida in tow as witnesses, takes Clare into the barn to officially make her his slave. That is allowed, he tells Maverick and Nerida, because it often happens when kings and queens and princesses fall; they either lose their heads or are made slaves. Since the traitor-magician Pito has deserted, and the princess abdicated, Judd may now take Sickface as his slave.

Maverick readily agrees to the justice of this, but Nerida is not so sure. Not long out of the wardrobe, the world still looks huge and strange to her. Even the barn seems like a giant, empty wardrobe, waiting for huge clothes to be hung up. She saw a book once about Patch-Pants the tailor who made trousers out of blue sky; those are the sort of trousers that would hang up in a barn.

Clare stands her ground and tries to stare Judd down, but this game is already lost. Judd takes out Uncle Honk's knife and lets the sight of it do its work on Nerida and Maverick. Maverick is completely won over by this daring theft but Nerida backs away from it.

- Y're not going t' tell, Judd says to Nerida.

- Maybe I will.

Judd leans across, grabs hold of Teddy with a quick easy movement and threatens to slice off one of his arms.

Nerida screams. Judd hands Teddy back. - You're not goin t' tell.

Nerida clutches Teddy to her breast.

Judd turns back to Clare. - Swear allegiance t' me now, Sickface. Since y' can't talk, all y' have t' do is nod y' head, like y' done earlier.

Clare does nothing. Giving in to Judd in the barn is one thing; this humiliation in front of Nerida and Maverick quite another.

- Just think of Nerida, Judd says. - An' I cn always cut out Croak's tongue, of course. Or 'is tail.

Clare lowers her eyes, and nods. Like any other slave, she will learn to bide her time.

- Y' see that? Judd says excitedly. - Y' see she agrees t' be m' slave. She's not Princess anymore, she's Sickface, the slave.

Maverick and Nerida stare at him.

- If y' want t' do anythin, y' have t' ask me first, see. Ask me first an' I'll say yes or no.

Later, before sundown, she escapes from the first of her slave duties, most of which involve chores Judd himself is expected to do, and runs over the lower Dog-leg to the broom bush where Pito's finger is buried.

She sits for a while by the little grave, hoping there will be some sign of him, something of his presence, but there is nothing.

She fights with her throat to make human sounds. Maybe the sky with its long arm of mountains will let her talk. There are no people around to pounce upon her words. No one to hear but the rock, the hillside, and a pile of mute stones. A sky turning mauve. She pushes the air past her throat, hoping for a noise, for something that could be built into a syllable. Nothing comes. A chill wind creeps across the ground and wraps around her ankles. She could stay here like this wrestling with her throat all night, and be no further ahead.

After a while, the chill creeps into her body and she gets up, stiffly, reluctant to move, stretching her muscles against her bones.

Below, to the west, the lights of the farmhouse come on. Grandfather's tower flashes like a tiny revolving crystal. Inside, in the kitchen, plates will be rattling, food smells soaking the air, but Clare faces her return with dread. A pit as big as the sky lies inside her, and it holds no stars.

After dinner, Clare decides to try to sleep in Mother and Father's room, on the floor somewhere; all she needs to do is approach Mother. The question of when and where is tricky, for she doesn't want to attract Aunty Pi's attention. Hoping that Aunty Pi and Grin have left Mother to do the dishes, Clare heads down the hall. Nerida passes her going the other way, Teddy clutched firmly in one hand, hardly appearing to notice her sister. It is an odd, awkward moment for Clare, the two of them passing each other like strangers. She hears voices from the kitchen and decides to walk past and take a quick look first.

She catches a brief glimpse of Mother, seated on a chair, Aunty Grin and Aunty Pi standing to each side of her. Aunty Pi is leaning forward and whispering, it seems, directly into Mother's ear, her eyes wide and fixed on Mother's face, the thin, hard line of her mouth hardly moving. She has a hand on Mother's bare arm, fingers tightly encircled, stiff white flesh showing either side. Aunty Grin stands straight-backed, her face set in a righteous smirk. Mother is looking down. As Clare goes past she glances up, her eyes like two great pale lilies.

In her nightdress and clutching her teddy, Nerida stands in the hall between the kitchen and the lounge, the children's room and the stairs, the bathroom and the back door, shivering.

Croak comes up and rubs his back against her leg. Absently, she bends over and strokes the cat.

In the lurching silence of the house, there are howls and moans that take the form of moving shapes and humping shadows; these are closest to the surface in the lounge where Uncle Honk is passed by fevered hands from nightmare to nightmare. At various intervals some semblance of sound grips his throat and choked obscenities emerge with spittle and foam.

She creeps past this door pressed against the opposite wall, as if that few feet of extra distance might protect her, like a moat protects a castle, from the flickering shades and violent shapes in the lounge. Croak accompanies her in short, brisk runs.

From the kitchen, she hears voices, adult voices, whispering low, both fearful and conniving, as if the adults were still awake and in conference, repeating phrases behind hands.

She races past the kitchen to the back door and moves quickly to unlatch it. Her hand, however, comes to a standstill a few inches above the latch. She had a dream once in which she had to open a door which contained an electric current. Every time she touched the door-knob, the current passed through her fingers and up her arm in a horrible thrill and tingle. Now she is back in the dream and cannot, will not, touch the door.

She lets her hand drop to her side and puts it out again as she has done a thousand times before, in a natural movement, and still she cannot touch the latch. Croak's no help; he does nothing but sit and watch her.

Behind her, the shadows have gathered. She hears a stifled giggle, the sort Clare might make when hiding in a game of hide-and-seek. Or Maverick's crazy baby-giggle.

There is a warm tingling in her legs and arms, like a warning, and suddenly a being from the blue world is with her, not in a body, but as a ghostly radiance which enters her through her skin and peers out at the world through her eyes. The being uses her eyes to survey the porch, the oilskins hanging in black folds, pairs of gumboots standing to stiff attention among shoes, odd bits of firewood and a handy-bag of tools.

- Don't be scared, Teddy says.

Using Nerida's hand, the blue angel reaches forward and tips the latch and Nerida slips through the door. Croak does not come with her, he is fastidious when it comes to the cold.

The yard and the paddocks beyond, the boulders of the river bed, are whitening; everything is growing a thin spine of frost. She can feel the crystals scattering under her feet. The blue being breathes deep in the chill air and departs. It is only a puff of mist, like a breath, dissolving on the air. Nerida looks up and sees the moon hard, bright and thin edged. She looks over at the barn. All is calm at the dog kennels. She can see the hump of the fallen dog growing its fur of moon-ice.

She advances as far as she can, keeping the house between her and Grandfather's room, and pauses. Her plan is to make a quick run to the tractor; from Grandfather's glass tower she will be no more than a brief ghost of white flitting over the ground.

Taking a deep breath, she runs, the ice and the mountains in her face. Her feet leave the earth and briefly she flies, like a creature of no mass, borne up by the chill air and the waves coming up out of the earth.

She crouches beneath the tractor, behind the rigid tyres and the bulk of the wheels. From here it is a short dash to the edge of the barn and beyond. The machine looms above her, solid and silent. Ice covers it too, all its working parts, with stiff white filings. Its mass and bulk, while protecting her, manifests an iron cold that offers no comfort. It is an inert, metal density that only dimly recalls its function, the drawing in and spitting out of fire. She knows the cold will reach into its cosmolined interior and grip it with an ancient rust.

A few feet away the great boar too glows with ice. His head is turned to her and she sees his eyes, still awake, fixed in her direction, cold, smooth and hard. Hawk feathers, like a shattered cloak of rank, adorn the shoulders and flanks. The eyes are sunk in a timeless, frozen gleam; the feathers stand up straight with frost.

Nerida runs.

She crosses the river, the clay-filled water swirling about her legs; in that torrent she can feel the inertia of the mountains, their precipitous height and density, the turbidity of rock and the yellow treachery of clay.

She doesn't feel the cold as she moves up into the beech forest on the flank of Sister Peak. Once amongst the shadows of the trees she looks back towards the farm house, far away and uninhabited. An invention of the frost. The wall of Grandfather's attic turns a blank, moon-glazed face towards her. Instinctively, she pulls herself back into the trees.

The beech trees are stiff and scrubby. This steep, straggly strip of forest between the riverbed and the rocky upper slopes and summits is as tough a stand of wood as you would find anywhere, according to Uncle Owl. Winds, snows, floods... the trees are as crazy as the people to live in such a place, he'd said.

Nerida begins to climb.

The beech trees grow more stunted as she ascends and there's more lichen the shape of tiny ears growing on the bark. Looking back from above the tree line, she is impressed with the peculiar flatness of the night scene. She can still see the windows of Grandfather's tower, facetted like the eyes of a fly, and the neat, dark oblong of the barn. She can even see the boar lying where it fell in the yard, a black dot the size of a flea.

To the southwest, Old Snowy, shaken free of cloud, stands out in all his glory, one pristine face towards her. She remembers Grandfather telling her his hair turned white when he washed it in the snow from that mountain. Behind it she can see the polished glare of further peaks. She takes a deep breath and draws the dark sky into her throat.

She has no firm idea of where she is going but as she climbs her purpose becomes clearer. Ahead of her lies the pure land of ice and rock, the land of the blue light.

The thought keeps her going until she reaches the snow line. There she sits down in the crisp snow and spreads her nightdress around her. Teddy she hugs to her so he won't get cold. It is easy enough to believe that if she climbs high enough the sun will turn blue. In that world, the ice will make lilies and vases and other fantastic shapes.

She thinks about that and watches her pale skin glow in the moon light.

She makes herself comfortable, and waits.

The next morning, when the children wake up, Nerida is gone. Frost cakes the window with spangled icing. The boys lie huddled in their beds while Clare runs about the house from the kitchen to the bathroom to the hall and back again. Finally, she creeps into her parents' bedroom to see if Nerida has slipped into their bed in the night as Clare herself hoped to do.

As soon as she sees Clare, Mother sits up in bed in alarm, her eyes as wide as her silent daughter's. Her beautiful long, fair hair falls around her shoulders. Beside her, Father groans and pulls the covers up over his head to protect himself from the long bombardment.

It is not long before the house and the barn have been thoroughly searched. Clare even checks the old dunny, where she and Pito used to meet. The place has a smell that comes back at her from her old life as Princess.

Aunty Pi receives the news tight-lipped. The first thing she does is check Nerida's bed to see if it is wet, deciding that the child is probably hiding somewhere to avoid punishment. She is puzzled to find the bed dry.

- You'll have t' go 'n look fr her, she tells the bleary-eyed Uncle Owl. She has noticed something the others have missed; none of Nerida's clothes are missing which means the girl must be running about in her nightdress.

When Mother says she'll go too, Aunty Pi raises no objection.

Nobody thinks about Grandfather until a package comes flying down from his window, spewing old fruit scraps into the yard. When it lands, the dogs chained by the barn swing their heads around and back up against their leashes.

Aunty Pi hardly turns her head, so Aunty Grin goes out to deal with Grandfather.

Grandfather's face is at the window above. - Where's Pi?

- Pull yr head in y' silly old goat, Aunty Grin calls out.

- Tell her t' get a rope on that pig.

Aunty Grin shakes her fist at the window. - Pull yr head in before somethin bites it off.

Her voice, which has no real timbre, sounds silly and childish. There is something empty and hollow in her threats.

- She won't get a penny, not six square feet of it. The lawyiz've already seen t' that.

Grandfather's head vanishes.

Her round, pinched face suffused with heat as if she were drunk, Aunty Grin turns and walks with erect dignity back to the kitchen where Aunty Pi awaits a full report.

- He might kill another dog, Aunty Grin says.

Pi gives a sour look. - He'd cut off his nose t' spite his face, she says.

Judd goes slowly into the lounge, into the brooding presence of Uncle Honk, who moves in and out of fever the way a monk passes in and out of ecstasy. There is a heavy, beery fogginess in the room and something more, something thick and rubbery which gives off a peculiar, rotting smell. The thing with the heavy, snake eyes of Uncle Honk is slow and stupid owing to the squeeze of fever, and Judd can get some advantage from it if he moves quickly enough.

The Uncle Honk creature blanks out all the colour around it, as if slowly erasing the room. Sometimes it snuffles like a pig, other times it grunts and moans like a man. - He'll be pickin us off one b' one now, unless we move, it says. - Like pluckin fucken feathers from a fucken chook.

Judd sucks in his checks. - Y' right there, he says thoughtfully, like an adult.

The fever has made Uncle Honk slow and ponderous. He delivers each word as if it's gone through a wringer. - An' when it comes t' starvin, we cd starve down here before he gets a tummy ache. Th old arsehole cn live on th smell of an oily rag. If we're waitin f' him t' die, we'll be here till hell freezes over.

- I gotta plan.

- Go play cowboys 'n fucken Indians, the thing snarls. Judd notices the rifle tucked down beside the chair, and the powerful arm that rests by it.

- And where's th little bitch?

- Who? Judd affects innocence.

- Nerida, the creature spits. - Where th fuck is she?

- Dunno. Reckon she's run off.

- Run off my arse. Where wd she run t'? The thing snorts.

- Dunno.

- Y' dunno fucken much. I'll find out soon enough.

Judd doesn't like the sound of that soon enough, and tries to steer the conversation back to the plan, suddenly wondering why he needs to tell Uncle Honk at all. The plan would work quite well without him, maybe even better; he can steal everything he needs, which isn't much. Christ! Sickface can steal it. Uncle Honk's diversion might be more trouble than it's worth. Still, with a few quick sentences he outlines his plan.

There is no sound in the room for a long time but Uncle Honk's ragged breathing and restless turning; Judd begins to wonder if he's even heard him or maybe gone to sleep. When his voice comes it is thick and slurred.

- If only Owl ws up t' somethin more than gettin pissed an' lyin dog-drunk on his bed all day. If only I had somethin better t' work with than a fucken schemin brat, we'd have old scrotum hangin fr'm a tree with th rats workin on him right now. We'd have th farm, we'd have th fucken works.

- I'm not a kid. Judd lets the silence pull.

- Y' could of fooled me.

Judd suddenly thinks he can identify the strange smell in the air. - But I cd do it, he says, wanting to get out of there. - Clare cd do it best. She took him up that pork pie, remember. That sets him up. - He'll never suspect his little white mouse.

- That's true enough. A mouse cn go through a rathole sure enough.

- An' yr not doin a hell of a lot here. Judd makes ready to jump.

For a moment, it looks as if the thing will move to strike him, then it relaxes. - Just rottin away. That's all I'm doin.

He makes as if to rise up, moving his stiff leg, and a muggy, close smell comes up. Judd has the sudden impression that he is with a blind person, that he could get up and flit around the room, poking into this and prying into that, but it is a dangerous illusion; the fever thing, even in its most hectic sweats, waits patiently for him to make a false move.

As Judd is leaving the room, he meets Aunty Grin coming the other way. She stops and gives him a suspicious look.

- I think he needs changin, Judd says.

Aunty Pi sits at the kitchen table deep in thought. Nerida's disappearance has violated the principle of fairness, a principle she has lived by all her life. As she says to Aunty Grin, - y' try t' belt some sense inta th kids 'n what happens? Yr damned if y' do and yr damned if y' don't.

- Y' don't get any thanks fr't, Aunty Grin says quickly, treading a familiar path, but true as this may be it is not what Aunty Pi has in mind. The source of her dissatisfaction is more obscure and goes deeper than the ingratitude of children. It is the universe itself which is ungrateful. If the universe itself is unfair, what is the use of trying with the kids? It's a bloody uphill battle anyway. Y' get up an' y' slave y' guts out fr'm morning t' night. You cook 'n you clean an' then y' get out on th tractor y'self. Y' work y' fingers t' the bone, fr what? A grocer's bill that never gets paid. A farm where all th fields're made of stones. A bunch of kids around y' neck. A mad old man with a bee in his bonnet. An early grave, like Mary. Off down t' hell with lips tight, fists clenched.

Aunty Grin, whose mind does not have such a large and powerful sweep as Pi's, nor the capacity for despair, is still lost on the trials that children bring. And now a runaway! She draws in a sharp disapproving breath and clicks her tongue.

- Yr damned if y' do and yr damned if y' don't, Aunty Pi says, facing defeat. - Y' can't win.

Grandfather's second ultimatum comes in the early afternoon, when the promise of another cold night is already in the air. It is delivered in a hoarse, flat voice shorn of any rhetoric. He will shoot anything in range that moves, anyone that tries to leave the house, human or animal. With the sole exception of Jack, who isn't in his right mind, as long as he doesn't try to bring food into the house. Drunks are not excepted, so Owl and Grin better watch out.

Aunty Pi takes the news sitting at the table, her face stony. Uncle Owl is up and around in the kitchen, drinking water and trying to organize himself to search for Nerida. Aunty Pi keeps looking towards the door as if the girl was about to walk in. - I'll thrash her t' within an inch of her life when she turns up, she says to Aunty Grin.

- A thrashin's too good f' her, says Grin.

Mother stands at the bench, her hands motionless in the sink, staring out the window, Clare by her side. She puts her arm around her daughter's shoulder and squeezes gently.

Grandfather's ultimatum stops Uncle Owl dead in his tracks. - I'm not goin out there with him snipin away at me. There is a craven whine in his voice.

Aunty Pi rises stiffly and heads for the stairs. - Get the ladder out, Owl, she says over her shoulder.

With Uncle Owl holding the ladder to keep it steady, Aunty Pi hoists herself up into the eaves and begins the climb. When she reaches the trapdoor into Grandfather's room she shouts, loud enough for everybody below to hear.

- Open up. I have t' speak t' y'.

The listeners below can't hear Grandfather's reply.

- Then I'll talk t' y' from here, shoot me if y' want. We've got a missin child… What? … Nerida. Let me in.

The trapdoor lifts a little. Even those below can hear his voice, faint and reedy. - My little Churchmouse's bolted. Good f' her. She's probably gone t' th Lester's.

- She hasn't. We already rung them.

- A little Churchmouse knows where t' hide.

- Owl an' th two boys'll be goin out t' search f' her.

- I'll shoot anythin that moves. I told y' that, Pi. Anyway, how do I know yr not lyin, pullin th wool over m' eyes. She's probably down there somewhere, locked in th wardrobe, maybe. You show me yr good faith by gettin a rope on that fucken hog. Then I'll let y' look f' Nerida.

Aunty Pi comes back through the ceiling and down the ladder with as much dignity as the situation allows.

- Let's rope up th hog quick, she says to Owl. - It's only meat. Her thin face is haggard with worry.

Owl shakes his head uneasily. - Honk's not goin t' like that.

- He cn like it or lump it. Get the ladder away. We got rope in th barn.

Aunty Grin looks shocked at this change of policy but, like everyone else, she knows that special tone Aunty Pi uses when she will brook no argument. Uncle Owl knows it too but continues to shake his head. - He's not goin t' like it.

Aunty Pi's voice is as sharp as galvanized iron. - We're findin Nerida before nightfall, Owl, even if we have t' tie up a dozen hogs.

- Then what'll we do about ol' Hoppy in there, glowerin out at the yard.

Aunty Pi swings around on Aunty Grin. - You can go in and hold him off, wash him or somethin. Steal his gun. Knock im over th head.

Turning from the stunned Aunty Grin, she leads the procession off down the stairs, her mind busy with the details.

Uncle Honk is standing at the bottom of the stairs, leaning hard against the door jamb, his rifle held firm against his ribs. His face has a drawn, bleached quality. His eyes have gone darker, smaller, as if the fever has wrung out something of their substance. His voice is not more than a whisper, a sound that might be coming from behind him or from the other room.

- You'll tie up that hog over my dead body.

From the tower above comes the sound of shots, and something smashing.

- That's ol' chief Sittin Bull blowin out th telephone, Owl says.

The second morning after Nerida's disappearance, a sheet of ice lies over the ground, making a sparkling hillock out of the body of the boar. The two remaining dogs get up, their chains break free from the ice with a dry, soda crackle, and slither about as the animals limp to their limit and back again. They have not been fed since Tonks was shot and are made sad by their hunger.

Before the children have got up and dressed, Judd goes to Clare's bunk.

He is full of excitement. - I want y' t' make a cake fr me, slave.

Clare looks puzzled.

- Y' cn bake a cake can't y'?

A cautious assent.

- Then bake one. I jus' have some special ingredients fr it.

Another puzzled look.

- You'll see.

There's a sly, triumphant look on Judd's face, but he lets her get up and does not taunt her about Pito. While she dresses, however, she can feel his eyes upon her, especially when she tries to hide the soft belt mother gave her. - How's them welts now, he says.

When she goes into the kitchen, Aunty Pi is sitting at the table, staring at the scrubbed surface.

Aunty Grin walks around, waiting for cues. - Th girl must be dead of exposure by now, she says from time to time, her voice tentative. - We have t' sit here twiddlin our thumbs while th farm goes t' rack 'n ruin.

As she talks she keeps an eye on Aunty Pi, testing her response.

Clare takes a bowl, pours some sugar and beef fat into it, and begins to quickly work the fat into the sugar with nimble fingers.

Aunty Pi is immediately on her feet. - What're y' doin, she demands. Clare points to the flour and the sugar, and Nerida's place at the table. She mimes Nerida eating the cake.

Considering the girl's mime, Aunty Pi sees an augury of a funeral, and her impulse to stop Clare is cut short. The prospect of a dead girl lies across as a heavy weight. She turns away from the sight to the window where the unchanging prospect of yard and barn greets her, dreary and tense.

Without wasting any time, in case Aunty Pi should change her mind,

Clare breaks two eggs into the bowl and mixes them up with the sugar and fat. She then adds water, laced with a little milk, a generous amount of flour, and mixes furiously until the mixture is at the right consistency.

As she works she suffers under the disapproving eye of Aunty Grin and it's hard to see how Judd is going to add his secret ingredient without her taking the mixture out of the kitchen, a move which would be sure to provoke comment. She leaves the room as if suddenly called to the lavatory, and finds Judd waiting in the hall for her. She holds out her hand for the secret ingredient but he won't hand it over. Instead he marches into the kitchen, head in the air, looking like he's in charge. He wanders straight over to the cake and peers into the bowl, at the same time drawing a paper-wrapped packet from his trousers.

- Keep y' nose out of there, Aunty Grin says, as much from habit as anything else. Aunty Pi's silence is beginning to unhinge her; without her cues, Aunty Grin doesn't know what to say, what note to hit, what theme to harp upon, what complaints to whine about.

- I just thought I'd tell y', Judd says.

- Tell us what?

- Uncle Honk's gettin worse.

- What d' y' mean?

- Moanin 'n stuff.

With a sigh she learned from Aunty Pi, Aunty Grin sweeps out of the kitchen. Judd takes the opportunity to pour some powder from his package into the cake mix.

- Needs a bit of a stir, he says to Sickface with a smirk on his face. - It's goin t' be a good cake I reckon.

It was Aunty Grin who, upon her return, spread the mixture in the cake tin and put it in the oven.

Late that afternoon, Judd and Maverick come into the children's room to find Clare with her hands underneath his bunk, pulling out the rat poison.

- Look't this, Mav, he says.

Clare is shocked by the look of triumph on his face.

Judd decides to waste no time blabbin. Quick as a cat, he jumps to her side, pulling out the knife as he goes, dragging her to her feet and shoving her roughly against the wall. The knife he holds up against her throat; if she moves, if she so much as swallows too hard, she will cut herself. His other hand moves to her body and up under her skirt. She flinches but the knife sinks a little deeper, enough to prick. Judd's face is choked with blood, his lips pulled into something like a sneer and his sharp, uneven breath is hot on her face. She closes her eyes and holds still as his fingers find her insides and claw around.

When Judd has finished he inspects his fingers. Her bleeding is nearly over and his fingers are sticky and streaked with a little blood. He wipes them carefully on her sheet, right in the middle of it, and then holds the knife to her throat again so Maverick can have a turn, and wipe his fingers on the sheets too. He is clumsier than Judd and hurts her more. She has to close her eyes again and sees huge blocks of darkness smashing against each other.

Clare goes up the stairs to Uncle Owl's room, trying to loosen her throat for the action of words, if only there were words. If she can't learn to speak soon, she may have to kill Judd, for there is no safety in her silence; rather, the deeper the grip of her muteness, the more vulnerable she becomes, the more likely a target for Judd's growing viciousness.

Uncle Owl lies on his bed, fully clothed, one arm dangling down, his mouth hung open, a rasping sound like Father's fence-mender going to and fro in his throat. Sometimes the sound stops right on the precipice of an indrawn breath and, just as Clare begins to fear he will never start breathing again, it resumes its unsteady course.

His other arm is thrown around a woollen coverlet as if he were hugging someone.

She glances at the pile of magazines around the bed, and instinctively across at Mut's empty basket, as if expecting the dog to be there, one alert eye cocked in her direction. Some of the magazines feature cartoons of men with rolled-up sleeves and peaked caps. One shows some of these men hanging from ropes by their necks while others off to one side, lean skeletons dressed in suits, count money. Another shows a man on a spit above flames, a pig dressed in a suit turning the wheel. Lying beside the bed, near where Uncle Owl's hand dangles, is the encyclopedia lying open at the Great Fire of London. The picture is from a woodcut, showing houses in flame with people fleeing, their backs bent under their loads.

Above the bed, slung over the bed-end, is Mut's collar, looking greasy and familiar. Clare stretches her hand out toward it, certain she will find it still warm.

Uncle Owl's fingers close around her wrist. One rheumy eye locks onto hers.

- What're yr stealin that for?

She makes gestures of innocence.

- Why wd y' want t' come sneakin in here just t' look't Mut's collar?

Uncle Owl is horribly awake.

Clare begins to cry.

With a groan, Uncle Owl sits up. He gropes around the other side of the bed and comes up with a flask, sniffs it and wrinkles his nose. - Why th blubberin? He takes a swig and sinks back against the pillows, his head resting on the bedpost, Mut's collar hanging above him like a tipsy leather halo. The flask drops off the bed onto the floor.

Clare wants to find some words in the knot of muscles in her throat. She knows the words are there, she can hear them in her mind, but knows too the uselessness of battering up against the barrier of flesh.

She sits down on the bed and, feeling her strength ebbing, rouses herself for a final effort, and mimics Judd with the knife. When it comes to showing what Judd did even her hands cannot find a language, but she tries, finally, in an embarrassed movement, using her own hand to mimic Judd's.

A look of alarm comes over Uncle Owl's face, and he rubs his temples hard, two fingers up each side of his face.

- What'd y' come t' me fr? Why'd y' come here? He shakes his head backward and forward as if dodging blows.

Clare shrugs helplessly.

- Why'd y' come t' me? he insists, a touch of aggression in his voice, as if there were something sinister in her intent.

Clare shakes her head slowly. The room rocks from side to side.

- Y' don't come t' me f' that sort of thing. Y' go to Aunty Pi. She takes care of those things.

He nods to himself. His left arm, which is drooped over the bed, begins to twitch as his hand feels around on the floor for the flask. - Y' go t' Aunty Pi. That's what y' do.

A childlike note has entered his voice, as if he were reciting a lesson. - She looks after that department.

Then, unaccountably, he giggles.

Clare puts her hands up in front of her face and stares at him through her fingers.

Uncle Owl takes another swig and recovers himself. Whatever has amused him vanishes as soon as he focuses on Clare.

- Then what about Honey an' Jack, yr own mum an' dad. Why don't y' go there?

She looks sad and mimics Father shouting.

- I guess Jack isn't up t' much. Owl looks on the point of being amused again. - But Honey's th one. She cn help y'.

There is no way she can simply indicate to him why she can't turn to Mother. Just thinking about Mother makes her want to cry. If she told Mother, that awful, lost look would come into Mother's eyes, her face would collapse.

Instead of answering Owl, she places her palms together, puts her cheek on them, then looks around the room inquiringly.

Uncle Owl's alarm increases. He pulls himself up in the bed. - Y' want' sleep here? When she nods, he rubs his forehead furiously. - Y' got t' sleep in yr own room.

Her eyes widen with terror and she shakes her head emphatically.

- Y' can't sleep in here. There's nowhere t' sleep.

Her looks becomes imploring.

Uncle Owl's eyes rove furtively around the room as if there was some escape for him there.

- Not in here. I'll tell y' what, I'll take y' back t' th kids room. I'll tuck y' up in bed. The boys'll see that yr with me an'll leave y' alone. He winks at her and nods to himself at the wisdom of what he is saying. - You jus' see 'f they don't. Boys're like dogs, they come in tough an' run off with their tails between their legs.

Clare shakes her head violently.

Uncle Owl gazes at her in perplexity. - There's no bed, no blankets in here, y' cn see f' y'self. Where would y' sleep?

Clare points to the recess where Mut slept. Mut's old blanket is still there, curled like a tongue into his familiar shape.

Uncle Owl looks shocked. - Y' can't sleep there, that's where Mut slept. There is a note of panic in his voice.

Clare tips forward onto Uncle Owl's bed. His room is remote; the piles of books march off to the horizon like a line of mountains. She dimly hears Uncle Owl cursing and swearing as he lifts her up and stumbles to the door with her. She knows where he is taking her but she is too tired to fight. She allows Uncle Owl to put her in her bunk. She hears him promise to skin the boys alive if he has any trouble with them. The boys don't open their eyes.

As soon as Uncle Owl has left Judd speaks, once.

- We know y're there, Sickface, he says.

Before she goes to sleep, Clare hears Father moving down the hall.

On the third morning after Nerida's disappearance, the sky lies close to the earth, blotting out the mountains just above the tree line. It's a black frost, Aunty Pi says, because new frost has gone down on old ice. The sky shape shifts just above their heads in endless eddies of amorphous grey, like the underside of a huge silent river.

When Clare wakes, Judd's face is staring into hers. - Y' blabbed t' Uncle Owl, did y?

Clare closes her eyes. Pito, Pito, she calls out inside her head, back into the dream space from which she's just come. Pito was there standing beside her, smiling and laughing. He was telling her that he loved her and his voice was full of sweetness. At the same time he was trying to tell her something, something that she should do to help herself.

- I said, y' blabbed t' Uncle Owl.

Clare shook her head.

- Y' did. I'm goin t' get y' f' this. I'm gonna pay y' back.

Maverick sits up in bed. - What're goin t' do t' her, Juddy?

- That'd be tellin.

- Why don't y' cut off one of her fingers?

- Yeah. I cd cut off one of yours t' go with it.

- Hey, don't go that way.

- Then shut yr stupid face.

Clare slips out of bed and goes to leave. Judd grabs her by the arm. - Where d' y' think yr goin?

Annoyed, she indicates the bathroom. He roughly fingers her breast. - Y' wear a belt round yr tits, he says, and laughs the way Uncle Honk laughs when he shoots an opossum.

As soon as he lets her go, she races to the kitchen to look for the poisoned cake, her feet hardly registering the floor. The cake has gone from the pantry shelf where Aunty Grin put it after baking.

She is heading back to the bedroom when there is a cry from somewhere in the house and a commotion upstairs. Clare changes direction and runs for the back door.

Outside the yard is calm, the sky still close to the earth, its sinuous cloud cover writhing. The yard looks like nothing has moved there for years, like one of those old fashioned paintings in which everything is frozen to dust. The tractor springs white, crystal blooms.

Walking across the yard towards the house, quite casually, swinging her teddy in one hand, is Nerida. In a nightdress and barefoot, singing quietly to herself, she passes the tractor and dead boar without a glance at either.

Judd and Maverick come up behind Clare and watch in silence as Nerida skips up to the back door.

They think of three freezing nights among the white boulders.

They think of the moon, remote and savage as ice.

They think of the dark that comes up out of the earth when the sun goes down.

They think of Old Snowy who kills whenever warm, moving things grow careless.

Nerida smiles at them. - What're y' lookin at?

It is her old Nerida voice, yet something has come into it the way death or fire comes into the body, from the outside.

Judd backs away, - How come yr alive?

- I wsn't cold.

- Izat so?

- She don't even look hungry t' me, Maverick says.

The adults crowd in past the children. Mother picks up Nerida and squeezes her until there is no breath left in either of them. Then, still hugging her, she swings around to Aunty Pi.

- This child never goes in th wardrobe again, she says in a loud, clear voice.

- Look who's givin th orders, Aunty Grin says, but Aunty Pi says nothing. For a moment, her mask drops and someone old, scared and frail stares out.

- Where'd y' go, Mother says, stroking the child's hair.

- I went up Old Snowy.

- She's lyin, Aunty Grin says instantly. - There's not a scrap of protection up there.

Aunty Pi has to agree. There are stories of strange things of course.

The sort of stories Grandfather likes to tell. A man fell from a plane onto Old Snowy and lived. A climber taken down from Old Snowy froze so quick that he still looked surprised. They took the block of ice to Christchurch, thawed him out and now he was up and walking around just like any other person. And John Dingwell saw a moa; he was such an ignoramus he didn't know what a moa was, and had to describe the bird which everybody except himself recognised. Then there was old Slash Harry who'd spent more time in the hills than any other man following the deer and who'd never touched a drop in his life; he saw a stagecoach, large as life and loaded with gold, come out of the solid rock and ride past him casual as you please. Miles from the pass, mind you. And no gold to show for it.

Humbug, all of it. Humbug.

The children stare at Nerida. It seems to Clare that her younger sister is different. Her glowing skin looks whiter, almost translucent, as if it has been bleached by snow. Her eyes are bigger and darker, as if the night has entered them. Her movements, while still gentle and Nerida-like, have lost their diffidence and have become calmer and more certain. She moves around the house gravely, and accepts food as if she were only mildly hungry.

While she is eating in the kitchen Uncle Owl shambles in and screws one eye up to look at her. Then he laughs.

Aunty Pi is not amused. - What's so funny.

- What'd y' bring back, little girl?

- Fr'm where, Uncle Owl.

- Fr'm Old Snowy.

- Nothin.

- Nothin? Y' got t' bring somethin back. Them's th rules with fairy tales. Thaz th trouble with ol' Slash Harry. He seen all that gold but didn' bring nothin back.

- I didn't see any gold, Uncle Owl.

- The dead can't come back out of th snow, Aunty Pi says with finality.

- Thaz easy. She spent three nights in th barn snugged up in th straw.

- That barn's colder than a fridge. We had eggs freeze solid there one winter. And there's no water. Yr not tryin t' tell me she went three days without water, freezin in the barn in a thin cotton nightdress that wouldn't keep a skeleton warm, not callin out or sayin anythin, 'cos if y' are then yr a bigger liar than God!

That shuts Uncle Owl up for a minute. He is pleased at the idea of being a bigger liar than God, but he is puzzled too. He tries to look at Nerida and get her in his focus, but all the time she slithers away from his eye, rotating through another moving space, making him dizzy.

- All that matters is that she's back, Mother says quietly from the table, where she is sitting beside Nerida. Aunty Pi looks uncomfortable. This is a point of view she'd like to share herself but there are too many niggles.

Suddenly Father walks into the kitchen and stares at Nerida.

- Hello Father, she says brightly.

- Hello, Father says. - You've been away fr a long time.

And he laughs before his face closes down.

Father throws himself on the bed and dreams of wheat, wide fields of it, rich and yellow and dusty with pollen. The colour of Honey's hair in the mirror when she combs it. A light wind sends shivers and waves through it, opening up the heavily laden stalks. To one side of the field, there are children with sticks beating thistles until they give up their seed; the dry thistle heads turn their cracked faces towards the snow when the easterly blows cold. When struck they explode sending a thousand seeds, each hanging from its own tiny gossamer star, out into the world to chance a crack in a rock or a fence line. Father did the same when he was a child, and beat the air when it turned thick with midges on a summer evening while his father dug in the garden and his mother peeled potatoes. It was more to leap with them than to kill them when he took to the air, but he didn't know that at the time. The dream wakes him, for the children are shouting and laughing as their sticks descend, and when he opens his eyes he can still see the seeds floating lightly through the air. Some of them land on the bed where they simply vanish the way soap bubbles do, in a sudden blur of colour.

He tries to talk to Honey but only his mouth will move. He wants to tell her that her hair is like a field of wheat.

There is a silence that feels like flawed ice, and looks that have no boundaries; Father feels the silence and the looks and they make him helpless. Before he left for the hospital, he heard the Sarge tell someone that he was a coward, and now, when he thinks of it, he hides his head under the blankets. The looks Honey can give him have the same effect, although there is no reproach in them; it is the resignation in her eyes that sends him scurrying for a pothole.

Forming the words to speak to her is like tying a knot, an act of intricate memory: left over right and under, right over left and under. Tighten. But no words emerge.

That night, at Uncle Honk's request, the family gather in the lounge for an announcement. When Judd hears that news, his face falls into the smirk that is rapidly becoming his habitual expression.

- You'll get yr orders, Sickface, he whispers to Clare. - You'll have yr part t' play.

- I don't like kids whisperin, Aunty Pi says as she shunts them all into the lounge. Mother is there already, standing at the empty fireplace beside Aunty Grin. There are marks on her face as if she's been weeping or scratching herself.

- It's a miracle, y' see, Hoppy. Uncle Owl puts out a hand to steady himself and finds nothing but empty air.

- Hallelujah! Uncle Honk says, pulling himself up in his chair at his accustomed place by the window, his leg up on a stool in front of him. He has declared his fever to be at an end, but nobody believes him. It looks as if it has just burrowed deeper into him, into his body, his sweating skin has a greasy, grey pallor.

- Lemme see.

Aunty Pi pushes Nerida forward. Nerida stands clear but does not approach. Uncle Honk leans forward, frowning. - Pull the curtains, he commands and Mother moves slowly to obey, her head held away from her brother.

With the curtains pulled tight across the window, the room is sunk into a stifling twilight, a seeping, fluid medium in which every object is embalmed. The silent, white face of the clock on the mantelpiece, the sofa with its arms worn shiny, the black cave of the fireplace with its eroded grate, each deep in the sepia vat of its history, and submerged in the deeper, formless shadow of the room.

Then they all see it, a glow around Nerida, like radioactivity. It makes her look as if her flesh has turned to glass. And around her head there is a nimbus, a scribble of bright blue as if a gas ring has been turned on.

- Pull back th fucken curtains, Uncle Honk shouts.

Aunty Pi hisses at his bad language, but Uncle Honk ignores her. In the time they have been in darkness, his temperature has risen sharply and the fever shines naked on his face. He says nothing but stares at Nerida until the tension rises up in their gorges.

Uncle Owl begins to hum *She'll be comin around the Mountain*.

- Where's Jack? Uncle Honk says, harshly interrupting Owl.

- Wanderin around as usual, fightin th War. Owl spits towards the grate.

- He shd be here, Honk says. - I don't like it, how he jus' wanders round loose all th time.

- I'll get a collar fr im, Hoppy, Owl sneers. - An' a chain. I think I got one handy.

He doesn't look at Honk, but keeps his eyes on the empty grate. The words come out of the side of his mouth as if someone else were saying them.

- Do that, says Honk. - It's high time y' did somethin besides sittin 'round drinkin piss all bloody day. Drinkin th piss in, an' pissin th drink out.

Uncle Owl forces himself to look at Honk. - An it's high time y' got down off yr high bloody horse, Honk. What makes y' think yr better than me, eh? Come on? What gives y' the right? The right t' kill m' dog. T' kill any fucken thing that pleases y'.

His voice is full of false bravado, and Uncle Honk's contempt is bottomless.

- Shud up, Owl, yr makin a fool of y'self. Yr actin like a ninny.

- Izat so? I've taken yr lip long enough, Honk. Had y' tellin me what t' do. Owl pulls himself upright and waves his arms around in an absurd fashion. - I'm sick of y' boastin 'n bellyachin. His voice, which had become screechy, now veers dangerously close to the tone of one of Aunty Pi's grand pronouncements. - I'm fed up t' th back teeth with it.

And he looks well satisfied with this utterance as coming from one whose word is not to be taken lightly. He pulls his stomach in and sticks out his chin, daring anyone to contradict him; he is a lawyer, perhaps, just delivered of a profound judgement.

Honk is rapidly running short of patience. - Yr right, Owl, yr very right. Yr right about th boastin 'n bellyachin, and yr right about th killin. We're goin t' kill someone right now. Deader than a duck. We're goin t' kill th old bugger upstairs before he kills us.

Uncle Owl looks as if he's going to interrupt again, but his voice fades into mutters before he has properly got started. - That'll be th fucken day, he says to himself.

With some stops and starts, Uncle Honk outlines the plan he's taken from Judd and is now presenting as his own. Clare will make a trip up to the old man's room with some poisoned cake. This will provide cover for the run Honk will make for the barn. He doesn't acknowledge Aunty Grin's sharp intake of breath or her significant look to Pi at his mention of the cake. Aunty Pi turns her stony face towards Clare. Uncle Honk presses on. Owl and the women will help Clare, who will give Grandfather the poisoned cake. - He'll be stuffin it inta his cakehole while I'm linin im up in m' sights, he says. - If I don' get im, th cake will.

He waves a febrile hand in the direction of the other children - The rest of you kids're goin t' have t' stay locked up in yr room.

Uncle Owl laughs. It seems surprising to him that nobody else finds the whole idea funny. Just looking at Pi, whose face is like a funeral, is enough to make him laugh. Besides, Honk is a dead man, any fool can see that, even a drunk fool.

- You're goin t' run over t' the barn, are y? What're y' goin t' run on? Yr hands? Y' front paws? He laughs again, that drunken laughter rich in appreciated ironies.

The fever beast draws a shotgun from the blankets beside it and levels the weapon at Uncle Owl.

Uncle Owl shakes his fists and screams, but his voice is hollow, as if he is just putting on a big act. He dances around the room like one on hot coals, a bad actor in a bad play. - Shoot me! Go on, shoot me! Cut me down in th dust like m' fucken dog! Turn me inta hawk meat, y' might as well. Finish th job good 'n proper.

Uncle Honk looks more puzzled than provoked by Uncle Owl's behaviour. He points the shotgun at his own leg. - Me a fucken cripple with gangrene or somethin because of yr fucken dog, Christ! Don't tempt me, Owl, don't twist m' arm or I jus might do it.

Hot dew stands out on his upper lip; spittle flies from his mouth.

- I'll show you what I think, Uncle Owl says, lurching into the middle of the room. He is beside himself. Exultant. His head is held up as if supported from above by an invisible rope, and he is suddenly possessed of that sense of high dignity that will overcome a drunk when he is challenged or attacked. He looks haughtily around the room, yet without exactly meeting anybody's eye. It is with the same ponderous dignity that he fumbles at his pants. Before anyone can say anything, he is pissing copiously on the rug in front of Uncle Honk.

Aunty Grin giggles. Coming from her mouth it is a blasphemous sound, horribly out of place. The kids know that Aunty Grin has been at the gin. Judd and Maverick are trying to stop themselves from giggling. It is like the game they play in the barn, only much worse. One look at either Uncle Owl, whose expression has achieved that sense of triumph known only to the righteous, or Aunty Grin, her hand up to her treacherous mouth, would set them off. Clare would giggle if she weren't so scared. Only Nerida, gazing solemnly at Uncle Owl, seems immune.

Uncle Honk stares stupidly down at the puddle on the floor as the stream dribbles away to nothing. Owl gives his cock a couple of contented flicks and pops it away.

- Clean it up! Aunty Pi comes forward. She looms up over Uncle Owl, her frame trembling, her fist out in front of her.

- Get down on yr knees and clean it up, y' filthy beast.

Before anyone can stop him, Uncle Owl has removed his trousers and is mopping the floor with them, tears rolling down his cheeks.

Uncle Honk makes his run before the moon gets up, when the yard is filled with shadows, not bothering to wait for Clare and the cake. He doesn't try any fancy route, he just runs from the back door to the barn. Dragging one leg, it is a peculiar, shuffling gait, but the wonder of it is his being able to move at all.

He makes it across the yard without a reaction from Grandfather. Then takes his time and drags himself up into the loft where he commands a fairer view of the tower. He sees what he thinks is the silhouette of Grandfather's head; his hands are too fevered to hold the gun steady. Yet soon he begins to pump shells into that room, shell after shell in a steady barrage, smashing every window.

His pleasure wanes, however, when nothing happens, nobody fires back. According to the plan, the girl should have climbed the tower by now. The old man would be taking the cake and stuffing it down.

He keeps firing intermittently for an hour or more until he half forgets why he is there and why he's firing round after round. He passes in and out of time as the fever carries him from the shadows to the light and back into the shadows again. He loses all sense of what he's firing at, the broken jewelled insect that squats on top of the house, or the shadows around it that won't hold still. Once, he thinks he sees a figure in the yard, a small, slight shadow creeping towards the barn, and he fires at that too, with no effect.

Finally, he runs out of ammunition, but there is still no sign of activity in the house. No signal from Owl that the job is done. Grandfather's room remains quiet except for the odd tinkle of glass.

In the still time before dawn, Honk's whole body begins to shake and his teeth to hammer inside his head. His tongue has grown huge and dry in his mouth. There is a sound in his chest like his bones are breaking open, a thousand voices clamour in his head for attention. The cold has crept in past all his clothing and the strictures of the fever, and there is ice water in his veins. He goes to stand up but only has one leg and his arms have lost the power of the shoulders. A band of ice and steel goes round his neck and begins to tighten; his throat fills up with something hot and slimy. He grabs for his pig knife to try and cut the thing away but the knife has gone from its sheath. In a moment of lucidity he knows that Judd must have stolen it.

Cursing the image of Judd he claws at the thing around his neck with his bare fingers. His fingers suddenly go dead. Below his neck, the rest of his body kicks and thrashes like a man on the gallows.

- He'll never eat it, Aunty Pi declares as they crowd into the kitchen.

- It may not kill him, Uncle Owl says. - That's one dirty big rat. And he giggles.

But no one takes any notice of Uncle Owl; since his performance in the lounge, he has become *persona non grata* on Aunty Pi's instructions.

- It's not fair fr a child t' have t' do this, Mother says to Aunty Pi. - Anyway, Honk's already there.

Privately, Pi agrees. Killing men is men's work, not for children, but she sees that the scheme might just work, even still. The old man has a soft spot for the child, and can't resist cake. Besides, they can't stay holed up in the house forever with the pig going rotten in the yard and the farm going to wrack and ruin, Honk is right in that.

- I don't care how many times Honk beats me, I'm goin t' fight it, Mother says. - You'll have t' beat me y'self, Pi. Drown me in th bath. I'm not lettin th child go up there.

- Lis'n t' who's gettin uppity, Aunty Grin says, heading to the pantry for the cake.

- You! Aunty Pi says bitterly. Now th worm turns! Now y' crawls fr'm under y' rock!

- I don't care, Mother says. As if by instinct, she has gone to her post at the sink, she speaks looking down into the eternal pile of greasy dishes, but when she turns around her face is haggard and obdurate, all the beauty leached from it.

Something snaps in Pi. A terrible ferocity takes hold of her. The children back away as she turns on Mother, screaming, her face livid. - You! Now y' start! If it weren't f' you, none of this would've happened. Shame! If I ws you, Honey, I wouldn't say too much about anythin.

Mother puts her hands up to shield herself, but does not turn her face to one side. - I have no shame, Pi.

- She never did, Aunty Grin puts in from the pantry.

- I never wanted it, Pi. I've nothin t' be ashamed of.

Uncle Owl puts his hands over his ears and indicates urgently for the children to do the same. Only Maverick obeys, and then for just a moment, after which he feels stupid for having done so.

- Ask Grandfather, he ws there.

- Ask him! I wdn't ask him th time of day. Anyway, I know what went on. I knew at th time. Y' led im on a merry dance fr months. Years fr all I know.

Aunty Grin comes out of the kitchen. - The cake's gone, she says, looking at the children. Clare looks at Judd. Judd looks back at her, a question on his face.

In the silence, they hear the first volley of shots from the barn.

They find the cake in the lounge, sitting on the table in front of Grandfather who is making himself at home in Uncle Honk's big easy chair. A rifle lies across his knees.

- There's a terrible stink in here, he says to Aunty Pi when she walks in. - Someone's been usin this place fr a lavatory.

His tone is almost casual, as if he's been sitting there talking to them for hours.

Aunty Pi stops suddenly, and Aunty Grin, following behind, knocks into her. Grandfather gestures with his rifle. - Come in, come in. It stinks in here, but there's nobody shootin at us.

When Aunty Pi speaks it is with barely a whisper. - What're you doin here?

- Waitin f' Honk t' finish shootin out m' windows. And f' him t' come back inside. Wd y' like a piece of cake while yr waitin. Maybe Grin cd put on a cuppa. Catch yr death of cold here.

Grandfather raises his eyebrows at Aunty Grin. Then he does a trick that has made Nerida laugh many times, he waggles his ears. This time, however, he does it without a trace of mirth or humour. Nerida, who's crowded in with the other children, does not laugh; she studies Grandfather with large, serious eyes, the way children do when they first meet somebody.

Aunty Grin looks speechless at Aunty Pi but all the wind has gone out of Pi's sails. The tension that holds her body together suddenly flickers.

- An' I'll tell y' why else I had t' come down, Pi. That's t' kill Honk. To spill his guts. It's somethin I shd of done a long time ago. I done wrong. I done wrong not t' kill Honk right at th beginnin, when it started. An then I done wrong not shootin you, Pi, when the butchery started. An' then I done wrong boltin up t' th tower like a scared cat after Mary died.

His voice breaks off.

- I'm glad yr here, Mother says.

Grandfather turns eagerly to his youngest daughter. - We stood by y', didn' we? We did all we cd. It killed Mary, I told y' that. An' it damn near killed me.

Aunty Pi gives a snort of disbelief, but Grandfather has the bit between his teeth. He turns solicitously to his daughter, - Lemme see y' Honey, come inta th light. What's them marks on yr arm. Lemme see. Lemme see what they're doin t' y', fr cryin out loud.

Standing calmly in front of them all, Mother takes off her blouse. There are dark smudges on her shoulders and breasts. Everybody sees them, even Uncle Owl who's working through one eye to keep the world steady.

- So it's still goin on, Pi, Grandfather says, not looking away from Mother.

Aunty Pi snorts again but says nothing. Clare remembers her brief glimpse of mother in the kitchen, the aunts on each side bending over her like avenging angels.

- Have y' got somethin up yr nose, Pi?

- Y' stood right by. Aunty Pi swallows hard. Her voice has recovered from its whisper but is strained to the limit. She has to use all the power of her body just to stand upright. - Y' stood right by. Y' thought it ws funny. Y' even watched him.

Grandfather doesn't look at Clare, who remembers the hunched figure stroking the finger bone of his grandson twice over; she remembers his moon-ridden eyes and their hidden gleam, and the sensitive fingers that crawled over her face in search of Pito.

- Y' got him t'kill th baby, didn't y', Pi. You were th one. He wouldn't've done't without you in there pushin him fr'm behind. Honk's like that. He needed y' in there, stirrin, yabberin at him night 'n day, bitchin 'n moanin til he just takes up his pig knife an' done it, jus' like he ws stickin a pig. It should've been you got th stickin. An' you 'n that harridan Grin dug th grave. That ws a pretty piece of work, Pi. Out behind th old dunny, scrapin away at th ground with Owl staggerin round. I'm surprised y' didn't just chuck't down th old long drop 'n fill that up.

The rifle is back across his knees, pointing in Aunty Pi's direction.

Aunty Pi is quiet for a long time. In her mind's eye, Honey still lies on the damp floor, screaming in the effort of childbirth, the head emerging, the head of an abomination.

- And I'd do it again, she says, her voice coming up out of the pit of her stomach, making dark knots of the syllables. - I'd do it again. But I'd do it different. I'd've cut it out while it was still in 'er womb.

Mother flinches.

- And I'da done it m'self.

In the silence that follows, there comes from the barn the sharp, futile sound of Uncle Honk still picking holes in nothing.

- What're they talkin about? Judd whispers to Maverick, thinking of the pig knife he has hidden carefully under his bed.

There's a rush of charged air in Clare's throat. - Pito, she says.

Father

FOR CLARE, sleep is a great cave whose hanging roof is like frozen cloud. Hours, days go by but no time at all, just a few hours. During that sleep there is a sunrise, and she sees Grandfather and Uncle Owl carrying Uncle Honk's body across the yard to the house, where he lies in state for eternity on a table in the lounge.

She hides in one dark corner while Grandfather throws useless curses at the corpse. The curses follow her whichever tunnel she crawls into and however far from waking she may creep. Judd and Maverick are with her, crawling into holes in sleep, the great cave dripping, solemnly, one drop a century. Only Nerida escapes, being able to walk through the walls of sleep and back without harm; it is a trick that Pito would have envied.

She has the use of Clare's voice too, and screams at Judd every time he calls her Sickface until Aunty Pi arrives and herds them into silence, her promises of beatings grimly sincere.

Then, down a long, deep tunnel she finds the world of wakefulness, smelling of broom and ice, and opens her eyes.

The first thing she sees is Judd's face bloated in sleep. One arm is under his pillow where he keeps his precious knife, doubly his now its real owner is dead. The first work to which he put it was the cutting up of Seth into tiny little pieces which he is secretly feeding into the stew.

Quietly, so as not to disturb him, she slips out of bed and gets dressed. From the kitchen she hears the fugitive sounds of Father making himself a cup of tea before the day's labour down at the fence line. Since fear has made him clumsy, Clare has no trouble following his movements.

The movements themselves make her curious for, by standing still by the door and paying careful attention, she can construct a picture of what he is doing; the rush of water into the jug, filled to overflowing; the rattle of the cup on the table as Father attempts to keep his hand steady; the long hesitations as he tries to figure out the next step; the squeaking of the teapot as he turns the lid seeking the slot that will allow it to pull free; the whine of the water boiling in the kettle… She can see the puzzled look on his face, the compulsive sweep of his hand through his thinning, sandy hair, and how his pale, washed blue eyes register the intricacies of his confusion.

She sneaks downstairs and watches him depart; his peculiar, uneven gait, sometimes brisk and purposeful, sometimes shambling and uncertain. Sometimes, too, he twists his body and jumps sideways, as if his feet had landed on some hot place.

This morning he has the thermos, and she guesses he is going to sit under the macrocarpa and drink his tea as the sun comes up. Already the mountains are glowing with that soft, almost internal light that presages a clear day. First to catch the glow, old Snowy stands above the lesser peaks in obvious majesty, apparently spreading the light around from its own radiance, reminding her of the morning she buried the bone.

Croak is sitting on the back doorstep, staring sleepy-eyed in the direction Father has taken. The air is chill in her lungs as she skips across the yard, grateful to be away from the house.

She approaches the macrocarpa tree and stops when she has a clear side view of Father. She watches as he attempts to unscrew the thermos, succeeding only when he realizes he has to put down the cup and use both hands. She thinks then that he is like her, having to learn to use his body all over again.

Fascinated, she watches the meticulous unscrewing, the hard concentration required to keep the cap moving in the same direction. With the cap off, a new problem presents itself; getting the tea into the cup. After a long period of consideration, Father picks up the cup and tries to co-ordinate a mid-air pouring operation, the result of which is half a cupful. Now both cup and thermos are in balance, and it takes him a while to make up his mind which one to put on the ground, deciding, wisely Clare thinks, that the thermos should go. The tea, still too hot, can finally be sipped, held steady in two hands.

As he goes through these motions, Clare goes through them with him in dumb show, practising for later, for an odd idea has occurred to her. If she were to perform this dumb show for him, would he recognise himself? Would he laugh?

She goes on watching as he sips at his tea, not wanting to spy exactly, but reluctant to step forward and break the delicate shell of solitude he has created for himself under the boughs of the macrocarpa, sipping at the steaming mug, gesturing every now and then to dead or absent interlocutors, sometimes making sharp, fearful noises in his throat.

Sure he will see her, she wonders if this is one of Pito's invisible spots. Eventually, however, feeling more embarrassed with the passing of time, she breaks the spell and steps forward.

Father stops very still and looks at her. She stops too and stares back. They stare without moving, as if they have just met or have encountered one another in a wild place. A magpie flies into their silence to perch in the upper branches of the macrocarpa. A moment later, it makes a familiar chortling sound.

- I'm Clare, she says, feeling foolish for saying it.

- Clare, he repeats guardedly, the word sharp and hard in his mouth.

Clare doesn't want to say any more. She sees Father reacting to words, flinching, the sound apparently jarring his ears as the stringent taste of a poison leaf will curl the tongue or a bright light hurt the eyes.

Seizing inspiration, she goes over to the wire-tightening machine, a large mechanical beast with a handle, and pretends to turn it, putting on all the appearance of strain. He watches her for a few moments, puzzled, apprehensive, but when she bulges her cheeks out with effort, he smiles. It is a smile that doesn't seem to come from anywhere and vanishes quick enough, but as soon as she sees it, Clare smiles too.

And runs away.

When she has gone, Father carries a few stones from the paddock to the ramparts he is attempting to make. After a few stones, he stops and the magpie takes the opportunity to fly down and land on one of the surviving fence posts nearby. Around him, the broken strands of the old fence lie in dissolute, rusty loops, half overgrown.

He plans to mend the fence or replace it with stones and has already built a massive buttress at the Scrubby Flat end of the fence line. Some days there is nothing else to do but pick up stones and wander around with them. Today he thinks of the girl and the silly face she pulled. Her smile reminds him of something that lies just around the corner of his memory.

Only half of Father returned from the war. The other half ceased to live in real time and still inhabits a hospital in France near the combat zone. The French hospital isn't a bad place as far as Father is concerned. People come and go like meals, like night and day; hungry children come up like ants from out of bomb shelters, their eyes like cracked saucers. Americans move in and out; they speak with lassos around their vowels. The mark of war is everywhere.

He wonders if he'll ever escape.

His hospital room has a view out over calm French fields with their neat hedges and fences. He loves the stone fences more than anything else because of their history, as if the human divisions of the land have grown out of the rock.

In his own country, the rock has not bedded down the way it has in France, or Italy, but is held loosely by nothing more than yellow tussock. He's seen the Waimakariri river bed whose channels never stay the same from one season to the next; there are miles of country like that, broom, gorse and the yellow grass. The whole plain is a big river bed.

Everyday people come and talk to him and make explosions in the air with their mouths. Sometimes, to get away, he will hide under the bed. Or pretend he can't hear or see them.

To begin with he couldn't sit down for longer than ten minutes, even to eat. There was a fierce monkey chatter in his head. When he tried to speak his teeth knocked together. He'd get up and walk quickly around the hospital ground two or three times before sitting down again. Sometimes he'd do that halfway through eating. He can't bear eating with the others anyway because they all eat like animals, slurping and snuffling over their plates.

The magpie heads for the old pine down by the sheep-dip where it can get an unobstructed view of both Father and old Wakefield. The bird tips its head around as if the world were not straight.

Father looks out across the stony ground towards the river, wondering if the girl will come back and make more silly faces. Across Scrubby Flat, on the western side of the river, loom the triple peaks of the Three Sisters. In the astonishment of these distances, a shout is a small thing, even a rifle shot is diminished. Somewhere in the tussock, a rabbit quivers. A hawk rides upwind. A rock cracks open under the sun. History pours out its pictures in sedimentary rock. Beyond, sheep graze. The sheep tracks stay level with the hill, and, staying level with the hill stay level with the eye, and, staying level with the eye hold over in the brain after the hill has gone down to twilight and the river piddles into a pot. He falls on the ground and covers his head with his hands. Combat practice; you never know when it will be the real thing, and the buzzing in his head will tear the sky wide open, pot or piddle, it won't matter; the scorpion hoists its sting.

Aunty Pi calls it shell-shock, lowering her voice to a double shush as if it were something that happened at the ocean, and should really not be talked about, but Father just sits and looks at the fence and the curled wire lying in the thick grass where sheep and fowls alike wander with indifference. Or at his pile of stones across which chickens hop leaving little white trails. Every now and then he gets up and energetically applies himself to the business of the machinery, the winding on of the broken strands. The collecting of a few more rocks.

The magpie keeps watch. It tilts the world backward and forward, keeping Father at the centre.

Father has one memory which never fails him. He was wandering down a street in some Italian town with his fellow soldiers when he was stricken with a sudden fear. He stopped before the corner of the street and refused to take a further step. He was ahead of the rest, two steps in front of his best friend, Lindsay, Linds he was called, when he reached the corner. - I can't move, he said as Linds went past. - Don't be a bloody idiot, Jack, Linds said, stepping out to cross the street, - there's nobody here... getting his head blown away in a flower of blood, his body taking a few more unbelieving steps, as in a Bela Lugosi movie, before falling into the ochre dust of a sunny Mediterranean afternoon, quiet if not reconciled.

- He stole your death, the soldier next in line said to Father.

- An arsehole sniper, the sergeant said.

- He stole nothin, Father said, walking backwards.

And he ran, holding his stolen life close to him. He ran down streets that had more eyes than walls. And there's never an eye so accurate that squints down the sights of a gun. He ran into hills that had no location but bare tussock and stones. That was the beginning of his madness. At that point he split into two beings, one who ran off with his stolen life, and the other who died. The dead one kept trying to re-enter his body, especially at night in dreams. The one with the stolen life was transferred to a hospital in France, and the dead one went with him.

Father throws down a few more stones and walks away. He can hear the explosions, rocks flying apart, lifting up out of their camouflaged beds to scatter death around. The hospital is not safe. The farm is just across the river from the combat zone.

One day Father will have to cross the river and return to duty.

A man comes to talk to him, gesticulating wildly as if Father were deaf. It is the children's Uncle Owl. His voice is full of holes, his breath full of alcohol. He points to the paddock where, Father understands, a man is to be buried; he has already seen them carrying the corpse of the arsehole sniper from the barn. Owl wants Father to help with the burial but Father doesn't stay to listen. His head is already stuffed with noises and corpses. He walks and walks until his legs are satisfied. Then he throws himself down on the ground to wait it out, chomping down hard on the stringy tussock grass, thinking of his wife who will be standing at the sink under the watchful eye of Aunty Pi, her hands greasy with dishwater.

When he returns, however, the funeral is still there, lying in wait for him. He walks around the side of the old dunny and there they all are, standing around a grave dug where the ground is softest.

It is an awkward gathering. Aunty Pi holds herself straight and correct, as if standing upright were simply a matter of willpower, not looking at anybody, her face closed off. Grin stands like a shrunken shadow behind her, the gin has made her tearful. Uncle Owl stands beside Grin, chewing on his gums. He's sober and trying to get used to it. The children stand together with Mother, a little to one side, their eyes riveted on the shrouded form of Uncle Honk, for the adults have decided to do away with the complication of a coffin since none of them is competent enough to make one. Mother is dry-eyed, her face the colour of greywacke. She holds Nerida's hand and stares towards the Dog-leg, pointedly absent from the proceedings.

At the head of the grave stands Grandfather, looking frail and uncertain.

Nobody knows a prayer.

Usually Aunty Pi steps in to take control of a situation like this, but now she stands as silent as the rest of them, ultimately just as embarrassed by death. Aunty Pi knows when she's met her match.

When Father approaches, Clare moves a little way to meet him, subtly piloting him to the graveside. Father looks down into the hole; it is deep, and there is nothing in it but white stones. The body lies on a pallet beside it, wrapped in sheets. He hums to himself, feeling almost content; the visible, outward signs of death an affirmation of what he knows to be true of war and combat zones. It is only the enormous silence of death that makes all this killing possible.

Clare, who is still standing beside him, takes his hand and squeezes it gently. Inspired by this touch, Father steps forward and salutes briskly, pronouncing,

- Blessed are th dead, fr they shall inherit th stones.

Mother smiles.

Owl steps forward to lift up his arm too but the salute dies in the making, collapsed by the brittle, now-focused gaze of Aunty Pi. Uncle Owl's salute turns into a hopeless shrug.

Looking down at the body, Father remembers an escapade in Egypt when a group of soldiers stole a newly slaughtered pig from the officer's mess by putting it on a stretcher, throwing a sheet over it, and taking it through the streets as if it were a corpse. It's a marvellous thing, the Sarge said, for the New Zealanders to teach the bloody wogs how to thieve. The Kiwis weren't known as Freyberg and his Forty Thousand Thieves for nothing. They walked along beside the stretcher with funereal faces, trying not to laugh; everybody stood to one side respectfully and took off their hats. The pig made a handsome corpse.

- It'll make a good roast, Father says aloud to the Sarge.

Mother's smile grows.

Aunty Pi turns her stare, grown more brittle than ever, onto Father. Her body sways, as if held to the ground by centripetal force alone.

Then it all goes out of her. Her shoulders slump, her body seems to cave inwards, her stare dulls over.

Still they all wait for her to make a move.

- Get im in th ground, she says, turning on her heel and walking for the house. Aunty Grin follows in train.

Grandfather stoops over the body, his face the colour of his hair. - We shd of had a coffin, he says.

The day after Uncle Honk's funeral Father gets up early again to make a cup of tea and Clare again follows him, stopping at the same discreet distance to watch him manoeuvre the mug and thermos.

This time when she approaches him, his moment of fear and tension passes faster. He disregards her and goes back to his tea. She positions herself a few yards from him, just under the boughs of the macrocarpa, not close enough to frighten him in his own territory, and begins her dumb show with the laborious unscrewing of the thermos cap. At first Father doesn't appear to notice, then he stops what he is doing and watches her with that alert stillness with which one might watch a wild animal from a hiding place.

Faced with her toughest audience yet, she puts everything into her performance, triumphantly finishing up with the cup at her lips.

When she looks up he is still watching her. - There's many a slip 'twixt cup and lip, he says in a voice which reverberates in such a hollow way she wants to laugh.

The next day the pattern is repeated, and this time when she shows herself he looks as if he expected her. She is half way through one of her dumb shows, when Father suddenly throws his hands up in front of his face and screams. He jumps up and runs around the tree, throws himself down and pushes his head against the ground.

Turning around, she sees Judd and Maverick standing a little way off.

- What d' y' want? she demands, a little of the old imperial Princess tone in her voice.

- Nothin, Judd says.

There is a buzzing in Father's ears that will not go away. Low as the rumble of artillery, high as a bat screaming, mindless as a blowfly, the buzzing is a torture built right into his head. Sometimes he rolls in the dust and holds his hands over his ears, sometimes he dunks his head into a barrel of water and holds it there, and sometimes he bashes against the side of his head with his fists; none of it to any avail. He shouts his way through the nights and by day lies in a stupor in the shadow and thick scent of the macrocarpa, staring at the fence and the machinery he's assembled for the assault.

The final assault.

He's assembled his army, dreaming of victory, the spoils of which will be silence; the fence will be fixed and the pile of rocks grow moss. Everything will settle, gratefully, back into its old forgetfulness, except the magpie who, with a touch of snow on each wing, will settle into watchfulness. There will come a moment not knocked sideways in the concussion of air, and words will find a silence fit to match. He will unlock the numbness in his mouth and speak to the world in straight syllables.

His weapons are the simple tools of a practical man, wrenches, screwdrivers, chisels, wire, spanners, drills, saws, set squares and hammers. When the girl and other children have gone he takes them out and goes through them, admiring the perfection of each one and trying to forget the buzzing in his head.

He has the crescent wrench which is thick and immortal and silver and gleaming. Its steel, lockjawed face can bite down on any nut, force its will upon even the most pervasive rust, turn the most reluctant screw.

He has a long, thin screwdriver, good for most ordinary size screws. It has a slender, tensile strength, an assured precision of purpose.

Together the wrench and the screwdriver are the bishop and knight of his attack. They are backed up by the steel sledgehammer, ultimately capable of reducing most problems to a single pulverized instant, but useful too for more oblique forms of coercing brute matter; and a long bevel-ended crowbar with enough leverage for a man to be able to jack half the sky up.

Then there is an array of nails, lesser wrenches, pliers, coils of bronze wire, a Phillips screwdriver, some safety pins, a nail punch, a tyre lever, some adhesive black tape and a variety of screws and washers. It is a whole army, a splendid array, and he watches them all from the scented shadow of the macrocarpa.

Despite the atrocity of the buzzing in his head and the constant need to duck, he feels something like a brief happiness. Everything is ready. All the components are assembled, along with the Queen of the piece, the fence-mender itself with its great wheel for cranking up tension on the wires. So vast are the forces it contains, so powerful its inner mechanisms, Father can only approach it with awe and trepidation. In this beast lies the key, the very solution to the mending of the fence.

Father believes that the buzzing comes from the sky, and not from his head as has been suggested; his head is not large enough to contain that sound. It is a sound that needs big, open spaces, peeled back and revealed, rather than muffled bone. It is the sound of a Messerschmitt in a steep dive, a sound that divides the air in half. It is the sound of a mountain falling apart. It is the ubiquitous monkey chatter of small arms. It bounces off every mountain, it comes from every direction, it is the Alpha and the Omega of sound.

Sometimes it is all he can do just to hang onto the earth, to crouch and cling; other times it grows faint enough to hope that he may, in the end, make amends with silence. Then he will be able to decipher the steel syllables of the fence-mending machine. Then he will be able to bring his spanner and his screwdriver and all the hosts of the legion of practicality into the battle and mend the bloody fence.

That evening Clare slips down into the cellar, taking a torch with her for fear the light might be noticed. The ancient, bound chests with their dust and mystery flicker uneasily around her as, with a little hunting, she finds the spot where Pito once showed off his vanishing trick. Upon one of the trunks she finds the thin case she'd noticed previously, takes it down and places it on the floor.

She hesitates before opening it, a little superstitious about what she might find; the place is suddenly thick with the presence of Pito and she thinks she can hear the trunks whisper to themselves in the silence. Her hands tremble a little as she thumbs back the clasps.

Inside she finds a butterfly collection, each butterfly neatly pinned and named. Her eyes are drawn to the red admiral, sitting quietly to one side, wings outspread with the rest. For a long time she looks at it with nothing at all passing through her mind, not even the thought of Pito or their day at the broom bush. Or the coy, delicate way it had lifted its wings to show a body which was born in a different world to its wings. Finally, a thought arrives and it is enough; it sustains her.

A butterfly puts all her expression into her wings.

A very Pito thought.

Carrying the case carefully, she goes upstairs and finds Father who is lying on his bed, his hands behind his head, staring up, moving his eyes slowly from one side of the room to the other, like a radar scanner searching a far horizon. He sits up on the bed and takes the case in his lap. Since he cannot work the catches, she opens it for him, and when the lid flips up, his hands leap back and his eyes spring wide as if the butterflies were about to jump through the glass at him. Then he stares closer, apparently at the pins in a butterfly's body.

She points to the red admiral, suddenly at a loss as to what to say, how to make it comprehensible to him.

He follows the line of her finger, locates the red admiral, and nods wisely.

- Fresh fr'm grave, he says with a zestful smile. - That ws Linds. He came up fr'm th grave with bloody coloured wings an' dirt an' leaves in is mouth.

Mother comes in and looks over Clare's shoulder. - Yes, she says to Clare. - It belonged t' yr Grandmother, Mary.

- They're very beautiful. Did Grandmother Mary collect them?

- Mostly. A little boy used t' collect them, too. He'd spend hours trying t' net them.

- Who ws the little boy?

Mother looks straight at her. - Yr Uncle Honk, she says.

In the days following she gets up and goes with Father to the macrocarpa tree, more sure now of her course. To begin with, Judd and Maverick try to follow and poke fun at her and Father, but she turns and repels them once she has drawn near him. She realizes, with scorn in her heart, that the boys are afraid of Father. It's his suddenness, his unpredictability, that strangeness in him, as if he's just arrived from another country.

Some days are better than others. He is with her, watching her, although not laughing, or he is tuned backwards to the crackle of gunfire and the drone of distant engines. The hospital grounds loom large in his mind, the bunkers are never far away, yet one way or another he begins to observe the children, especially the girl who makes faces, and images race up through his body to the surface of his mind. He sees his children come and go, sometimes laughing sometimes crying; the urchins of war, they all have the same hunted look. They rise up out of a lake into the luminous air, their voices making shapes in his ear. They want him to play. Hide-and-go-seek. Ring-a-ring-a-Rosy. His children are booby traps, waiting to explode when he draws near them. They hold out their hands to him. They jump on the snow. They laugh and run over bridges. They laugh and jump over stones. They cry and hide in the barn. They laugh at him and run away, inviting him to follow.

The sight of the children arouses in him an ancient torment. It is death to follow them. They have their secrets and their haunts and they live in a foggy land beyond the fence, beyond the river, beyond the black stump.

And the girl is one of them.

They call him Father and laugh. They have guns in their hands. They jump across the fence, the border he is trying to make with a double strand of wire and a heap of stones. The machine guns chatter in his teeth. The stones in the ground shake against one another. The bridges fall upon their knees in the dry river beds. The children run away. Like sheep, who run in front of a car, the children run in front of machine guns.

Father can do nothing but huddle in the tent of his own uncertain flesh, watching the number eight wire curling away through the grass, and the stones piled up as if over a grave.

Secure borders are everything; the fence a Maginot line facing a barbarous night, facing the stars that creep through the long, silken wire that threads one world to the next, facing the alien hills, the formidable shapes that lie beyond the Dog-leg; expansive and spare, the great sloping peaks, the endless exchange of earth and sky, the membrane of sunrise, the combustible air.

Father goes mad in an ecstasy of breathing. Lying like that, terrified, close to survival, he sucks the air into his lungs so desperately he tears apart the filaments of the body and fills his whole skin with air.

In the moment of his dying, when the sniper's bullet has gone through his throat, he knows who he is and what he has been and done. He's tasted the sands of Egypt in military issue wrapping. He's heard Beniamino Gigli lift the roof off the La Scala Opera House in Turino. He watched the ancient monastery at Casino dissolve in the space of a prayer. He's seen the Colosseum from the turret of a tank. In Milano he saw lines of orphans trudging through chill rain, searching for their parents. Dawn over the mountains. *Bastardo!*

Like the taste of sand, like the colour of the sky, like the howl of a woman who's just seen her child on the end of a bayonet, it can no longer be kept away and he cries. His tears make the stones glisten. They run into the ground like the blood of children and make mud out of dust.

He gets up and begins to operate the lever of the wire-tightening equipment. No wire is attached.

The girl is nowhere to be seen.

The ratchet spins hard against the cogs.

Father knows there is a better place to be than the hospital. As a child, he was taken to a clear pool and shown the miraculous sight of a rainbow trout, a huge old grandmummy, flicking from one existence to the next with a twist of her tail. She looked up at him with an eye older than the world, and vanished, leaving a rhythmical pattern of light on the shuffle of stones which seemed momentarily to have absorbed her colour.

He believed then that the ancient fish had come up out of the depths through a great fountain at the centre of the world. Here was a world in itself, a world that did not belong to the unbreath or fall within the compass of death, a world that had shed itself open to the sky. Somewhere there was a fountain that had not surrendered to stones; somewhere there was a raft of bliss wheeling upon a great river. There was a woman's voice calling out across the wheat. There was the taste of sunshine on the tongue. A place where the four quarters were tied to the stake of the earth, neither the hospital nor the farm nor any place on the broken borderline between.

These things he knew as a child, staring down into the clear stone pool where the trout flickered. When his parents moved off a little, he knelt by the pool and slipped his hand into the water with the ill-defined impulse of becoming a part of it, a part of the trout, a part of the world of refracted light. He got a shock when he saw his hand, once in the water, apparently dislocated from his wrist and bent at a sharp angle.

This memory, bright as a polished coin, comes to him as he stands under the macrocarpa and gazes over to old Wakefield. Gazing at the placid animal stills the blood and brings restless feet to a halt. He forgets the buzzing in his head. Forgets the combat zone. Forgets even the Great Trout of the world. The movement of Wakefield's jaws is monumental, his weighted stance classic, like the Parthenon.

While he is busy forgetting, the children creep up behind him, make a loud noise, and pretend not to snigger when he jumps up, throws his hands upon his head and runs about in circles as if stones were falling out of the sky.

The girl comes and shouts at the other children, screams and goes red in the face until they go away.

Clare joins Father when she first hears his noises in the kitchen and watches him for a few moments, waiting patiently for him to acknowledge her. When he does, with no more than a flicker of his eye, she joins him and begins to silently mimic his actions.

At first he is puzzled but when she practises with the thermos lid he gets the idea, able to follow the direction of her turning fingers rather than his own, which tend to forget which way to go. This way his hands screw the lid on and off several times without difficulty. After this he looks at his hands, turning them over as if they were new to him.

As they walk down to the macrocarpa, the light coming up in the valley, Clare feels that something special is going to happen; there is a quality to the morning, bright, intense, the feeling that she could simply step up into the air so lightly does the world bear itself. Croak joins them and trots along in front, tail up.

She has brought her own mug and holds it out to be filled from the thermos once they have arrived under the macrocarpa. Father stares as if he does not remember what it's for, then pours without spilling a drop. Croak lies near them, stretched out along the root of the tree.

The magpie lands on the fencepost, pretends not to see Croak whose tail gives a twitch or two, and favours Father a cock-eyed, knowledgeable look. A look that is full of calculation. It is an understanding that Father and the magpie have; they have seen orphans of war crawling out of the dung, gulping fear-soaked rinds of bread and ash. The white-winged crows know the smell of blood.

Once, driving through a devastated Italian town Father saw a little girl like this one, whose own body did not seem to belong to her. Everything was shut down, the shops the hospitals the churches the faces of the people the posture of the dogs, all reduced to density and mass; every move another step in a funeral procession that would last the rest of their lives; except for this one girl who smiled at him, the first and only smile of the war, opening everything up.

It's a comfort to have her sitting there by his side, for unlike some children she knows how to be quiet, and how to speak with such a light softness he can close his eyes and see the feathers of a rare and exotic bird.

Suddenly Clare gets up and begins to mimic Father, the way he runs around holding his head, falling on the ground and beating his fists. She looks so funny doing it, like an ungainly bird, that Father has to laugh.

The laugh comes easily, as if he's been laughing like that for years. He's on his feet then, imitating her imitating him. He dashes about holding his head, braying as loud as a donkey. Then he falls on the ground and gets up, laughing, and does it again.

Quite put out, and already having second thoughts about Croak, the magpie takes off; Croak watches it go without any apparent regret.

Now different kinds of laughs are jumping out of Father's body as if his ribcage has been sprung open. From throaty chuckles to silly giggles. For a moment the laughs, not all of them belonging to him, multiply alarmingly in his chest, but he laughs them through and they are gone, like creatures of the ether.

Clare sits down and applauds and he goes into a new one, a dumb show of his own devising. He shows her he and Linds walking down the street of that Italian town, and Linds is swaggering along in a manner peculiar to soldiers, only to have his head blown off in the middle of a laugh. He does this last bit by opening his mouth and his eyes as wide as he can and falling on the ground.

Clare claps and raises him up from the dead again.

Father comes up off the ground laughing. In the middle of the laugh, the buzzing in his head goes away, vanishes for just a few, pure moments.

He doesn't even notice.

Under the macrocarpa, his tools spread out before him once more, Father turns in his midday sleep, dreaming of gunfire and laughter all mixed-up together, as if the firearms were laughing and the people spitting bullets. Without waking properly, he leaps to his feet. There is a special smell, thick with memory, he associates with death and the combat zone, and he smells it now. He started to smell it when Linds' head got blown off and it has never gone away. He can smell it in the tussock and in the precinct of the barn. He knows that war has passed through here, destroying laughter, leaving in its wake an apathetic stupor which presses heavily on house, yard and barn. The odour of death saturates the wind.

As he wanders into the yard he sees Pi standing in the doorway, looking across at the barn, and Father recognises the slumped defeated angle of her shoulders. He's seen a thousand farmyards like this one, blown to bits. Babies casually bayonetted and thrown into open graves. Women lying in the contorted grotesquery of the last rape. Men lying face down, soaked in the bloodied shame of their deaths.

He finds himself looking down at a big black pig covered in flies and hawk's feathers. He's seen bodies before; bodies everywhere, churned up in the slushy wake of tanks or stacked stiffly in rows like firewood.

Like a swift acting poison, a sweet pain enters his heart and he sits down in the dust and cries. It's all the girl's fault that I feel like this, he thinks. He remembers his own mother, sitting on the balcony of some house, shelling peas, her fingernails passing swiftly down the seam of each pod. What is her name? He sees his father in the garden planting carrots, his back stooped, the spade upright beside him.

It occurs to him that now he is crying sensible tears. His mother told him there are two kinds of tears, silly tears and sensible tears. Silly tears are naughty tears, shed when a little boy doesn't get his own way. Sensible tears come out of grief, because it is sensible to cry when something dies. With laughter it is the same.

Now, looking down upon the pig's seething mantle of flies he imagines that he's finally found the real source of the buzzing in his head. That sound is none other than the sound of flies upon dead meat, the moan of their pleasure, the whir of their ecstasy, the thrum of frustration; if he could but silence this roar a huge quiet would settle over the earth, guns would fall silent and aircraft drop out of the air without a sound, like paper darts.

He flutters his hands towards the carcass; there's a brief flurry in the dark shifting mass and a deep disturbed sound. A few flies land on him and grope around in his clothing.

Father looks across at the skulking children who are watching him. He can no longer feel the sniper's bead on the back of his neck, but it doesn't matter. Linds is already dead. The sniper is dead, strangled by fever. Father looks down at his hands. There is an inheritance in them, there is truth in the fingers and the way they move. They are hands that were once capable, able to hook a sheep or mend a fence or lift a woman, and now they are useless things full of their own uncertainty and trembling.

He decides to lie down in the dust and emulate the boar. Pulling the boar's shadow protectively across himself as if it were a blanket, waiting for the mantle of flies to settle on his corpse, he can feel the pig's massiveness, its density, and also the weightlessness of its death. It makes the stones beneath his body cold and hard and eternal; it makes the multitudinous hum of the flies a Gregorian chant to hunger. It makes death itself full of illusory stillness. It makes laughter a ladder. At the same time, since he lies within its long shadow, it will protect him on his trip to the land of the dead, which is full of soldiers, and snipers with rotting fingers.

He has to tell his old friends that he is still alive.

He digs his hands into the skin of animal earth and puzzles at what he finds there; cold shrapnel, the flinted cries of magpies, his body's own fugitive odours, and a history of floods, the great song to gravity that opens up the plains from the stony guts of the hills. He sees his father again as he whirls past, a tall, stooping man, bending over and pulling the carrots from the ground. They come up with small sighs. Threads of dark earth hang to them like a beard.

- Mother is dying, his father says.

But the tall, stooping man who is patting the earth as if it were a pet, rolling dirt into the holes the carrots have left, is wrong. Mother is sitting on the balcony where she has always been, shelling peas. She takes a pod between thumb and forefinger and peels back a translucent cellulose film. This she discards into a bowl for the fowls. Her movements are quick and dry. Now the remainder of the pod is fit for the soup. The fowls get only the peels, tips and stalks upon which they tread fastidiously.

Beside her, on the table is a sewing box, and inside the sewing box is a tangle of thread of every different hue. There is a little cloth man with a rotund belly full of needles; there is a thimble which contains, in its hollow interior, a brass sun; there is a small tin which contains a thousand bright-eyed pins. Nearby, honeysuckle creeps up the balcony, heavy with scent. A kingfisher lifts its head to drink. Its eye is enclosed by a pool of clear water in which a trout moves in depth and secrecy.

From where he lies in the shadow of the boar, Father turns over and pushes his tongue into the raw, dry earth. He hears the listless dead moving in the ground underneath him. The sound of their voices comes up out of the ground but he ignores them. He is concentrating on the hectic slide of the earth through the seasons, and the sharp, mineral images it generates.

- Mother is dying, the tall, stooping man says, lifting the spade. Father grips the earth and sees that it is true. Where the tall man peels back the earth, blood appears, and when the woman on the balcony opens her mouth to talk, he hears a far off sound like the cry of a gull lost inland. Father wants to dig himself a hole but there is no time, the ground is already beginning to shake and quiver, the stones in the earth knock together like violent castanets.

A horse rides out of the earth carrying a rider, a woman dressed in armour with wings on her helmet. He sees that she is a dreamer visiting herself in a dream, and that she inhabits a city that smells of lilies and cypresses. Dead children cling to her coat as if they remembered their lives. She is one who has breathed with the living and lain with the dead and Father is afraid of her because she knows everything about Linds, and how Father stole Linds' life. She reigns in the wide valleys of stones and emptiness and she has no rival. He can't tell her he is alive when she might, with the pure gesture of an adept, scoop the little life from him with a fluid movement of her hand.

He grips the earth harder and breathes into it until it makes a moaning sound. The rider dismounts and approaches him, carrying a cup. Inside the cup there is a fragmenting depth which fills with fire, hills and the quick stone. He is amazed at how rapidly the air fills up with earth, lightning leaps from out of the mountains, and the plains leap from the foothills. This is the earth that holds the spade upright, this is the fire that percolates in the earth. This is the air that gives suck to the fire. This is the dreamer from the valley of the Asphodels, where the rusting body of a tank points to the sky a single eroded finger.

She kneels to give him the cup, smiling and encouraging. The liquid has an odd, astringent taste. It rushes into his blood where his wounds are carried. His hips jerk and his pants fill with sticky seed. Memories drop down on him out of the air above and rise out of the earth and slip into his body. He remembers when the rivers still had muscles and the sky was clean. He remembers what it was to be a child, to draw a face on the glass with holes for eyes, and to watch the world pour through the holes; he remembers climbing a tree and having to fight a magpie. He remembers when he was a pig and rooted the earth with strong tusks.

Memories cover him like spring blossoms.

He feels his own body with disbelieving fingers, as if his fingers could invent something like this; the body, a cup of blood held in the circular flesh by strings of bones looped through the air, filled with lightnings and chilled spaces, staked to the earth by a shadow. It makes him laugh.

He stands and the flies rise with him, undulating like a cape. Evening shadows have lifted above the Dog-leg and begun their creep across the plains. The children have gone and around him the valley of stone is filling with dark air.

He moves slowly, one foot carefully placed in front of the other, the flies deserting him as he leaves the boar. It takes a long time to reach the house, but finally reaching the door he makes a bolt for the shadows inside.

The house has a cold, hollow feeling as if all life has been sucked out. In the hinged shadows of the hall, sitting at the bottom of the stairs, his head in his hands, he finds Owl, who's sweating in the effort to 'dry out'. He barely looks up as Father goes past. - At ease, Jack, he murmurs.

Father walks with the same care to the kitchen. Honey is there, silently facing a pile of dishes and staring through the window towards the river. He knows this is Honey, his wife, but she has been nothing more than a shadow to him. Sometimes, at night, when his legs want to run, her hands soothe his face and cheeks and sometimes, when the memory of the rich, dark red Italian wines is strong, he will climb upon her and in a few swift, fearful strokes, bring himself to collapse.

Now it is different. He wants to know her, to bring her out of the shadow and see her face. The buzzing in his head increases as he tries to concentrate, but he ignores it for as long as he can, screwing up his face in the effort.

- Hello, Jack. She speaks in the same voice she uses for the children, light, friendly and without condescension.

The girl, restored to her proper form, comes into the room and looks up at him earnestly. - You cn talk t' me Father, y' know who I am now, don't y'?

The word comes from far off and when it appears it has a taste, sharp, tart, like the blade of a knife on the tongue.

- Clare, he says.

Impulsively she puts her arms around him and kisses him. There is a blessing in the kiss of a child, he thinks.

A few moments later, when he sees Grandfather, he runs and hides under the table.

The next day Father does not go down to the macrocarpa but hangs around the yard all morning, staring from time to time at the corpse of the boar. Clare watches him from the back door. It is always like this before an attack. The air has a purity. Everything trembles, as in a heat haze. Ran lifts his head dispiritedly and looks at him, eyes full of resignation and the ancient grievance dogs bear mankind.

Father looks towards the boar, which has become a hollow vortex of flies, and back towards the dog. His eyes fill up with the world and empty again. He looks up at the glass tower but of course there's no sniper there now, no attack due. No need for the prickle between his shoulder blades.

Yet here in no-man's-land time stands still around noon. It's the silence that falls before a sudden mortar barrage. He moves on at his own speed, half run, half shuffle, until he reaches the barn door. There he stops, thinking of the girl. Suddenly this girl has a name. His tongue finds the sound again and rings it like a small bell in his mouth.

He turns back to the house and calls out. - Clare!

The girl at the back door jumps up. There is a brief sketch of joy on her face.

Father throws his head back and looks up. The buzzing in his head cuts off, leaving a great cliff of silence. The sky is one great empty bell-jar.

That night Father dreams of the burial of Linds. Half the platoon is there, half the army, it seems. They'd got a proper coffin for him and draped a flag over it as if he were a General; Linds would have been tickled pink. Then they all stand around with their hats off and the wind in their hair while the Parson says some words. As the coffin is lowered there is a deep growling from the earth.

Father listens to see if the buzzing will return. Nothing happens, and he gets up and goes to the window. There is a long moment while the air stirs. In the yard, upon the dead boar, the flies are singing deep inside their bodies. He cannot understand the calm of the sky; at any moment it must crack open and the scorn of bullets pour through.

This doesn't happen.

- We have t'bury it, he says, looking at the boar.

Honey rolls over and looks at him. - That's right, Jack, she says, casually.

Clare takes Father by the hand and gives him a guided tour of the house as if he's never been there before and is, perhaps, some prospective tenant. Father is happy with this temporary identity, looks with interest at everything, shows the appropriate response, and comes to feel that indeed these rooms have been hidden from him, another wing of the house perhaps, or one seen so long ago its nooks and crannies have become myths. He agrees to see them again through her eyes and have them unfold from the palm of her hand.

The lounge he finds the hardest to accept. He has a memory of an open room with the afternoon sun streaming in the window, the carpet glowing, the fireplace and the mantelpiece standing deep in its dignity. Now he finds a room saturated with death. Heavy curtains are rolled over the windows and the air has a stagnant, stale quality with a faint lingering foulness.

In the great easy chair, where Honk spent his fevered, fraught hours, sits Pi, upright and rigid, so still she might have been sewn to the shadows. Pi is only a shell of her old indomitable self; since the death of Honk she has taken to mourning, draped a shawl across her shoulders, and has developed an uncharacteristic quiver in her voice. Having abandoned the day-to-day running of the house to those far less competent than her, she restricts herself to occasional sallies into the kitchen where she will snarl, carp and moan and give a series of elaborate instructions before retreating to the lounge with a dissatisfied twist of her shoulders.

In a less grand chair opposite is Grin who, having nothing better to do, has also taken to mourning, with the added comfort of a gin bottle under her blanket. She sits there most days feeding Pi's bitterness and hatred back to her, but sometimes she takes time off and goes up to Owl's room, steals from his remaining bottles and tries to convince him that he should get off the wagon and drink with her. Owl, however, has developed a terror of alcohol and screams and shouts at her when she tries to drink in front of him.

After a brief look around the room, Clare takes Father out but he cannot remove from his mind the picture of the two women facing each other in the dark and turning themselves into shadows. This picture quickly assumes the proportions of an icon in his mind; the lounge a shrine to stasis and death.

Grandfather and Mother are talking in the kitchen. Judd and Maverick are there pretending not to listen. When he sees his Father, Judd's face takes on a contemptuous leer, but nothing more than that. Since Clare can talk again she doesn't make such an easy slave, and Judd has to keep his knife hidden from Grandfather in case the old man confiscates it. But there is a memory from his brief reign of power which he holds dear; Clare, pushed up against the bunks, the knife at her throat, her insides hot and wet on his fingers. It is not a memory which will go away quickly.

Grandfather and Mother are talking about selling the farm and moving to Christchurch. Grandfather himself, as he points out, is too old and bloody tired to start running a farm and Owl is no use, drunk or sober. And Jack, well...

Father listens and tries to piece the words together in the new silence of his mind. He's been in hospital, but that was quite a long time ago as the mind flies, just after Linds died and the shadows of snipers jumped at every window. Even the Sarge, who could swear better than the Chaplain, caught his one day; he opened his mouth to shout a command and blood came out instead of words.

Now, while words and sentences do not fly apart the way they once did, he still has difficulty finding purchase among them. There is an atmosphere in the room however that impresses him with its gravity. Grandfather looks grave and solemn enough, standing by the kitchen table with his snowy hair and grey shingle-fan beard which he will take, occasionally, in one hand and squeeze.

After a long pause, he says, - We cn take Ran 'n Billy t' Lesters. We might get a bob or two for im.

- Lester won't have any money. Aunty Pi says from the door, - so you cn scotch that idea right away. Unless of course you're goin t' give away th dogs. Suck up half a gallon of petrol takin im there. Bloody typical.

She walks across to the sink and has a glass of water, looking with distaste at the dishes still not done on the sink bench. Bloody typical.

Grandfather dithers. Safe in his attic, the only decisions he faced were when to rise, when to eat and when to brood. Decisions are like landscapes that can be viewed from many angles. Pros and cons pile up with no prospect of a resolution. Going to Christchurch, for example, would see him off the farm and away from prickly memories. But it might also see him in an old people's home, chomping on a brand new pair of false teeth he'll have paid for himself in some roundabout way. The world is full of robbers and cutthroats, people who will call themselves friend or family and clean you out for every penny you've got. And as they walk out the door with the last of your things they'll tell you what a mean, miserable old bastard you've been all these years. In his heart of hearts he can't believe that he won't be fleeced in some way with this move to Christchurch. Pi herself, standing right in front of him, heaping shit upon his head, would not hesitate to take advantage if one were in the offing. The more cornered a woman like Pi is, the more cunning she will become, at least in her own mind, and the more elaborate her schemes. He saw her, the other day, get Grin to change the position of a photograph of Mary on the sideboard a dozen times before Grin got sick of it and was roundly cursed out by Pi for ignoring her. Imagine trying to get some kind of legal settlement out of someone like that.

Grandfather hardly has the strength left for such a task. He was better off up in his tower, gettin food sent up at the end of the rope and shootin pigs when they came trottin into the yard. Never faced with any decision from one week to the next.

Coming down from his tower was Grandfather's last shot, and the last of his strength went in carrying his own son, bloated with death, across the yard from barn to house. Digging a grave and burying him without even a coffin. The exhaustion he felt after has never quite gone away. Whenever he stands up he can still feel the unholy weight on his shoulders, still see the staring, fever-cooked eyes that would not close. He doesn't say anything, however, for whatever he might say would only be seized upon by Pi and turned against him in some way.

For herself, Pi doesn't see it in those terms. She sees a bunch of no-hopers trying to decide what to do with the property when they can't even do the dishes. It is enough to make a bloody cat laugh. Honey's washing her hair and walking proud but she'll be slaving her guts out twice as hard before you can say Jack Robinson. She'll learn. And there is poor Jack of course, standing around gaping as if he knew what was going on. He and Clare spend their time down by the macrocarpa, giggling like a couple of ninnies, cackling like a pair of magpies; it is all well and good for some. It takes one to know one.

- We cn work those things out later, Grandfather says. - We shd ring Christchurch.

By Christchurch he means Dot and Merl, whom most of them would prefer to forget. Anyway, Grandfather shot out the telephone lines, so what is he talking about? The old man is losing his grip.

Pi downs her water. As it hits the back of her throat, she becomes aware of a silent scrutiny; secretive but intense. It is the child Clare, her hands across her face protecting her mouth. If only this stupid child had been able to let the dead stay buried, they could of choked the old bastard out in his tower of glass and got the lot, stones, ice and all.

The water has a faint bitterness to it, suggesting that someone hasn't cleaned out the tank lately. She's not about to say who that is. It's not her place any longer to point out the obvious. Her best cue is a dignified exit, but her conviction remains; let the kids once get the best of you, like they do with Honey, and poor old addled Jack, and you're a gonner; give them an inch and they'll take a mile.

She leaves with the peculiar dignity of the defeated; she's perfected by this time the tense, negative cast of her back. Be it on yr own heads. It's yr funeral.

Father listens, but his ear is made of a different shape, with a different topography; this splits the words into their component syllables and back again, spliced sound, glottal and sudden. He looks for help to Clare who is silent and solemn.

As she goes through the door Pi turns and throws Father a baleful look. He puts his hands up to his eyes, palms outward; protection against a blinding light or flying shrapnel.

Father approaches the boar with a spade in his hand and Clare by his side. The corpse has by now been completely gutted by flies, and when Father passes the spade across it, almost in benediction, the flies lift revealing a white writhing mass in the boar's body cavity.

When the smell hits them, Father knows it but Clare turns away and makes puking motions. Ignoring it, Father walks around the body until he reaches the spot where he lay down and visited the dead, and there he begins to dig.

From a safe distance, out of the range of the stench, the boys and Nerida gather to watch. They are soon joined by Uncle Owl who walks as if all the bones in his body have been broken and knitted together again.

Father digs into the stony ground, making little headway. After a while, Clare moves back out of range of the stench. As each stone comes out, Father's load lightens, for he senses that he is taking them out of his own body, clearing a cavity inside himself in which to bury this death. Neither the smell nor the slowness of the work is important, only the rhythm of it, the steady sense of enlargement.

Watching him, Owl rubs the back of his hand over his chin. - Why don't y' just pour a bit of petrol over im an' set im alight. That'd be a lot easier.

Father doesn't stop. Owl shrugs, as a person does in the face of bloody-mindedness. His eyebrows go up and down. The children soon get sick of watching and wander away, except for Clare, who keeps a lone vigil a few yards away.

When dusk falls and the light goes on in the kitchen, Father is still working. Sometimes they hear the steady clunk of the shovel, at others, a silence as he removes larger rocks by hand.

Pi and Grin come to the window of the lounge to take a look. - Mad as a meat axe, Grin says ritually.

Pi says nothing. She's not so sure. Of course she's never seen Jack finish anything he started, but then she's never seen him dig for half the day and half the night either.

When darkness falls Clare goes inside to the kitchen window, where she can continue to watch him. Mother is at the table with pen and paper, writing a letter. She writes slowly but determinedly with big, sloping, oblong letters, frowning with concentration. Later that evening, she hustles Clare to bed, having allowed her to keep her vigil by the window, with Croak, far past her normal bedtime.

Father digs all night, hauling the stones out under a pale, first quarter moon. The dark and the cold have sent the flies away, but the corpse of the pig still vibrates with maggoty life. The stones are pale in his hands, like moons in themselves, their darkside turned to the earth.

Come morning and Father is still digging, although the hole is near big enough. A huge pile of stones lie beside the new grave. After breakfast the children file out to take a look at him finishing the hole. Judd and Maverick get near enough to look in, and confirm that it is indeed big enough to hold the still massive carcass.

Grandfather doesn't come out, nor show any reaction to the digging; he is not going to give anybody that satisfaction. The loss of the meat rankles, but he makes up for it by slipping himself a couple of extra chops from the last of the sow's meat and a bottle of home brew from Honk's last batch. He dropped the beast with a single shot, no one will forget that. Dead in mid-stride, just as if it had run into a wall. Everybody seen it.

Finally, the hole is dug. Father jumps up out of it, singing an Italian song. He has a loud, clear baritone which carries right across the yard where the sound of it, filtered by the heavy curtains of the lounge, brings a frown to Pi's face.

When the time comes Owl appears, sweatingly sober, to help Father haul the beast to the hole. Now everybody except Grandfather, Pi and Grin, gathers around as the body is slung into the hole.

Father stands, swaying, his face ringed with grime, his hair full of dust. He wishes the Chaplain was here to give a prayer, but Christians do not pray for the souls of pigs. Then he sits down as if the air were a cushion, a smile on his face, while the children fill the grave with rough soil and stones.

When the grave is finished and piled high, Father goes into the house and sleeps the sleep of stones. He sleeps all day and all night without a single murmur, wakes an hour before dawn, gets up and dressed, goes to the window to look out over the yard and the new grave.

He knows where he is. He is not in a hospital in France. He is not in Italy, he is not in the desert, nor in the underworld with the dead. He is home on the farm, and he's been trying for years to build a fence between the land of the living and the land of the dead. He has even fathered children who rose up before him, their breaths hanging pale in the air, wanting him to play with them. - You promised, they cried. - You promised.

And he has not slept. When people thought he was asleep, he was living other lifetimes, harrowing events through which he always maintained the hope that, in the end, all would be disclosed and made well, all evils reversed. Bullets would speed back down rifle barrels, blasted children would re-convene their limbs and leap back into the womb, Linds would get up off the Italian street and walk backwards into his life, the world would reassemble out of its scattered fragments; a world in which fish learn their colours from stones and snow burns the light.

He's seen that world himself as a child; a world in which fish learn their colours from stones and snow burns the light. Into that world he was born, from that world he was dragged, through the saliva of history, to be dropped in the combat zone.

This last thought propels him down the stairs and out into the pre-dawn darkness of the yard. When he reaches the barn he hesitates. There is a buzzing in the sky, distant at first, like a lone blowfly weaving across the tussock. As it grows louder it comes in waves, phasing in and out in rhythm. Father doesn't move. He knows the barn will be no protection. Not even the bare ground.

The sound is loud enough now to shake the air, throbbing and ubiquitous, but Father does not clap his hands to his ears and roll on the ground yelling; instead he goes still and gently closes his eyes. This sound, the sound of heavy engines, now enters him and makes his flesh vibrate; the bones rocking in their beds of sinew and muscle.

Then it fades. He opens his eyes in time to see something heavy and dark block out the stars. When the sound has finally gone the air is completely empty. Father breathes into this emptiness and it breathes back into his lungs. He knows this was a real sound, a real aircraft, and not in his head, for it has left his ears clean, purified of sound, everything except the residual blackbody background hum of creation.

A little light is coming up out of the stones, making the riverbed glimmer as he goes into the barn.

After a thorough inspection of Honk's Bedford, Father goes to work again.

In the morning the word loses no time in spreading itself through the house. Pi and Grin come to their window and twitch the curtain aside to confirm for themselves. The big double doors are wide open to show Father at work on the Bedford.

Pi stares for a very long time and, finally, cannot make up her mind. You never know with Jack, you never bloody know.

But Grandfather understands it, and for him it is an ominous sign, bringing the prospect of Christchurch a step closer. He retreats up to his room for a while, hungry for the view across the barn to the river bed and the whiteness of Old Snowy. Hungry for the days of his exile.

Mother understands it too, and for her it is an emblem of hope. She watches from the bedroom window, trying to determine how purposeful his actions are. Presently she goes downstairs and joins him.

- This is th distributor, he says in a grave voice. - This is th distributor cap, an' these are th points. These are th sparkplugs, caked up with carbon. This is th carburettor. This is th starter motor. This is th head. This is th engine.

- You know a lot about engines? she asks, pushing her hair back off her face.

- Not much, he says modestly. - I have t' listen t' see how't works.

She nods and watches him work. Soon Nerida, Clare and the boys join her. After a while Judd and Maverick get bored and wander off. Uncle Owl, still sober, comes up and watches, rolls a cigarette, smokes and watches. He removes the cigarette, leaving a few threads of tobacco hanging from his lower lip, and says - Y' need a crescent wrench fr that kind of job, mate.

Father works all day and by afternoon has the engine running. The sound of it wakes Grandfather out of an uneasy slumber in which he has been dreaming of the ghost child, Pito. He has asked Clare just what Pito looked like and he dreamed him the way she described him; dark haired and sallow with big soft eyes. This would have been the child of his two children, more like Honey than Honk by the sound of it, but in the dream the boy has hold of Honk's pig-knife and is stalking Grandfather across a bare, windswept mountainside. In the same dream, he sees Pito strangling his father with fingers of ice.

He goes to the window in time to see the Bedford edging out of the barn. There's something wrong with the muffler and the thing is making enough noise to wake the stones.

Sitting in the cab, the steering wheel in his hands, Father finds himself at the centre of the same huge throbbing sound he heard by the barn that morning, the same sound that now jolts up his elbows and sets his bones jumping. It doesn't matter. He can turn the key and the sound dies.

After easing the truck out of the barn, he puts it in neutral, pulls the stiff, creaky handbrake on, jumps out of the cab and walks around the chugging creature, checking out its exhaust and having a closer look at the tyres.

Judd is impressed despite himself, and when Father lifts the bonnet to see how the water is faring in the radiator Judd climbs on the bumper to look in the engine. The engine is big and tough and oily. Maverick leaps up beside him.

To Father, Judd says, - Cn I drive?

Father laughs. The truck blows up under him, again and again in a flaming fireball, but he is still unhurt. So he laughs and the truck blows up and he laughs and the truck blows up but still the truck keeps running, the motor bouncing up and down, Father laughing.

After fixing the Bedford, Father goes to sleep. He lies on the bed fully clothed, still as a corpse, his chest barely moving, but when he wakes his head is clear. Honey lies beside him, her wheat-coloured hair spread across the pillow breathing deeply in sleep.

He steals over to the window whose changing scenes have become a sequence in his mind. It is deep night and he can see Snowy Peak, its sides pure with snow, standing free of the clouds. Tonight the peak is clear and calm.

When he sees the moon, he thinks of deserts. And how he would cry and cry and cry, filling the sand with tears. That is the territory of memory. It doesn't change. A tall man is there, stooped over a garden. There is the smell of honeysuckle, the royal purple of thistles and a corpse with the grinning face of war; so he has to start again, along the line backstends, grove and river, balcony and house, pines, nasturtiums, thistle, cockabully. The future precipitates out. Father comes up through the ocean. His mother crosses the room, her hands on fire, his father stoops over his unfolded heart and dies among the silverbeet and the potatoes, lying face down beside the upright spade.

He will move on from here. Below him the Bedford sits silent, waiting for the turn of the key. On the other side of the yard, the boar's grave shines, already looking like a relic.

He looks down at the macrocarpa, secretive and dense. He has spent so many hours there, dreaming of mended fences and communing with the magpie. That was in the combat zone. He's heard the shooting and the sound of falling glass. And he's heard the silence which follows the burial, the dumb mouths moving in a show of prayer.

A great sadness and grief shakes his body which is too frail to contain it. Tears as big as pennies roll down his cheeks. His mother comes back into the room, climbs out the window and flies away. His father follows, holding a rifle. He turns and fires again and again at his cursed son.

One day, he hopes, everything will fall silent like this. Like a great blanket of snow that so purifies sound. Silence, he decides, is a kind of purified sound, and in that medium the pieces of the sky come together, fit into the frame of one world, and everything makes sense again. The Messerschmitts cease their screaming, the cries of the dying turn into stones and the smell of the dead gives way to cut grass.

He leaves the room and wanders down the stairs, walking slowly past the children's room. There is silence within but it is not the silence of sleep. The children are awake, wondering where they will be going in the Bedford. He walks past Owl's room and hears a loud, sober snoring. Around him, the house creaks its joints, like an empty church. There was a church in Italy where he took refuge with Linds. As the bombs came down, the church began to shake as if a train were passing through the building. Suddenly a plaster saint, attached to the wall, turned serenely towards them, one hand held out in benediction. Then its head fell off and rolled on the floor.

There is a step from the common language of sleep to the dialect of wakefulness, and Father has taken that step before he knows what he's doing. He feels the breath in his chest and the slipping of skin over bones as if he has been given a new body. His tongue explores his mouth and the uneven line of his teeth as after a long absence. His eyes slide around in their sockets, feeling out a space for themselves.

He's reached the main hall and has no idea why he woke, or where he thinks he's going.

Croak the cat sits by the back door apparently waiting for him. When he sees Father, he rises and arches his back in a yawn, as if to tell him what a long vigil he's kept. It seems to Father that the animal has some supernatural power, divination perhaps. Now, it seems, Croak wants him to go outside.

He pauses by the window. In it, there is an outline, barely decipherable as a face, but he can read familiar features into the dark pools and humps. His face is waiting for him there, behind the shadows. Behind yard and barn. He opens the door, Croak scoots out, and Father steps into his newly-coined bones, looks up and sees the clear sky. His eyes are elongated with tears but he holds onto his seeing; his grief, once wide as an ocean, has shrunk to the compass of the human heart. His mind begins to work again.

After a long absence, Father returns. Dawn across Scrubby Flat. The river bed whitens under the frost. The mountains pull up black into the sky; fir trees stand on their lower slopes like unlit candles.

Children sleep.

A dog barks.

A hillside barks back.